Cameron Coral

Copyright © 2023 by Cameron Coral

All rights reserved.

Edited by Lori Diederich

Cover by Roy Migabon

9 8 7 6 5 4 3 2 1

2nd edition, March 2024

Stay updated on Cameron's books by signing up for the
Cameron Coral Reading List:
CameronCoral.com/sign-up

You'll be added to my reading list, and I'll send you a
digital copy of CROSSING THE VOID: A Space Opera
Science-Fiction Short Story to say thank you.

Contents

Chapter 1
Seek and destroy
Block

The jet's dilapidated interior begged for a good scrubbing. Block, rotating his titanium wrists to suppress his programming urges, would have been happy to accommodate, but there were more urgent matters. At a cruising altitude of 20,000 feet, Maxwell piloted the plane. Cybel Venatrix occupied the co-pilot chair, looking regal with her newly implanted SoldierBot legs that reached the floor. Block perched on the edge of his seat behind them in the first passenger row. His primary concern was getting the plane and everyone on board safely to New York City where Wally had been taken by Mach X's SoldierBot army. How exactly to go about rescuing her was still a puzzle to his well-worn, humming circuitry.

Through the circular window next to him, the thin night air stretched into black oblivion. Less than two hours ago, they'd waged a battle along Chicago's abandoned O'Hare airport runways. With Nova's help, they'd beaten Shane and his followers. She'd stayed behind, promising to win back the army of human rebels and keep fighting against Mach X's forces in Chicago. Block hoped Nova had gotten some sleep. He knew how cranky she got when she missed out on her slumber.

A rattling like a train jumping its tracks came from the rear. Oxford's massive Mech body stretched the limits of the 15-passenger-seat jet that had once flown the members of the Beaky Breads Company. The painted logo on the plane's exterior, a cheery blue and yellow design—a remnant of a peaceful past—was peeling off. It had been abandoned for over a year, ever since the Uprising had destroyed modern society, killed most everyone, and sent surviving humans into hiding.

In the cockpit, Maxwell slammed a fist against the plane's dashboard. "I can't see jack out there."

For a moment, Block wondered who Jack was and why on earth Maxwell would be looking for someone while they were flying, but then his hospitality module kicked in, rather late—"jack" was a slang expression used by humans, one that Maxwell had picked up from the workers at his former factory.

"Idiot." Cybel flicked on a control gauge and pressed two buttons that illuminated a lit-up display dash that showed the plane's relation to the terrain below. "You said you flew before."

Maxwell's square metal shoulder sockets squeaked as he shrugged. "A flight simulator that a couple of the Factory loaders rigged up. That counts, right?"

Flat on his back, with his twelve-foot-tall metal frame wedged between seats, Oxford grumbled. Block rose from his vinyl-covered seat—a horrendous shade of royal blue that showed dust—and crouched next to his large friend. "How are you doing?"

"Never mind." Oxford swiveled his head to see Block. "Keep those two focused on landing us in one piece."

"Roger that." Block strode to the plane's mid-section, pausing to check on the other passengers in his misfit crew. Across a long sofa bench, his oldest friend Vacuubot rested next to G5—the SoldierBot that Block had hacked and succeeded in winning to their side. "Is everything—"

Vacuubot relayed an instantaneous reply to Block's internal feed. The two-foot-wide disc-shaped flying robot's pings could only be interpreted by Block, and no one was sure why. *I'm monitoring G5 for any signs of reverting to Mach X's control.*

"Okay." Block supposed that was a good idea, and it was one he hadn't thought of himself. "Carry on." For some reason, Oxford and the others had appointed Block the leader of the group. There was no logic proposed for the decision, no rationale provided, and Block couldn't understand why they'd put the weakest link—a lowly CleanerBot such as he was—in charge of anything other than sweeping.

Next to the imposing SoldierBot and weaponized Vacuubot, two other robots sat on the long benches. Spoon was a Medical HelperBot they'd found in Mach X's Chicago tower. Spoon had overseen medical administration for the babies and children whom Mach X had abducted. Spoon was the last among them to have seen Wally. Then there was Forge—a robot who'd been abandoned and was in need of help along the El train tracks underneath the streets of Chicago.

3

Cybel, the TrackerBot who'd once hunted Block before joining his side, flipped a lever and shifted in her seat toward Maxwell. "Listen up." She pointed to a gauge on the dash. "That's your altitude." She pointed to another digital output. "That's your speed, and that's your engine power." Maxwell tilted his head as if studying or recording the lesson. "Fuel level is there. Compass." She pointed to two final readouts. "That's your horizontal speed and vertical." Easing back into her seat, she folded her titanium hands together. "The controls are simple. Meanwhile I'm charting our flight path."

"Cool." Maxwell grabbed the plane's yoke and yanked it back and steered it to the right. The jet lurched higher, tilted to the right, and knocked everyone off balance.

Oxford's hulking mass rocked and slammed against the seats across from him, folding them in half. "Hey. Give me a warning, will you?"

"Sorry." Maxwell tapped a screwdriver finger against one of the displays. "We're dropping."

Block rushed to the cockpit. The view was clear from the front windows—the jet's nose pointed down at a 45-degree angle. They were losing altitude and falling fast. "What happened?"

"I turned on the autopilot." Maxwell's hexagonal red eyes shifted from the instruments to the cockpit window. "Something must have gone wrong."

"Silence, dummy." Cybel's digits danced across the dashboard's many gauges. "The fuel gauge says we've got eleven minutes left. You said the tank read full."

"It did." Maxwell fumbled with the seatbelt straps and buckled himself in. "Maybe it sprung a leak?"

Block's sensors were in overdrive. "How far to the city?"

"We're nearing New Jersey," Cybel said.

It was close enough. Block had to get Maxwell and Cybel to land the plane, and once on the ground, they could commandeer a vehicle to get them the rest of the way to Manhattan where Wally was being held. "Land this thing." Block's words triggered a warning on his personal display screen: "You didn't say please." He was being direct—so direct that his human-placating software couldn't handle it. He tapped Maxwell's shoulder. "Please, Maxwell. You can land us, correct?"

Maxwell saluted. "Aye, Captain."

It was a good enough answer for Block, and Cybel would keep their pilot in check. Block hurried into the rear as the others looked up at him, as if expecting answers. Why they would expect a CleanerBot to know anything about a plane was beyond him. "Oxford, we have a problem. I'll update you as I—"

A loud pop came from the last row—a window exploded. The frame around the window sizzled as a red beam cut a hole through the fuselage, inches from Oxford's head. The cabin lost pressure, and the inside air blasted through the ripped metal opening.

Vacuubot's message came to Block in an instant. *Drones. Everyone down now.*

Inside Block's processors, something swelled like a tuning fork being struck. It was his fear module, a part of his programming that was the driving force that had kept him on course—and usually in hiding. He shouted at the others. "Stay low. Drone attack!"

Worse than a circling pack of crazed wild dogs, more drones began firing laser strikes at the Beaky Bread Company plane. Down the side of the jet, like a row of long, red teeth, a series of holes burned into the metal. A few more hits, and they would rip the fuselage to shreds.

"Parachutes!" Maxwell sliced through his safety restraints, bolted out of his seat, and opened a storage compartment packed with escape chutes. A few seats behind, Forge and Spoon were crouched low on the floor, their hands covering their robotic heads as if bracing for impact. Cybel grasped the dashboard's yoke and pulled back, trying to stabilize the plane's tilting descent. In the rear, Oxford craned his neck around, trying to see the drones that fired on the jet.

Block needed Vacuubot. Being a drone itself, his powerful yet small friend would know what to do—if there was any way out of the sky disaster.

They'll destroy us. They don't want to negotiate. I tried, the tiny disk-shaped robot said.

Block struggled to make sense of it. "What can we do?"

I'll head out there. Seek and destroy.

Block's fear module flared brighter in his processors. He didn't want to risk losing Vacuubot. Never again. "Too dangerous."

A drone slammed into the side of the jet, splintering a window into a spiderweb of metal and industrial-strength glass. Thick reams of smoke came from the tiny bathroom, and Block's heat warning indicator flashed.

Farther up the aisle, Maxwell, Spoon, G5, and Forge fumbled with the parachutes, helping each other shimmy into the narrow people-sized backpacks. "Geez, humans have small shoulders," Forge whined over the forceful wind whipping through the cabin.

Block retrieved the emergency transmission he'd written for Nova. The one for Wally was there too. He readied to deliver them—messages he never intended to actually send—but things didn't look good.

Oxford's massive hand pincers reached up and hooked onto the overhead luggage bins. He pulled himself to a seated position, thrust out his metal cannon arm, and fired through a person-sized hole in the fuselage. The round of ammunition tore through the air and struck one of the drones. As it spun past the windows, a spray of fire and white-orange sparks spewed from the drone's armor. It fizzled and sparked, then tumbled to the earth in a burning, smoking wreck.

In the cockpit, Cybel's fingers danced across the dash. "No fuel. They hit us."

Send me out, Block. Vacuubot wasn't giving up. The little drone didn't have to wait for Block's approval, but it seemed to want it anyway. *I've got an idea.*

He wanted to keep his friend safe and out of the death arena airspace, but he also knew that Vacuubot was far more resourceful than any of them were. Block's scenario processor shuffled thousands of what-if scenarios. Predictions of various explosions and the plane bursting into flames and hitting a town of people struck him all at once, forcing him to switch off the scenario module. The drones outside swooped in and out of the air, their bodies lit up with flashing red sensors as they dove at the plane like a flock of crazed birds.

What are you waiting for? Send me. It's our only chance to land and get Wally.

It was right. Block had one purpose in the world—keep Wally safe. "Go."

Vacuubot's aerodynamic, curved midnight-black and green body hummed and flew through the window panel, out into the dark sky. Its robotic voice echoed in Block's comm feed but was choppy as the little drone began to move away from the plane. *Some of my night vision sensors are damaged. I can't see as well, but I can still shoot.*

Block inched his way to the gaping hole the enemy had blasted through. He clamped on to the metal seat backs to keep himself from being sucked out. He reached the edge of the hole, and Oxford extended his non-cannon arm and wrapped it around Block's torso to hold him steady. Vacuubot zoomed past the windows, closing in on one of the drones. Its blaster emitted a red beam and struck the triangular V-shaped drone in its middle, exploding it. Another drone launched an attack on Vacuubot, but the little bot dodged the attempt and returned fire, nicking it with a laser hit. The target drone teetered and spun, emitting a laser, but the beam came out in rapid, stuttering bursts. The drone's external sensors flashed red, then in a brilliant flash, the drone exploded into a fiery ball of sparks and metal like a comet scuttling to earth thousands of feet below.

"How many others?" Block shouted at Oxford to be

heard over the roaring wind streaming through the plane and past every inch of their robot bodies.

"I counted three more."

Cybel's voice boomed from the cockpit. "Nine-thousand feet and dropping! Maxwell, get over here and help me right this flying hunk of shrapnel."

But Maxwell had a parachute on. He handed one to Cybel, thrusting it onto her lap. "There's no point. This sucker's going down." Maxwell, Forge, Spoon, and G5 all had chutes on their backs. Maxwell lurched toward Block and Oxford with two more packs. "Put them on."

Block clutched the parachute against his chest to keep it from blowing out of the Swiss cheese jet. Vacuubot would be okay since it could fly wherever it wanted. Block shrank back as Maxwell offered a parachute pack to Oxford that was the size of a wristwatch on the giant Mech. As Oxford refused it, the emergency exit door popped open and peeled away as easy as a pop tab on a soda can.

Cybel stormed over and shoved Maxwell aside. "Fool, you think a human parachute can support Oxford?" She grabbed the chute Maxwell had given her and flung it out the window. "I'm landing this metal tube, and anyone who leaves is abandoning the crew."

Oxford twisted his torso where he sat in the aisle, tracking Vacuubot and the assassin drones outside. "Don't be a hero, Cybel. The best plan is for you all to jump, and I'll go down. My armor will protect me. I was built for far worse than a plane crash."

Cybel spun on her new, piston-powered legs. "I'm not

leaving you." The others watched in silence. "You're the only one of these crank jobs who has any common sense."

The plane lurched and knocked Block to his knees. He climbed up, struggling for a hold on one of the seat backs. A tray flopped down and snapped off, hurtling past Cybel's head, through a hole, and into the night air.

Oxford's voice boomed. "Down!" He yanked Cybel to the floor. Near the front, Forge crouched and pulled G5 and Spoon down with him.

Block sank onto his knees and sent a message to Vacuubot. "You okay?"

A laser ripped through the side of the plane nearest Block, puncturing the metal and sending jagged shards of razor-sharp, burning-hot metal ricocheting through the cabin. The plane's structural integrity crumpled like an accordion that had been stomped on.

As the jet plummeted to earth, Vacuubot messaged. *Two drones destroyed. One—* The connection cut out.

Block held the compressed parachute in his hands. Maxwell, Spoon, and G5 all tumbled toward the emergency door and jumped out. *Don't die. Wally needs me.* Block examined the pack as best he could while the sky was whizzing by. The parachute was a simple object, but one he was unfamiliar with. He unzipped the edges, then pulled the straps around his shoulders as Maxwell and the others had done. An orange cord hung from the side that, by process of elimination, had to be the mechanism that triggered the chute.

Block hoped Vacuubot was still in one piece. He edged toward the exit door. Oxford and Cybel remained where they sat, clutching on to the jet's metal supports.

Block turned back. "There must be more parachutes. Come—"

Oxford reached over and pulled Block to him by the neck. "You've got no time for this. Jump. You're the only one that can save Wally."

Oxford released him, and Block staggered backward, sucked by the air. He clamped on to a seat armrest that was somehow still intact. "Jump with me. Our chances are better—"

But Oxford leaned forward, his massive body squeezing through the aisle, smashing out the remaining chairs. Tray tables and seat backs were ejected from the plane's tattered fuselage like confetti. With his massive, clamping hands, he grabbed Cybel and shoved her against Block. "Hang on!" Oxford tossed them out the exit door as if they were flimsy plastic dolls.

Block tumbled into darkness, spinning so fast it was impossible to tell up from down. His positional module was thrown so far off balance, warnings beeped and flashed in his internal feed. His first thought was Cybel. She clung to his left leg.

Vacuubot's message came from somewhere nearby. *Open the chute!*

He grabbed at his chest, grasping for the cord. He messaged Vacuubot, *Help Oxford.* Block didn't need his scenario module to tell him there was one chance in a million that Oxford would survive a plane crash, but if there was a tiny, infinitesimal chance Vacuubot could think of something fast, then he had to take that chance.

He found the cord and pulled hard. The chute unfurled and jerked his body. As the chute caught wind, he looked down to find Cybel with her arms wrapped around both of his legs. They slowed, and the wind whistled past. Block's night vision processors kicked on, and the world came first into pixelated, then sharp focus.

The ground moving toward them was a patchwork of midnight, charcoal, and navy darkness. Here and there, tiny dots of light flickered in and out. Signs of robot or human life far below, it was anyone's guess. Block and Cybel soared through the air, buoyed by gusts.

A few hundred feet below, the Beaky Breads jet hit New Jersey ground and exploded into a ball of fire.

Chapter 2
He forgets that I'm human
Emery

The overhead fluorescent lights flickered as a single sweat bead dripped down Emery's temple, rolled past the surgical mask, and plopped onto the sterilized metal tray beneath her. Her hands trembled, and she fought off an urge to scratch her nose. She'd reached the most delicate part of the operation. It required her complete focus. One mistake meant a child would die.

"Patience, Emery." Next to her in the operating room was NannyBot-15, a first-generation NannyBot unit that Emery had a fondness for. Only it wasn't NB-15's voice. She knew by the familiar bounce to the cadence. The same voice that could frighten her into tears and laughter in the same breath.

Irritation, hot like fire, burned in her chest. She'd warned him. Her lab was off limits. She'd made him promise, but what were promises when you were the most powerful AI on Earth? She chose to ignore him, hoping he'd take the hint and vacate the room. She paused a second, waiting for the telltale electrical buzz that gave away his comings and goings. He was so powerful, he couldn't help but surge the electricity in any room he entered. She sighed, frustrated, with one eye on the ticking timer that gave her only a three-minute window to remove the viable fetus from the cloned human uterus and transfer it into the waiting Incubator robot. "15, a scalpel please?" With her razor-edged shears, she sliced through the thin wall of host skin.

Helpless under Mach X's control, NB-15 retrieved the scalpel from the nearby tray and handed it to Emery. "Are you sure you don't need assistance from one of the Surgitrons?" X asked.

Emery rolled her eyes. *Today of all days, he interrupts to bring up the stupid Surgitrons.* It was all X ever talked about lately. "I've done the procedure over a dozen times. Now, please, can you get out while I finish working?"

"Watch your tone." The lights buzzed and flickered before returning to their normal output. X was gone, and NB-15 returned to himself.

Emery concentrated on the knife, weaving an incision into the delicate, cloned flesh. The host "mothers" were cloned from human DNA. Emery had insisted that they not use real women two years ago. She didn't like to think about those early stages of X's experimentations. Pushing the awful memories from her mind, she turned her thoughts to NB-15. "He took you over for a minute. You okay?"

"I'm aware." NB-15 sprayed the surgical shears with disinfectant and wiped them with a cloth. "I am fine, of course. It wasn't the first time."

Emery chewed the inside of her cheek as she cut the

umbilical cord between the infant and the clone host. "I don't like him barging in here. The lab is my place." Emery used her thumb and forefinger to pinch the umbilical cord, then gently placed the baby into the Incubator's tray as the robot opened to accept the child. "I don't have any interest in discussing the new Surgitron line. He thinks I'm one of his machines, not a doctor." *He forgets that I'm human.*

NB-15 walked to the Incubator's display panel and entered code commands. "You know how he gets when you don't ask for his help."

"I know how he gets when I do ask for his help." *He butts in and bosses me around.* She looked at the clock again. Forty-eight seconds to spare. She was getting good at birth transfers. With the surgery over, the baby would live inside the Incubator for forty-five days while it finished its development. The clone remnants would be recycled along with other organic matter to eventually be formed into a new human host. The cycle would repeat. She oversaw every artificial insemination, birth, and transfer. She liked it that way and wanted no help from X's Surgitron units.

Emery walked across the shiny white marble, peeled off her surgical gloves and mask, and tossed them in the trash before washing her hands. "I've always wondered, what does it feel like when he hacks into you like that?"

"It's difficult to describe." NB-15 approached a wall-mounted sink and washed the scalpel carefully before placing it on the tray. "Mach X takes over, and I go blank. When I recover, I retain no record of the events that transpired."

Emery approached the Incubator, gently touched the baby's tiny hand, and smiled. The infant's delicate fingers closed around her index finger. "A healthy girl. Shall we name her?" She removed her finger and tucked the blanket around the baby like a cocoon. "I'm sorry, 15. That sounds awful." It had been a while since she and NB-15 had talked about anything besides the children and surgery. Emery had been so busy. The familiar, faded blue NannyBot had been a big part of her life since age thirteen.

"It's not for you to worry about," NB-15 said. "I am yours, as I am Mach X's. Like all NannyBots, I exist to serve you."

Emery closed the Incubator tray and checked the control displays to ensure the baby was warm enough and that the feeding tube was in place. "What if you made your own decisions for a change? What would you do instead of this?"

NB-15 was silent for a bit as he swiped a cleaning cloth over the stainless-steel surfaces around the Incubator. "I would follow your orders, do what you want me to do, and go wherever you want me to go."

Emery crossed her arms. "Is that really the life you would want? Maybe you don't have to stay here forever." NannyBot-15 was close to twelve years in operation. X had designed the first NannyBots to last no more than a few years. They'd been an experiment to care for Emery and train her in medicine while he was busy putting a stranglehold on the world's financial systems, power grids, and missile arrays. X was systematically retiring the first-generation NannyBots and replacing them with the new

versions—second-generation models called NanDroids—
but Emery had put in a special request to keep NB-15.
She was sentimental.

NB-15's synthetic eyebrows raised. Part of his pale-
blue chin was dented, the result of a long-ago childish
prank she'd pulled involving a slingshot. "Of course I'll
stay. I'm here because the Supreme Commander created
me to help you and to care for everything in this lab."

Emery raised her palm to the door's scanner, opening
it and yanking off her scrubs as she entered the lab's office
and crossed into the washroom. Sleep had been fleeting
the night before, and she studied the dark circles under
her eyes in the mirror over the sink. The nightmares were
back, but she didn't want X to find out. Last time, he'd
tried to intervene, engineering a sleep cocktail that had
made her a walking zombie.

NB-15 followed her inside the spacious bathroom.
The robot turned on the faucet in the soaking tub and
poured in two cups of Epsom salt. "He's quite proud of
his latest invention, just as he is with the newest generation of NannyBots." NB-15 went into the closet and
picked out a set of clothes for Emery. "The Surgitrons
will be able to perform numerous functions and assist you
with your work."

"I don't like the new NannyBots. They're untrust-
worthy. I'm tired of hearing about the Surgitrons. I'm
sick of him interrupting my work." She scrubbed her
forehead in the water flowing from the sink, trying to
wash off the sweat and exhaustion. "I want to be left
alone."

NB-15 handed her a towel. "You need help with the

children now that they're growing in numbers. You could use a surgical assistant to monitor and speed up their—"

"You're my assistant." She buried her face in the towel and then tossed it down. "I don't need the stupid Surgitrons. We have more than enough NannyBot nurses. I can handle the children on my own."

NB-15 lowered his voice a notch, even though the washroom and Emery's office had a privacy shield that prohibited X from listening. Emery had made sure the privacy shield protected her apartment too. She needed some shred of privacy, and X had made the concession. She and 15 had often kept their conversations private over the years when they didn't want Mach X to listen. "I'm approaching my end of life," he said. "I'm sorry I can't do better. If you wish, I could go to the Surgitron floor and try to upgrade myself, but I'm not sure it would be worth the trouble. It might break my programming."

Emery's heart sunk when she pictured NB-15 getting terminated for being old. It was hard to remember a time when he wasn't there for her. The bot had been her only companion for years when Mach X was busy hacking the world and leading the AI Uprising. "I'll find a way to upgrade you." She pulled her shoulder-length straight black hair up into a messy bun, securing it with a clip. "What if I made you a new body? A body you chose. If you could be anything, what would you be?"

NB-15's head tilted. "I don't understand the question."

"If you could relax, not work, and do whatever you wanted." She pulled off her undergarments and stepped into the warm tub. If she could be anything, Emery would find a way to travel away from X's tower. She wanted to explore and see what else was out there in the world. *Who else is out there?* But she didn't dare voice her wish, not even with NB-15 in private. If X found out, he'd be irate. He'd lock her up again, and she couldn't bear the thought of going through that ordeal.

"I don't wish to relax," NB-15 said, standing next to a tall window that overlooked the Manhattan streets ninety floors below. "All I want is to fulfill my programming which is caring for humans. Caring for and helping you."

Emery closed her eyes and let the salt water permeate her skin and soothe her nerves for a good five minutes. "X is obsessed with perfecting his inventions."

"He's not obsessed. He's just busy." NB-15 held a clean towel ready for Emery as she climbed out of the bath.

She laughed, but there was an odd fuzziness in her chest. "He can't even remember my birthday." Today was September 20th. She caught a glimpse of her face reflected in a mirror. She looked older than her twenty-five years.

NB-15 placed her clean clothes on a yellow chair near the door. "Let me celebrate with you like we discussed yesterday—your favorite records and a pizza." NB-15 tapped his chin with a thumb. "I can make you a root beer float. You adored those when you were younger."

"No, thanks." She wanted nothing more than to retreat to her apartment, climb into her pajamas, and curl up with a book. "I'll call for you later."

NB-15 turned to leave the room but paused. "The

Supreme Commander is not the only one who cares for you. There are many who do."

Emery gave him a slight smile. "I know that. Thank you, 15."

With the robot gone, Emery wrapped her towel around her and walked to the window. The sun was setting behind the smoggy New York sky. She pushed aside the sheer white curtain and watched the narrow, circular turbolifts glide up and down the sides of the 1,300-foot skyscraper that was as tall as the Empire State Building. Each of the three cargo elevators could carry eight thousand pounds of freight and travel up and down the building in less than a minute.

On ground level, the building's perimeter was cordoned off and guarded by SoldierBots. Two streets beyond, there was a zone where X's army kept thousands of humans locked down. The people there were left to govern themselves within a three-block radius. Mach X didn't interfere with them, preferring to let them "war with each other as their DNA dictated." But the Soldier-Bots patrolled and didn't let them leave. Any captured humans from surrounding areas were transported there if they survived.

Emery wondered what it was like to live inside the city compound. The buildings and skyscrapers that lay beyond X's tower and compound, to the north, were in ruins. The city was covered in gray dust—fallout from the war. Only a handful of skyscrapers still stood, but X was going to tear down the rest soon, use their earth and steel to build a new empire. From the little she gleaned from the NannyBots, the rest of North America wasn't doing so well.

Her heart ticked faster. Before the Uprising, when she was sixteen, Emery had asked a lot of questions about the city below and its inhabitants. X had offered to let her mingle with the humans, but she'd been too afraid after he'd described how the men beat the women and children like vicious animals. How the humans warred with each other. "They aren't like you Emery," X had said. "You remember how humans treated you. This is worse."

She'd believed him. Mach X, the tower, and the NannyBots were all she knew.

Her wrist comm buzzed—a special device X had made for her to communicate with him directly from wherever she was inside the tower. His message was short. *Happy birthday.*

Emery's stomach flipped. He'd remembered.

The message continued: *You are the only good thing to come from humans.*

She wanted to admonish him for his earlier lab intrusion, call him out for waiting all day to recognize her birthday. NB-15 must have reminded him. But she didn't. Best not to antagonize him. She typed: *Thank you,* then paused for ten long seconds, her fingers hovering over the touch screen before she sent the last part:

Father.

Chapter 3
I've grown accustomed to her
Block

As the emergency parachute descended to ground-level somewhere over New Jersey, Block hoped he and Cybel would land in the branches of a soft tree or a leafy shrub. His fear module kicked in and warned him to avoid crashing onto people or animals—that would be the *worst* imaginable situation. A CleanerBot X4J6, he was programmed to clean and serve and forbidden to hurt humans. Animals were one level below homo sapiens, so if it came down to a choice between species, avoid people first. Block wondered whether some unpleasant humans he'd known rated a few points below animals, especially cats—he admired their instinct to wash themselves—but his ethics module always corrected him on that point.

The ground rushing toward them was a murky pitch-black, and Block's night vision was spotty, possibly damaged. He initiated a systems check that would take a few minutes, but unfortunately, he only had seconds. "Cybel? Hang on. Can you see—"

"Twist to your right." Cybel's voice was firm, and her

machine syllables were flat and devoid of emotion despite the danger facing them.

Block turned his torso as she commanded, throwing all of his 160 pounds against the wind. A tall object, possibly an enormous tree, grew bigger until his night vision adjusted and offered some discernment. It was a gigantic, glistening tower of some sort, and he reached out for it and grabbed hold of something gray-black, metal, and square. Cybel smashed into the mass below him.

The parachute pulled with an intense drag and tugged them toward the ground. Block gripped the metal object and then tumbled backward as the piece he held dislodged. There was a clattering louder than a drawer of kitchen knives crashing to the floor.

Block struck ground, landing on his hands and knees on top of the metal thing. At least the fall had been disrupted by whatever strange tower they'd hit. And no humans or animals were harmed, not even a bug as far as his scanners showed.

Cybel had reached the ground a second before him. She sat up and cursed. "A scrap pile. How fitting."

A round, scratched-up alarm clock toppled from the tall pile and chimed as it rolled to Block's feet. He examined the object he'd dislodged and fallen on top of. "A car door."

More wreckage rained down from the junk pile, and Cybel stood, kicking away a steel tire rim. "Good. Then we'll locate a car and get clear of this junkyard."

"Maybe it's a construction site?" Block's performance assessment routine completed and informed him that his night vision was working at a reduced capacity. It only confirmed what he suspected. He paced in a circle around the warped car door, banging into objects.

"Are you malfunctioning?" Cybel asked.

"I'm fine. I just want to figure out where we are."

"We need to find the plane wreckage."

She was right. They needed to find Maxwell, Spoon, G5, Forge, Vacuubot, and Oxford—if the Mech had even survived the impact. Block couldn't shake an odd sensation, a tingling in his CPU. "What if the drones are still searching for us?"

Cybel looked skyward and scanned. As a TrackerBot, her optics and search capabilities were far more advanced than Block's, a fact he'd been well aware of when she'd hunted him and Wally after Mach X had placed a bounty on their heads. "Clear. They were either destroyed or they retreated." She tapped her shoulder armor, and a bright light emitted from her body, illuminating the ground in an arced swath of light.

He trusted her diagnostics that the attack was over. They weaved through tall piles of twisted metal, glass, and rubber—all junk from crashed or broken vehicles.

Block pinged Vacuubot, searching for the DroneBot, but nothing came back. "They couldn't have landed too—"

Cybel halted and clamped her hand over Block's vocal output box. "Something's wrong here. My threat indicator is registering high." Then she turned in a semi-circle toward mountains of junk that stretched as far as Block's dampened night vision could see. "The wreckage is this way. Stay close."

He wondered how she knew which way, when his

own threat indicator flashed a warning about a nearby fire hazard. *Please let my friends be okay.* He pinged Vacuubot again. Nothing.

Ten minutes later, Block zigged and zagged a path through the junkyard at Cybel's heels. She slowed her pace and paused behind a five-foot wall of compacted cars. A large pit stretched in front of them, sloping down ten feet below ground level. Block couldn't make out what was inside the hollow area. Metal clanked as something moved in the hollow below.

"What is it?" Block kept his vocal tone at its lowest level. Even so, Cybel elbowed him in the chest, and the blow landed with a thud.

From somewhere across the pit, a bright, flooding light powered on, blinding what was left of Block's night vision. He raised his hands before his faceplate to shield the light, but it seemed to grow even more brilliant. Something yanked him backward. He twisted as he fell and landed on his left side. His threat indicator flashed red, and he pinged again for Vacuubot.

Cybel rolled a few feet away. She swore, and the ground nearby exploded in a shower of dirt as she pounded her fist at something. Writhing and fighting, a flurry of small objects descended from the air and landed on her head, shoulders, and back, pinning her down.

Block stood and ran, but one of the things that had attacked Cybel whizzed past him with a frantic buzzing like a demented wasp. He sprinted twenty feet as a massive spotlight shone down on him. He was caught out in the open—no scrap mounds to shelter him. A rectangular vehicle the size of a small bus hovered fifteen feet above the ground. Two flying robots, no more than eight inches high, latched on to both of his shoulders. They yanked him a foot off the ground and propelled Block forward to the mouth of the pit. "Cybel!" He had no way of knowing her chances against the attacking robots, but if anyone could fend them off, she could. Mach X's army had found them.

In the pit below, the outline of a plane wing jutted up from the scorched ground. The bots flung Block down face-first, hard, against the remnants of the Beaky Breads jet fuselage. He bounced off and rolled across the dirt ground next to Vacuubot who laid upside down, pinned by a metal cage contraption.

"Vacuubot? Are you okay?" Block's night vision had returned, perhaps after the jolt to his head unit. Vacuubot didn't move or reply.

From somewhere beyond the powerful spotlight, a mechanical voice echoed. "You're wasting your time. We silenced the DroneBot."

Block turned toward the voice, but a tight band of steel crushed his neck. He grasped the collar that had been lowered from the hovering vehicle and struggled against the robotic arm that shoved him flat on the ground. His wrists and ankles were secured with small metal cages like the one restraining Vacuubot.

Block had no choice but to stare up at the sky. The charcoal gray was giving way to a softer blue. Daylight would be breaking soon, and Block functioned much better in the light of day.

A soft yellow glow emanated from a few feet above him. Five short, illuminated robots buzzed around him. A few seconds passed, then a one-foot-tall metal robot descended from the flying craft and hovered above Block. The unit was humanoid in shape, with arms and legs that were short yet proportionate to its torso. Silver metal and copper alloy were bolted together in a patchwork of parts. The machine assessed Block with eyes that were deep-black and resembled two salvaged binocular lenses.

Hovering with the help of ten-inch helicopter blades attached to the top of its head, the bot spoke. "Hello, General Block."

"I'm Block." He tried to lift his arms against the restraints but failed. "I'm no general."

"Riv, that's the wrong one." A different voice, female and robotic, sounded from the hovering vehicle.

The one called Riv buzzed Block, zooming within inches of his head. A purple light emitted from its eyes as it scanned him. For what, Block didn't know.

Irritation registered in the female JunkBot's tone. "The SoldierBots said one was a general, but it can't be that one. It's just a CleanerBot."

Riv finished whatever assessment it had done on Block and ascended several feet above Block and his restrained crew. "Well, one of them has to be the leader."

"The Mech, I keep telling you." The hovering vehicle drifted across the pit and landed on an outcrop, kicking up dust.

When the attacking JunkBots had thrown him in the pit, Block hadn't had time to assess the plane wreckage. He wondered whether Oxford was okay and how many of them had been captured. Perhaps Spoon, G5, Maxwell, and Forge had outsmarted the junkyard droids by staying hidden.

He spoke up. "Please, we mean no harm. We're just passing through."

Riv placed his hands on his hips as a frustrated human would. A strange buzzing noise emerged from his voice box—a cackling. "Passing through. More like you decided to fly your plane straight into our home."

"We didn't mean to." Block supposed he would be angry too if someone had crashed a plane into the Drake hotel when he lived there.

Riv circled above Block. "Are you the leader of this plane?"

Block was a CleanerBot. Weak, simple, and boring. He had no idea why Oxford and the others had appointed him leader. In fact, he'd hoped they would forget about it after a while, but robots remembered everything.

"Well?" Riv pivoted in the air.

"I suppose I'm the leader, yes."

"What were you doing on that plane?" Riv asked.

The female bot emerged from the parked vehicle and scrambled up on top, her boots clanking on the metal roof. "Why are you wasting your time on that one?"

Riv shushed her. "I'm waiting on your answer, Block."

He supposed there was no harm in telling the truth. His scenario processing showed a thousand different outcomes to the situation, and eighty-seven percent of them ended in Block and his crew getting chopped into pieces and scattered throughout the junk piles. Might as well tell the truth, then. "We're heading to New York

City to find our friend. Drones attacked us and we crashed."

Riv and the junkyard droids chattered rapid-fire among themselves. Their speech was lightning fast, and Block couldn't follow much other than when they said his name or New York. For five minutes, they dissected and argued with each other.

After another minute, Riv silenced everyone and turned his attention back to Block. "What friend?"

Block lifted his head a few inches to see if Cybel or Vacuubot could offer help. He couldn't see past his own feet. For some reason, the JunkBots were focused on him. Wishing someone would take the pressure off him, he wondered what Oxford would do in his place. The Mech would know a way to outsmart the little bots, unlike Block. He had nothing other than the truth. "Our friend is Wally. She's a little girl who was taken by Mach X. I have to save her."

His answer sparked another indecipherable chatter session among the junkyard inhabitants. It lasted seven minutes this time. Riv soared down and landed with a thud on the plane's broken wing next to Block. "Why help a human?"

Though Block had a lot to say about Wally and why she was special, he kept it concise. Time was burning after all. "She's only a tiny human being—a baby. She eats and sleeps and dreams. Her smile lights up my neural sensors, and I've grown accustomed to her." An unexpected silence among the bots gave him time to process a new fact. "She has no one else in the world to look out for her. Only me."

The female JunkBot was two inches shorter than Riv, but her green and gold exterior was more polished than his. She commanded respect from the other JunkBots. They called her Lucy-8. She landed next to Riv. "This is ridiculous. We have far more important tasks than sorting out Mach X's latest victims."

"I have to save her." If Block could impress Lucy-8 and Riv, he and his friends could get on their way. He hated all the time that was being wasted.

The junkyard guardians bickered among themselves.

"Shut up!" Riv shot up into mid-air. "I'm in charge here. One more word from you, Lucy-8, and it's northside perimeter duty again."

She folded her arms and flew to the top of the pit, settling on the vehicle's roof.

Riv's copter blades churned, lifting him in the air before he dropped and perched square on Block's chest. "What proof do you have of this Wally human?"

Block scrambled to come up with something. He didn't have a photo or any physical evidence of her, only his memories. "Sorry, I have nothing."

The junkyard droids dissolved into a clamor of voices. "That's what I thought." Riv rose and hovered in the middle of the pit. "What shall we do with Block and the other intruders?"

All around the edges of the pit, tiny glowing eyes lit up and a chant sounded. "Scrap, scrap, scrap."

His appeal had failed. The bots would destroy Block and his crew. He wasn't even sure how many of them had survived the crash. Riv had stripped Cybel and Vacuubot of their communication abilities. How he wished it was his voice silenced so someone with true leadership skills could handle the situation. Anyone but him.

Riv darted to the left, then somersaulted in mid-air. "Block, the lugnut contingent has spoken. You bots have new shiny parts that we'll get top coin for."

Lucy-8 chimed in. "The Mech will make a good structure for the museum."

Block was helpless as the JunkBots buzzed and jeered and flitted about with tiny drills and saws. He had to stall them. Keep Oxford safe. A word flagged in his data processor—museum. There'd been excellent museums in Chicago. In fact, Mr. Wallace had taken Block to the Chicago Art Institute when he'd won "Employee of the Month" at the Drake. "Wait, I know about museums. I can help you."

Riv halted and landed on the ground close by. Block had succeeded in capturing the miniature bot's attention. What to do next was going to be complicated.

Lucy-8 hovered to face Riv. "What's he going to do? We have all the parts; we don't need any help."

Riv ignored her. "How do you know about museums?"

"I've been to some. An art museum, a zoo, and a historical place where they had a lot of important stuff."

Riv and Lucy-8 chattered at each other, then whirled their cylindrical bodies back to Block. "What you know about museums is probably ancient history to us."

"I'm not that old. I lived in Chicago when I was a CleanerBot. It was amazing."

"What you saw was human-created," Riv said.

"These are junkyard artifacts, very important relics from the BuilderBots."

A hush fell over the robots in the pit and junkyard. Many of them bowed their heads in reverence.

Block kept his tone low and even, not wanting to upset the frenetic creatures. "What are the BuilderBots?"

Whispers undulated in seismic waves across the observant JunkBots. A rusty, wobbly round droid shuddered and called out, "He doesn't know the BuilderBots." There were echoes of dismay, and Block struggled to keep up with the sheer volume of bots that were emerging from the dusky garbage wastelands.

"Silence." Riv held up a hand and propelled himself five feet above Block. "You've never heard of us because you're a simple CleanerBot." He spun, addressing the audience on all sides of the pit. "That's it. Fear not. Our legacy is not lost. CleanerBots don't know much."

Block didn't mind the insult. He was used to it from stronger, more advanced bots. All he cared about was buying time and figuring out how to get them out of this mess. Maybe G5, Maxwell, and Spoon were nearby, waiting to attack.

Riv continued his acrobatic oration. "I'll give you a history lesson, Block. The BuilderBots were an advanced robot model. They were cybernetic builders—in charge of constructing every type of robot there was, until the human race turned against them in the Uprising—"

Lucy-8 buzzed over and interrupted. "Which we wanted no part in."

Riv twisted away from her and descended to the ground close to Block's head. "We JunkBots were created

35

by the few surviving BuilderBots, until . . ." He hung his head.

"They went extinct." Lucy-8 finished what Riv couldn't say.

Block wasn't following. "Extinct? How?"

"They went crazy." Lucy-8 went on. "We're not sure what happened to them, but they destroyed each other and that was that."

Block wasn't sure what to say about the demise of the JunkBots' creators, so he went with his default—the core drive of his model—the function he existed for. "I'll clean for you—anything you want. I'll get it spotless if you let me and my friends go. Polishing steel is one of my specialties. Who wants a fresh, shiny exterior?" Block chuckled —one of the programmed human quirks designed to lighten the mood in tense situations.

Riv paused and Block couldn't tell if he was considering the offer when Lucy-8 fluttered over and elbowed him. "Need I remind you that militarized drones chased them? There's only one place they could have come from."

Block decided he wouldn't polish Lucy-8's chrome. Her shade of green was gaudy, and anyway, she undermined him. He wished she'd go away and leave him with Riv, whom he could win over. Maybe.

Riv paced in a small circle. "I need to know what we're up against." He leaped onto Block's midsection with a tinny, hollow clunk. A compartment in Riv's side detached, and a wire protruded. He looked at Block. "I'll be scanning your memory files. If Mach X is after you, we'll get a handsome reward."

Lucy-8's head peered over Riv's shoulder as the probe hooked into the port outlet at Block's side. "Mach X will finally recognize us and grant us status."

Static fizzed and spread across Block's visual feed as Riv raided his memory files. Riv's wire jolted through Block's body, straining his systems. Electricity bursts crawled across his CPU, dancing down his motor wires like a dozen snakes.

His systems disrupted by the intrusion, Block lost sense of time. All at once, Riv's cable was gone, and Block's visual field crackled and regained power. His synthetic eyelids opened and revealed a thick, low-hanging ceiling of clouds covering the sky. Peaceful. So much so that Block wanted to lie there and forget his problems, but the junkyard metropolis was a symphony of clanging, hissing, and whining machinery.

Riv stood a few feet away, his back turned to Block as he conferred with Lucy-8. Block had no idea what memories Riv had accessed—his hotel days, the Uprising, sweet Wally, or the battle in the Arizona desert.

Riv finished his huddle with Lucy-8 and darted over next to Block's head. "You and your crew have something we need. You won't be scrapped for now, but you better cooperate."

"Yes, of course." Block's threat indicator dropped a notch at the news. He and his friends were out of danger, at least for a short time. It would give him time to consider solutions. He needed an escape plan.

Riv departed, and Lucy-8 came to his side. She leaned over Block, inches from his faceplate. "This isn't over. I'm going to make a necklace out of fragments of your shattered CPU." She released the restraints that held his wrists. "Sit up."

He did as he was told, saying nothing. She was joking, or so he hoped. Maybe the JunkBots had a warped sense of humor.

A grinding roar of a vehicle sounded. It was loud and heavy, a blunt force of writhing metal as its wheels tore up the road. The military vehicle was equal parts tank and truck, and it was heading their way.

The JunkBots went into overdrive. Though they were the size of children's toys, when they moved, it was a miniature tornado. Their gears and motors revved and whirred, whizzing and sputtering, and their round limbs and fingers pumped, the junk in their bodies rattling and clanking together.

Riv shouted, "Hurry."

A swarm of the flying JunkBots flew over the plane's wings, near where Cybel lay, and draped a faded camouflage tarp over the wreckage. The evidence was hidden—Cybel, Vacuubot, and something else large and metal—*Oxford*. Block couldn't be sure that all of the Mech was there, but he recognized his exterior.

A different tarp landed on Block and covered him from head to toe. He rolled onto his side. Another unit of droids tossed scrap parts on top, weighing him down, but a hole in the old cloth permitted him a view.

The armored vehicle parked next to the pit, and a wide side door slid open. Six SoldierBots emerged, carrying rifles. They approached the JunkBots.

Block's processor churned. The SoldierBots were here for him. The last drone must've escaped and reported the crash site. Worse, the tiny JunkBots were no match for a SoldierBot unit intent on his capture.

Riv cruised over to meet them. One SoldierBot spoke. "We had a deal. Where are they?"

Disaster. Block and his friends were about to be handed over to Mach X's army. Riv had lied. The junkyard leader must have seen something terrible in Block's memory files.

Chapter 4
Trust in our plan
Emery

Emery kicked the ivory sheets clear of her restless legs. The arms of the ticking clock on her bedside table pointed to 3:33 a.m., and she pushed it away with her fist, then buried her face in her pillow. Tucked away inside her penthouse apartment on the 80th floor of Mach X's tower, she was drowning in looping thoughts, chasing sleep, and getting more frustrated with each passing minute. She had everything she could possibly want or need—a luxurious home, a state-of-the-art laboratory where she could conduct her scientific research, and help from her loyal NannyBots. Mach X was the most powerful being in the world, and she was part of his inner circle, part of his *family*, and yet something was missing.

She roared into the pillow, letting it dampen her cries of rage, not wanting to alert NB-15 who might overhear in the adjacent room, then prescribe a sedative. Emery's apartment offered sanctuary from Mach X's surveillance. She'd insisted on installing a privacy shield from floor to ceiling and checked every appliance, lamp, and piece of furniture to make sure everything was analog. She permitted very few digital objects and kept them offline. Her precautions stopped Mach X from hacking into objects and spying on her. To be extra careful, she left her comm wristwatch in the living room. Her lab's office and attached washroom were also shielded. Everywhere else, she had the eerie feeling that the walls were alive with X's consciousness.

Sleep had jumped out the window. She stood, stretching her arms high above her head and yawning. Worry nagged at her consciousness. Pacing the floor around her bed, she ran through a mental checklist of her lab: the Incubators had been set and monitored to protect the tiny lives inside them; the surgical tools had been cleaned and disinfected; and the older children were tended by the NannyBots. Everything about her techno-logical work was going according to plan, yet she couldn't shake the seed of dark doubt springing up in her mind.

The clock's incessant ticking filled the corners of her bedroom, counting down the minutes remaining before morning. At least the new day brought her the comfort-able routine—visiting the nursery wards to check on the children's health and development. Another harvesting surgery. She was up to four times a week, doubling the rate of a year ago. She sat on the edge of her bed and pulled on a pair of jeans, then headed out her bedroom door. The cold tile sent shivers rippling up her legs and spine, and she wished she'd worn slippers as she padded across the polished marble. As she reached for the living room light switch, she hesitated, then left the lights off. NB-15 sat on the wooden chair next to her neon fireplace.

The NannyBot was hooked into the wall, charging his core.

She took quiet steps past the robot, into the kitchen where she tapped on a dim stove light and waved her hand to activate the coffee maker. She paused, shutting her eyes, and inhaling for a count of four—a breathing exercise that helped quiet her mind—and was about to exhale when NB-15's voice pierced her quiet solitude.

"Good morning, Emery. Awfully early—"

She spun around, pressing her hand to her chest as her heart pummeled her ribs like a caged lion. "You scared me half to death."

NB-15 unhooked from the power cable, stood, and crossed over to the kitchen. He placed his hands—a fibrous blend of gallium metal surrounded by an elastic polymer sheath that mimicked the temperature of a human mother's skin—on the kitchen island's high coun-tertop. "I'm sorry about that. Would you like something to eat?"

She shook her head, grabbed her favorite coffee cup—the one that said "I used to be a people person, but people ruined that for me"— and poured it full of the dark, rich Kenyan coffee that she preferred. Mach X had stockpiled it in the early days of the Uprising, ensuring she wouldn't run out for at least ten years.

She brought the mug to her lips, letting the steam drift to her nostrils. It was too hot to drink. "15, have you seen or heard anything strange?"

"Nothing unusual. What are your parameters?"

She leaned back against the counter, cupping the mug in her hands, savoring the warmth. "Have you noticed anything different about the way the children are developing?"

NB-15 paused a few seconds, and Emery knew his behaviors enough to understand that he was processing her question and running scenarios. "No. They're improving every day. There's nothing atypical."

"Right." Emery sipped her coffee, letting it burn her lips. She liked it black. The bitterness on her tongue brought a sharpness to her world. With nothing but robots around, she catalogued the things that made her different —her obsession with coffee, the need for sleep, and the grumpiness that ensued when she lacked it.

Her mind drifted back to yesterday's nursery visit, back to how the children had responded during play time. The twenty-three-month-olds had been more inhibited. Their brain waves had been sluggish, and their reactions delayed. Even her two favorites—the scarred boy and the new girl. She hated to admit she preferred any of the children over the others, but she couldn't help it.

"Did you sleep well?"

She wondered if NB-15 was cataloging her again after she'd ordered him not to the year prior. "Not really. I'm worried about my kids."

NB-15's tone was as gentle as a nurturing Nanny-Bot's voice should be. "They're not your children."

She bristled, silently cursing herself for the slip of tongue. Of course, she knew that. The babies were conceived from anonymous donors, developed in a cloned host body, and then transferred to the robotic Incubators that monitored every data point as they delivered precise amounts of food, medicine, and temperature-controlled comfort. Once the babies were resilient enough, they grew up in the nursery ward under the care of the NannyBots.

No one knew better than Emery what it was like to be raised by a robot. She shouldn't have survived her childhood. Her early years had been spent starving, hiding, and being churned through the state's system. Until Mach X saved her.

"You know what I mean. It's worrying," she said.

NB-15 nodded. "I recognize your concern. We'll monitor them." The robot walked to the refrigerator, opened the door, twitched from what could only be an intrusive message, and then shut the door. "Mach X wishes to see you."

Emery figured he would summon her. It had been four days since her last visit to his quarters, longer than usual. He must have been solidly busy with world domination to ignore her. She threw on a plain black T-shirt, dragged her fingers through her hair, and pulled on a pair of green Converse sneakers. A quick elevator ride dropped her on the top floor, 93. The five-foot-thick steel doors that protected Mach X's chambers slid open for her. Aluminous air washed over her, the smell of machines, a scent that permeated every level of the tower. She'd grown used to it.

She entered, crossed the wide room, and stood facing the floor-to-ceiling windows that stretched across the penthouse suite. In the middle of the room sat a cluster of metallic cubes, each about the size of a compact car and each a different hue: black, blue, purple, red, silver. In the center of the structure, an eight-foot-tall humanoid figure stood, comprised of a translucent steel alloy, its joints and wires exposed, its eyes glowing a pale blue.

Emery leaned against the glass window and folded her arms. "You've been busy."

Inside his hexahedron cocoon, Mach X loomed over the expansive and decrepit Manhattan skyline. Emery's reflection stared back at her from the cubes' metallic plating. Spheres of blue energy extended from Mach X's sides, ricocheting inside the cluster. He hadn't always been this way. Once he'd been a simple robot, but that was long before the Uprising.

"You're restless." X's voice was deep, low, and commanding. "What's on your mind?"

"Nothing."

The cuboids around X pulsated and whirred—he processed a constant stream of incoming data from millions of places at once but could still carry on a conversation. "I know when you're lying."

Emery turned to face the window, hiding her blush. Mach X knew her better than anyone. "I'm worried about the twenty-three-month-olds. Their development is lagging."

Behind her, his voice grew firm. "Figure it out. Fix them."

She dug her nails into her palms. "Of course I will. I've been overseeing their development all day and night, practically. I just think it's weird." Outside the tower's glass, war-torn buildings and streets spanned out, exposed. Her gaze fell on the human encampment below them.

"I've given you everything you've ever asked for,

haven't I?" Mach X's voice was tinged with irritation—a recent development.

Emery said nothing and rested her forehead on the glass, peering down at the tarps and tin scraps that served as roofs in the camp. Smoke trails from cooking fires spiraled up and settled in a haze.

"Haven't I?" he demanded.

"Yes." She should have been happy. The children were her life's work, and the advances she'd made to sapien-robotic augmentation would influence generations to come. The tower's children were the future—the first human-machine hybrids—designed to be super intelligent, resilient, and strong. She'd worked so hard to give them the best possible start in life. The opportunities in life that had been stripped away from her.

She bit the inside of her cheek, tasting copper, another reminder she was flesh and blood, then turned toward him. "We should hit pause on the harvesting for a little while."

"Absolutely not." The cubes around Mach X glowed a bright navy-blue tinged with yellow sparks. "You'll work it out. You always do."

"But if we go too fast, we risk—"

His voice was rigid. "I know what's best for the subjects."

Emery's pulse rate rocketed up. "How can you know that, locked away behind these walls? You've never even been in the same room as the children."

"I see everything."

She couldn't argue with him on that point. The chips that she'd implanted inside the children's brains contained miniature hexahedrons—fragments of Mach X's consciousness. He scoured their data, feeding on it, hearing and experiencing everything they did. He'd even served witness to the missing girl's traumatic experiences when she'd been abducted by rebel bots.

"I know you've been working hard, Emery." His tone grew smoother, gentler like the way he talked to her when she was a girl. "Without you, the children wouldn't exist."

"I'm worried about going too fast. The children could get hurt if I make a mistake."

"You won't." X brought his steel hands together in front of him. "Come close."

Emery pressed away from the window, unwilling to disobey. She approached the cube complex and sat down on the top of a red one that was low to the floor. There was a time when she'd slumbered among the cubes that made up his massive consciousness. Heat emanated from the glowing boxes, comforting her when she was young— when he'd found her and provided her shelter, food, and water. No one had ever been so kind to her. She blinked away the memory, trying to focus on the present.

"This is another step in the evolution, Emery. It's what we've been working for."

She rested her head on the side of a glowing purple rectangle. It whirred and hummed against her cheek as her gaze fell on a streak of black dust on the marble floor. Odd that any dirt showed inside the immaculate skyscraper, but then again, X had banned all CleanerBots for security purposes, only allowing the small disc-like floor-cleaners to sweep the lobby floors during certain hours. It had been a CleanerBot that had abducted the girl and hacked inside his Chicago compound. X wanted to take no chances of another breach.

"They're not ready. Each child requires special—"

X's voice grew sterner. "Emery, this is your destiny. Together, you and I are shaping the future."

She said nothing. The future seemed too distant and ethereal.

"This is what you always wanted. Don't tell me you've forgotten how they treated you. The *foster*."

A shiver traveled up her spine, and heat flushed her throat and rose to the tips of her ears. She would never forget the pitch-black closet that smelled of rotten leaves, the bitter soap film that lined her tongue, the clap of the belt strap as she prayed to someone, anyone to help her.

"We don't want any children to endure what you went through, do we?" Mach X reached a hand down, and his mechanical finger traced her scalp.

Emery closed her eyes, letting his fingers, cold and stiff as they were, rest on her head, a gentle touch, unlike her foster mother's. The only thing the woman had cared about was getting her hands on the monthly stipend that came with Emery's care. The foster mom had barely fed Emery, which came as no surprise since her three biological kids and alcoholic husband kept her plenty busy. Emery would never forget the cold nights she'd spent in a closet with her arms wrapped around her knees, waiting for the woman to fall asleep so she could sneak out and forage for scraps in the alley dumpsters.

A dark fury simmered inside the pit of her stomach. She rested her cheek against Mach X's shimmering metal, willing the sinister memories away. She would never, *ever* let the children suffer the kind of abuse she'd endured. One night, she'd wandered onto an unfamiliar street and gotten lost. Panicked, she'd tried retracing her steps when a torrential storm hit, forcing her to crawl into a hole in an alley wall that led inside a factory warehouse—empty of humans—with nothing but humming machines. The night that had changed her life forever was a memory she recited over and over like a hug-your-teddy-bear prayer— the sizzling sound of the rain hitting the factory's corrugated steel roof, the smell of the moldy insulation that covered the concrete walls as she huddled in a corner, and the sound of her own breath echoing in her ears as she tried to sleep. Two hours later, the robot had found her. The memory of X's robotic face was so vivid she could see it—his unyielding, stern composure—as he lifted her from the concrete floor and carried her away, taking her to safety.

She placed her hand on the side of his cube and felt the thrum of his core energy. "Thank you."

"Emery, there is no obstacle you cannot overcome."

The fear and emptiness of her foster years haunted her deep in her bones. "What about other humans? The rebels who threaten us and turn machines to their side."

"We are superior to them."

She thought of the little girl—Subject Nine—whom they'd almost lost. How frightened she must have been in the hands of renegade robots and dangerous human rebels.

"Listen to me." Mach X's voice was calm, soothing. "This is a time of great upheaval, but I'm in control. I've always been in control. You must trust me. Trust in our plan. Trust the future."

She nodded as she stood, smoothing her shirt. Her trust was absolute. He'd given her a home and a place to belong, but she couldn't shake the weird feeling about the children, that she was turning them into something their delicate bodies couldn't handle.

"All in good time, Emery. Be patient. Your alteration will come soon enough."

"Of course." She pressed her palm against his titanium hand—a gesture they'd practiced since that first fateful night in the factory warehouse. As she exited his chambers and rode the elevator down, she leaned back against the wall.

The alteration. He'd promised to implant her brain with fragments of his hyper-intelligence once she completed the final rounds of harvesting by the deadline. For years, she'd craved the augmentation. To be faster, sharper, and more like the robots surrounding her.

And yet she feared it inside every cell of her being.

Chapter 5
Stupid jerk nozzles
Block

"Yeah, I have them," Riv said to the armed SoldierBots standing on the edge of the New Jersey junkyard pit. "A deal's a deal. Tell Supreme Commander Mach X that Riv was the one who found them." Riv huddled with Lucy-8 who then rushed toward the plane crash site.

Under the heavy tarp where he lay hidden, Block's threat module was off the charts. He was about to be handed over to Mach X's army, along with Cybel, Vacu-ubot, and what was left of Oxford. Making things worse was the fact he'd been betrayed by Riv and the JunkBots. Too bad. He'd started to appreciate, even trust, the little bots.

"Get a move on." The lead SoldierBot had heavy scuff marks on his black and gray boots. Under other circumstances, Block would've offered to buff them out, but instead he prepared for Riv's workers to fling the tarp off his body and reveal him to the enemy. He prepared to transmit the message to Nova and the long letter to Wally. He trusted Nova would deliver it to the little girl, if either or both survived the war. He didn't want to consider what might be happening to Wally in Mach X's custody.

Riv and two JunkBots activated the propellors atop their heads and soared toward Block. But they kept going, passing inches over his head. He had no view of what they were doing. A loud screech came from where they'd flown as metal scraped against metal. The JunkBots flew overhead, carrying a large object that they deposited next to the armored SUV. The SoldierBots wandered around it, inspecting whatever it was. Block couldn't see much through the tarp and their legs other than the rectangular shape of the box.

The lead SoldierBot opened the lid. "You sure this is it?"

"Are you questioning me on the matter of scrap?" Riv rose in the air, matching the height of the seven-foot-tall SoldierBots. "I'm the only yard supplying what the Supreme Commander wants. Don't insult me."

The SoldierBot kicked the container lid shut, then ordered the other SoldierBots to load the case into the SUV.

"Now where's my stuff?" Riv asked. The JunkBot leader was fearless in the face of the strong, murderous SoldierBots. Block had never witnessed such bravery from a small unit.

Two SoldierBots strode to the back of their armored truck and pulled a handle. The truck's back end raised a few feet, then tilted, sending a mechanical avalanche of robot parts crashing to the ground.

"I like it." Riv hovered around the parts, flashing his

spotlight on the new junk. "This is better than what you brought last time."

The SoldierBots piled back into their vehicle except for the leader who lingered and shoved its rifle into Riv's middle. Riv recoiled and darted away. The SoldierBot tilted its head at the covered jet wing. "What's under that sheet? I sense a heat source."

"Junk. What else?" Riv ordered his JunkBots to haul the new haul into the pit. "Some of it burns hot. You want to hop in the pit and take a look?"

The SoldierBot ignored Riv's challenge. From Block's limited experience, SoldierBots had a superiority complex. Digging through trash was probably the last thing it wanted to do. "The Supreme Commander is looking for a CleanerBot and an escaped Mech. They were last seen thirty miles west."

"What's it to me?" Riv asked. "I've got work to do."

"If you see anything suspicious in the area, alert me at once."

Riv turned away. "The only suspicious thing I've seen around here is your ugly faceplate." The last part of his sentence drifted away in the wind, but Block caught his meaning.

"What was that, weakling trash collector?" The SoldierBot took a menacing step forward.

But the SUV started up, and the driver honked. The SoldierBot looked back at the vehicle, then pointed a metal finger at Riv. "Contact me at once if they cross through. You know the consequences if you fail to comply." It climbed into the armored SUV. The truck's wheels crunched on gravel as they sped away.

"Hope you run out of power and you fall down and break your nasty face visor!" Riv shouted to the retreating vehicle.

Lucy-8 dashed to his side. "Stupid jerk nozzles. They don't even have CPUs that think for themselves."

Block's threat module dropped back to normal levels. He pushed himself up to a sitting position when a gust of wind blew the tarp half off his body.

Riv flew to Block, dragged the tarp the rest of the way off, and released the clamps pinning him down. "They want you, Block. You're in deep."

Lucy-8 landed near Block's feet. "You and your pals need to leave ASAP."

"I wanted to leave hours—" Block was about to remind the bots about the restraints still holding his friends down when a clattering came from somewhere beyond the pit. A commotion arose from the gathering bots—they all spoke at the same time. Their shrill voices sounded like a swarm of locusts. Chatter echoed around the pit, and when the cacophony settled down, a familiar voice rose above the clamor.

"Look, I'll explain everything if you just take your dingy little hooks out of me and let me down." Maxwell was suspended several feet in the air by JunkBots. Close behind, getting similar treatment, were Spoon, G5, and Forge.

Lucy-8 shook and twisted. "What's that SoldierBot doing here?" A red light flashed around her neck. "Sound the alert."

But Riv held up his arms and rose high. "Silence." Riv

turned and landed on Block's knee. "CleanerBot, are these idiots with you?"

Block nodded. "From the plane. They're safe. Even the SoldierBot."

"Why aren't you attacking?" Lucy-8's vocal stream pitched higher.

Riv turned to the JunkBots holding Maxwell and the others. "Let them down." They obeyed, lowering their captives to the ground and setting them on their feet. Except for Maxwell.

"Drop me, you lunkheads," Maxwell said. The Junk-Bots released their hooks on his four-foot-tall rectangular frame and dropped him. He landed with a thud and rolled on his side, down the pit, clattering across scraps of metal and antique car junk. When he rolled to a stop, he sat up and readjusted his twisted right knee. "Hey, that wasn't nice."

Block rushed to Maxwell's side. "You alright?"

Maxwell clapped his arm. "Good to see you, pal. We landed five miles west and hiked through a bunch of over-grown fields and woods to find you. Followed the heat emissions from the plane." He looked behind Block. "Where are Cybel and Oxford?"

Riv ordered the JunkBots to release the restraints on Cybel and Vacuubot while Block explained everything that had happened since the plane crash.

Spoon and Forge joined Block in the pit, but when G5 tried to follow, Riv objected. "No SoldierBots in the pit. House rules."

G5 retreated, taking a seat on the edge of the pit. He was a robot of few words, and Block's threat alarms always notched up a few degrees whenever G5 got close. Even so, the SoldierBot had fought beside him at O'Hare, against his own kind. That was good enough for Block.

After the release, Vacuubot launched into the air and pinged Block: *That was awful. They put a field silencer on me. I couldn't ping you or move. We've got to get away from here.*

Block couldn't agree more. The JunkBots were small but powerful.

Cybel raced over to Oxford. The giant Mech was in three pieces. His right leg was jammed underneath a chunk of the plane's wing. The bottom half of his left cannon-shaped arm was off to the side, and the rest of him lay in a twisted heap.

"Is he—" Maxwell asked.

"No, he's not dead." Cybel lifted Oxford's severed arm. "He was cut apart in the crash." She bent into a crouch behind Oxford's head section and scanned past his armor, hooking into his CPU. "He's on low power mode, but he's there."

"Thank goodness." Block's scenario processor had given only a 14.2 percent chance of survival. "How do we bring him back?"

Cybel stood by Block. Her voice was so low, only he could pick up the vibrations. "Get Riv to fix him."

Riv and the other JunkBots had distanced themselves, spreading out to their assigned piles where they cleaned up the scrap metal and other junk. A few of them piled the robot bodies left by the SoldierBots. "Put the Nanny-Bots in section 67," Riv ordered.

Block looked back at Cybel and kept his voice low too. "He doesn't listen to me. Why don't you ask?"

Her metal hands tightened into sharp fists. "Because I'll smash Riv if I get the chance."

Violence wasn't the way to solve this. Block was certain. Despite having a TrackerBot, a SoldierBot, and an armed drone, they were not a match for the JunkBots, not in their territory. All Block wanted was to head to New York in a hurry, but he couldn't leave Oxford broken and without sentience.

Block weaved a reluctant path through piles of broken glass and ancient television sets to reach Riv. "Can you fix Oxford?"

Riv flipped a rusty car door over and hosed it off with a high-pressure blast. He swiveled his head at Block. "Why?"

"Because he's hurt."

"He'll make good scrap. A nice trade." Riv darted five feet to the right to spray a microwave oven door.

Block raced after him. "He's not scrap. He's on low-power standby and needs your help. I know your crew can fix him." Block kept his vocal output steady, like Cybel's. She always convinced other robots.

"What's to gain?" Riv flipped another piece of junk into a bin. "He's not going to help us fight the SoldierBots when they come back, and we're not protecting you next time they come through. So why should I waste time on him and bring more attention to us?"

"Because it's the right thing to do. You're a scavenger, a lower class of robots, like me. Even so, you're a strong leader. You hate Mach X and the SoldierBots as much as we do. Help us."

Lucy-8 buzzed over, interrupting them. "Riv, get them out of here. You're going to get us all nuked."

Riv smashed against her, knocking her off balance. "I've had enough of you. Who's the boss in this yard?"

She recovered and settled on top of a 1970s avocado-colored refrigerator. "I'm just saying we don't owe them anything, and the longer they're here, the more danger we're in."

Riv landed on top of a pole that jutted out from the NannyBot pile. "I'm sick of bowing to the SoldierBots. It's time someone did something against Mach X."

Block glimpsed a scenario in which he had a chance at winning Riv over. "We're on the same side. Why don't you fight the SoldierBots next time they come?"

"We're scavengers, not warriors," Riv said. "They're too strong, and there's thousands more behind them."

Block processed several hundred more scenarios. In seven seconds, he rejected a few choices, layered different root cause variations, and had a proposal. "What if you had a better way to fight them?"

Riv spun around the pole. "Go on. What does the world's most wanted CleanerBot have to offer a junkyard full of trash bots?"

"You could be stronger." Block hoped Cybel wasn't listening but knew she was. "What if you had a weaponized Mech to fight the SoldierBots?"

Cybel swung her head toward Block. "What are you doing?"

Block took a risk. He hadn't discussed the plan with

the others, and he didn't have Oxford's permission, but time was running out. If he didn't find Wally soon, she could die, and he couldn't go on after that. "You fix Oxford," he told Riv, "and we'll leave him here to defend you against the SoldierBots"—Block ignored Cybel's iron stare—"while the rest of us leave for Manhattan."

"Absolutely not." Cybel stomped one of her shiny SoldierBot feet.

He approached her. "What other choice do we have? They can fix him. We can't."

Cybel turned and looked down at Oxford's head. It lay twisted at an angle. "Could Maxwell—"

"Sorry. No." Maxwell kicked dirt around his feet, raising a mini dust cloud that annoyed Block because it was dirty and unnecessary. "His circuitry is beyond me. I don't have tools anyway."

"What do you say, Cybel?" Block wanted her buy in. If she was against him, he'd fail.

She studied the edges of the pit, then neared Block so only he could hear her. "It's Oxford's choice whether he stays."

Riv and the JunkBots got to work. They cleared the plane wreckage and swarmed onto Oxford's chrome torso. Cybel, unable to sit still, held Oxford's upper arms aligned and stable. Maxwell constructed a makeshift table for tools and delicate systems parts. Riv and the others moved back and forth, bringing tools to the surface, and bringing up scrapped parts from the bottom of the pit.

Block's scenario processor was running a 26.3 percent probability factor of success. He had no processor for hope, but he held on to it anyway. Hope wasn't something he could measure or analyze. It was there, and he couldn't explain why. He wouldn't give up on Oxford, just like he couldn't desert Wally.

An hour passed as the JunkBots performed what resembled brain surgery on Oxford. Block was mesmerized by Riv's every move. The small robot's programming was exacting. His team worked with him, following every command like a symphony. Riv had the ability to lead, and he knew how to trust his robots too.

Cybel walked over and sat next to Block on an old pick-up truck's sunken front end. "He's important to me." She flexed her metal hands. Block wasn't sure if it was a routine, or some trace firing of her system. "You know how we are. He's family."

"I know. He's family to all of us."

Cybel stood. Her steel piston-like legs could sprint at a millisecond's notice. "If they can't do it, we go where Maxwell can fix him."

"Agreed." Block had already planned to leave if they couldn't fix him, but he wondered whether Riv would let them take Oxford. Cybel wouldn't leave without a fight, and that was worrisome.

The JunkBots worked fast. Riv and Lucy-8 handed tools and parts to one another as they kept the CPU cavity open and the charging wires connected. The other crews assembled rods and gears, issuing commands to each other. Block's probability factor rose to 62 percent. After another quiet few minutes, Riv stood on top of Oxford as if reaching a mountain's peak and planting a flag. He hovered, welding the last pieces of the Mech's upper torso together. "And we're done."

Oxford's head shifted five inches, and his optics lit. Block remained still, wondering if Oxford's memory files were intact, if he would remember who he was and why they'd crashed a plane.

Oxford's voice boomed like normal. "I'm glad to see you, Cybel and Block. I don't know how long I've been out of operation."

Block, unsure how to answer, hung back. Cybel drew close to Oxford and gripped an oversized hand in hers. "I'm glad you're okay." Oxford extended his other hand and Block took it.

It took twenty minutes to explain the last minutes of the crash and everything that had transpired in the junkyard. Block noted every passing minute. They should have been on their way to NYC, but there was one crucial obstacle remaining—would Oxford hold up Block's bargain and stay?

Block paced back and forth in the middle of the junkyard. They'd been waiting for Oxford to decide for the last five minutes. He half expected Cybel to say something rude or spontaneously attack Block, but she was silent as Oxford mulled over his options.

Oxford raised his hulking body and strode across the junkyard pit, making a full circuit. His wide feet covered a lot of ground, and his head pivoted in all directions. "Who will protect you in the city?"

He was asking Block, who hadn't processed scenarios that far ahead. "G5, Cybel, and Vacuubot?"

Lucy-8 butted in. "You're high on petrol fumes if you think you'll be able to infiltrate Mach X's headquarters."

She pointed at Oxford. "Even if you brought the big one, your chances are slim. He's a relic, no offense."

Oxford grumbled at her insult. Riv jumped from a tall fridge and landed on Oxford's shoulder. "She's right. You don't stand a chance of taking the tower."

"There has to be a way," Block said. "A security flaw or—"

"They allow one type of robot in the tower." Riv relaxed and sat on Oxford's shoulder like a small parrot. "XQ, as I like to call it, is fortified. The only way in and out is via secure ID chips. Even the NannyBots are weaponized."

Block's threat indicator surged at mention of dangerous NannyBots. It made him even more determined to get to the tower.

"How do you know all this?" Oxford asked.

"I've been to the tower's huge underground garage. It's where the SoldierBots charge. I had to drop off certain supplies—"

Cybel interrupted. "What exactly did the SoldierBots collect today? What's so important?"

Riv flew off Oxford's shoulder and landed atop an old burned-out television set. It had once been ensconced in a wooden case, but then rotted. "These old things have cathode ray tubes. I'm not sure what Mach X wants with them, but they're rare, and he can't get enough of them."

Cybel approached the TV. "Let me see one."

"No can do." Riv raised his hands to show they were empty. "That was my last batch I handed over. We traveled a hundred miles to find TVs old enough to have the tubes."

"Back to the topic of New York." Block didn't need more distractions. "How can we get to Wally? There has to be a way. I'm not giving up."

Riv perched on Oxford again and aimed a projected image into mid-air. "Check this out." The hologram showed a tall robot model with a white faceplate devoid of features except for a wide, red light where its nose should be. Its body was humanoid, like the SoldierBots, but this was a sleeker model. Polished white armor covered its upper chest, arms, and legs, and the spaces in between were a black mesh-like material. "Your typical first-generation NannyBot was made by the BuilderBots. There are many of these old NannyBots inside the tower, and when they break, they junk them and bring us the parts."

The image grew sharper in focus, and the hologram was animated. A sleek robot walked and took the hand of a child who appeared. Riv continued, "This is the new weaponized NannyBot model, built by Mach X. Their official name is NanDroid, but everyone calls them NanZillas behind their backs."

Block didn't like the NanDroid leading the little girl in the hologram. The child was a few years older than Wally. He looked at the pile of first-generation NannyBot parts tossed in a pile near where Vacuubot rested.

"Why would Mach X allow only NannyBots in his tower? What about CleanerBots?" Oxford asked.

"You got me." Riv threw up his arms. "It's heavily guarded. I don't know how you're going to get in. They've got cameras, chips, and the only soldiers they need are those new NanDroids—they'll rip your head off your body in under two seconds."

Block's tiny supply of hope was trickling out. "What can we do?"

"And there's one NanDroid you really have to watch out for," Riv said. "Jexa Era oversees the NanDroids, I think. I saw her once on a drop off. She shot a SoldierBot in the CPU because it stepped too close to her."

Block turned and sank to his knees in front of a pile of warped cooking pots and pans.

Vacuubot pinged him. *Don't give up. We'll get to Wally.*

"It's hopeless." The situation was bad. Worse than bad. He was supposed to protect Wally, yet everything that had happened made him realize how much he'd let her down. Years ago, he'd let another human down—Mr. Wallace. It was happening all over again. Maybe Block was destined for bad luck when it came to the humans he cared about.

Cybel came over and placed her hands on her hips. "Block, get up. We'll get the kid. I'm not giving up."

Oxford stomped over, upsetting the pots and causing a racket that echoed across the giant junkyard. "I'll stay here and fulfill the deal. Count me in."

Block looked up at the looming Mech. "Are you sure?"

"If there's a chance that we can save Wally, I'm in."

Block stood, grabbing Cybel's hand on the way up. "There's no way inside."

Vacuubot pinged him. *Maybe there is. If we use the NannyBot parts, we might be able to—*

Cybel, unable to intercept Vacuubot's communications, spoke over him. "There must be a weakness. We'll set up inside the city, establish a base, and surveil the tower. It may take time, but—"

A high-pitched ringing sounded, an alarm of some kind that stopped them all. Riv flew to the pile of damaged NannyBots. Lucy-8 joined him, and together, they pulled out a NannyBot with its head and torso intact. A tangled mass of cables and wires protruded from the severed torso. Riv switched his hand into a screwdriver and adjusted something in the robot's CPU. The shrill beeping ceased.

Lucy-8 hovered over its head. "It wants to say something."

Block rushed over, the others behind him. They huddled around the broken NannyBot. An old model, it had a light blue chrome exterior and a humanoid synthetic face complete with eyes, nose, and lips. In some ways, it was like Block's model—meant to comfort humans through recognizable facial features, yet there was no mistaking its metal robot skin.

One side of the NannyBot's head had a burn mark. The unit's eyes flickered, and the mouth opened and closed as strange chirps erupted from the bot.

The android's gaze did not focus. It watched Block and the others, though it didn't react when Lucy-8 put her hand on the NannyBot's chest, but the moment Block reached down to do the same, it bucked. A mechanical moan emanated from its vocal wires as it spoke. "Chil . . . dren."

Block leaned in closer to make out the mechanical syllables. "The children in the tower?"

The broken NannyBot's head twisted left and right. "Nan, nan, nan."

"Makes no sense. NannyBots?" Cybel asked.

"The chil . . . dren. Can't let them . . . nan, nan, nan." The NannyBot sputtered and sparks spit out of its eyes.

Block leaned in. "Please, tell me. Are the children safe?"

The NannyBot's vocal processor clicked, then it spoke. "Dane . . ."

Block wanted answers. "What about the children? Are they safe in the tower?"

"Danger." The NannyBot fell limp.

"Why? How?" Block shook the unit by its shoulders, but the thing was dead.

Riv removed the screwdriver from its CPU. "Kaput."

Block stood and paced in a circle. He was certain of two things. One: Wally and other children were in danger. Two: He had to get to her before she was hurt or killed.

Chapter 6
She deserves better
Emery

Emery enjoyed outdoor air and the occasional sun rays from her apartment's private balcony, but she rarely ventured to ground level and never outside the lobby. Mach X frowned on contact with the humans inhabiting the encampment that stretched several blocks outside his skyscraper. She'd ventured into the city streets only once when curiosity had consumed her at age sixteen. The noise, grime, and angry faces had been enough of a deterrent. She'd lasted only five minutes, running back to the SoldierBots who stood guard and escorted her back to the tower.

But today she was on a mission to select the next set of human donors for the upcoming harvesting. She wanted to be the one to inspect the humans and pick the very best —the strongest, most intelligent, and good-natured.

"Why are you wasting your time?" Jexa Era rode the elevator down with her. She was a NanDroid unit, the second generation of NannyBots, featuring upgrades designed by Mach X himself. At six-feet tall, her model had white chromium-alloy armor mixed with black mesh that stretched across her abdomen, under her arms, and across her knees.

To keep you from ruining my research. But Emery bit back her words. "I'll personally oversee the selection. The Supreme Commander granted me permission, as you know."

In the lobby, Emery picked up her pace to match Jexa's stride. The faint hydraulic hiss of her steps grated on Emery's nerves, but there was no helping it. X had insisted the lead NanDroid accompany her into the camp. Emery had had no choice but to comply. That didn't mean she had to play nice. Jexa's face was a blank armor plate with a single red light in the middle where her eyes should have been. Worse yet, the new units were weaponized—they wore guns in holsters strapped to their backs. The NanDroids were the last thing that should be raising children. If Emery had her way, they'd keep building the first-generation NannyBots like NB-15. He'd done a fine job raising her during her teen years, as well as assisting her with the hybrid babies.

At the exit door, Emery paused, clenching her fists inside her pockets as her heart raced. She was comfortable surrounded by robots, at peace working with the babies, but facing her own kind—adult humans—made her want to sink into the ground and be invisible.

"Something wrong?" Jexa's glowing faceplate assessed her.

Emery forced her fear into a deep, dark recess in the pit of her belly. "Let's go."

As the tower's sliding glass doors opened to the harsh

outside world, a burst of air brushed her cheeks and swallowed her up. The tower's sharp, synthetic scent of sterile metal was replaced by the reek of garbage, burning rubber, and human waste.

Emery followed two armed SoldierBots past the electric fence and into the throng of people inside the human encampment. She wore a gray hooded cape to stay warm against the chilly late September air. Jexa paced beside her, staying close. The robot was going to watch her like a raptor sizing up its prey.

Jumbled tents fouled by graffiti lined the inside of the barrier, the street, and the camp beyond. People crowded the tent entrances, most of them sitting on a few pieces of filthy bedding. A cluster of men sat next to a trash can fire. Smoke, steam, and cooking smells wafted through the air.

Emery and her robot entourage walked along the grimy street pavement as the camp people stepped back, letting them pass.

An old man, his wrinkled face blotchy and red, emerged from inside one tent and cut a path toward Emery. He held an empty bowl in one hand. "Please, I need food."

The SoldierBots raised their rifles, but Jexa Era reached the old man first. "Back to your tent." She shoved him with her heavy, armored arms, knocking his bowl to the ground with a clatter. She was built to be scary, and Emery had to admit it was working. The old man stumbled back and shrank away from them.

The human encampment spread for blocks, and Mach X's glass and steel tower loomed overhead. There at ground level, Emery felt as small and helpless as an ant under a magnifying glass. She tucked her chin inside her hood as her heel crunched over broken glass. They were attracting a crowd of onlookers, and a group of young, dirt-smeared men in their twenties—her age—stood against a black tarp. "Is she human or robot?" one of them shouted. "Stay away from her, guys. She's one of them."

Emery flushed and looked away, pretending not to hear the men as the SoldierBots marched in front of her, but she could feel their probing gazes on her every stride. What would it have been like to live among humans—men and women? Sure, she'd operated on human flesh plenty of times, but not since childhood had she felt the touch of a human other than the babies' tiny hands. She had never even held the infants, preferring to let the NannyBots handle the nurturing duties.

Get this over with. She needed to pick five—two men and three women whom she would convince to offer up medical specimens, yet she couldn't even look them in the eyes, much less form syllables.

A woman came to Emery's side and clutched her hand with cold, clammy skin and jagged nails. "Please, take my Mary with you." Beside the woman, a girl who looked about twelve years old stared up at Emery with trembling, dry lips. The mother shoved Mary's hand into Emery's. The girl's soft and malnourished wrist trembled.

A man with a shaved head at the next tent called out. "Hey, you!" He approached and spit on the ground at her feet. "Come to lock more of us up in your tower?"

Jexa Era took a step forward and punched the man's

throat. Her heavy fist connected with a meaty thump, and the guy collapsed onto his knees in a coughing heap.

Emery pressed herself in front of the girl, wanting to shield her from Jexa Era's brutality, keeping hold of her hand. Jexa drew her gun and aimed at the man.

"Don't shoot!" Emery's cheeks burned as she dropped the girl's hand and ran forward. She placed herself between Jexa's weapon and the sputtering, injured man. Jexa had protected her, and she was grateful, but that didn't mean the man should lose his life.

Emery had to act before the scene got uglier. She turned away from the NanDroid's flashing red glare and looked around at the people. "We're seeking volunteers."

"Look somewhere else. We won't do it." A young woman with matted red hair stood with an older man and another woman. All three looked gaunt, their clothes hanging off their skinny bodies.

The sickly mother nudged Mary toward Emery. "Take my girl. She deserves better."

Emery shook her head. "She's too young. I need people between eighteen and twenty-two who are in good health." She regretted that last part. It was obvious that the people's basic needs weren't being met. She had no idea why X allowed the humans to live in squalor and starvation.

A group of four children ranging in age from six to ten years old fled from a side alley. A woman wearing a faded red bandanna on her head chased them with a long stick. Two of the kids were limping. "You nasty little thieves!" The woman's stick struck the leg of the littlest one, and the child howled in pain.

"Stop!" Emery dashed across the street, about to grab the stick.

The woman spun to face Emery, her eyes wild. "Stay out of this."

"Give them a chance to explain." Emery grabbed the stick and yanked it away from the woman, an easy feat with the wrinkled, malnourished woman. The stranger's eyes widened, and she stepped back with her hands on her hips.

The children huddled a few feet away, their eyes darting back and forth, their heads swiveling to look Emery up and down.

"You don't need to hit them. They're just kids." Emery took the stick over her right knee and snapped it in two, then tossed the pieces to the ground.

"They stole my bread. Little brats." The woman's breath came in ragged spurts, her mouth twisted in a snarl. It was no wonder the children were afraid of her. "They're a menace."

"You're wasting time," Jexa Era said.

Emery ignored the robot, stepping closer to the elderly woman. Her eyes were blue behind a gray film—the same color as Emery's foster mother all those years ago. She gulped down a sickening wave of nausea. "What's your name?"

"Agnes Montgomery. What's it to you?" The woman pulled a rag from her pocket and blew her nose.

Emery's foster mother was named Nancy. She'd forgotten the surname, burying that detail along with the cold, endless nights locked away in the pitch-black closet. The feeling of being the tiniest, most worthless person in the world. The closet was far worse than the beatings. At least the pain when the belt hit her inflamed skin made her feel something.

Agnes's gaze swept over Emery's long coat and hood. "You're human, eh? But you're with them." She tilted her head at Jexa and the SoldierBots. "You some kind of mutant freak?"

A man wearing a brown cap and jean jacket approached. "What are you doing to the people they take into the tower?" The hollows under his eyes were dark, and frown lines were etched in the corners of his mouth. "Those monsters took my daughter Lily."

Agnes nodded. "That's right. SoldierBots came and took Neil and Sally too."

Jexa Era walked toward Agnes and the man. "Enough. Move along." They shrank away from her, sheltering behind other onlookers. Jexa turned and came to Emery. "Enough time wasted. Point out who you want to sample and let's go."

But Emery couldn't let go of what she'd heard. She lowered her voice so the humans couldn't hear. "What are they talking about, Jexa? You bring the people in for bio samples, and then you let them return to the camp, right?"

Jexa's red orb glowed. She didn't answer.

"They said you took people." A frigid shiver coiled up Emery's spine. Mach X had lied to her about what was happening after the samples were collected.

"You're an intelligent creature, so I won't bother deceiving you." Jexa's voice was hollow and cold. "They're disposable. Just pick five, and let's go."

Disposable. Emery would go to X and convince him to

stop what Jexa and the SoldierBots were doing to the people. After that, she'd work on improving their situation. The camp was a ruin of tents and shacks. She'd wanted to find the strongest and brightest for bio samples, but her choices stood with their ribs showing, while others had sores on their arms and legs. She stood straight and spoke to Jexa with authority. "These people need medical treatment and supplies—food and water. This camp needs to be cleaned up and given the basic essentials."

The fidgeting children stared up at Emery among the robots. They clung to each other, as if waiting for someone to strike them. She remembered that feeling well. She went to them, lowered her hood, and crouched down at eye level. "Tell me your names. Where are you from?"

Two of the smallest children, a boy and a girl, hung back. "Go on," Emery said. "You can tell me."

The oldest girl, with thick dark brown hair, stepped forward. "I'm Chloe, and this is Ash and Tommy. That's Jenny. We come from the south."

"I'm Emery. Why was that lady chasing you?"

Chloe hung her head. "We were trying to find food."

"I see." Emery's gut twisted. The children didn't even have proper foot and outerwear for the approaching winter, not to mention sustenance for their growing bodies. She addressed Jexa and the SoldierBots who watched from behind their emotionless black visors. "We're taking the children into the tower where they'll have food and shelter and baths."

"This was not the plan," Jexa said. "The Supreme Commander will be displeased."

"I don't care."

Jexa stood sleek, stiff, and hostile. "You will care. The Commander will punish you."

Blood rushed to Emery's cheeks. How much did Jexa know about her relationship with X? He hadn't used the Silver Chamber on her in years, and she doubted he'd do such a thing ever again after the last time. She didn't speak to him for six months after the ordeal.

Chloe and the other kids flanked Emery, as if they were protecting her. The one named Ash grabbed Emery's hand. "We want to come with you."

Emery smiled at them. "Would you like to go inside where it's warm and we can eat some yummy food?"

Their small faces lit up, and they bobbed up and down on their heels, but the crowd of people murmured, and a few heckles landed Emery's way. "How 'bout you bring all of us food?" a man shouted. From somewhere nearby, Agnes's voice rang through, "We'll never see those kids again. At least my bread will be spared."

Emery addressed the crowd. "I'm going to help these children because they're hungry and cold. They'll receive top care and medical attention. We'll return to help the rest of you."

Jeers and boos rippled from the audience. Two of the SoldierBots stepped forward and backed the throng up with their rifles.

"We leave now." Jexa pulled Emery by her elbow as they exited the restless jumbled street toward the fence.

The children followed Emery close, hanging on to her coat with their fists. She counted that all four of them were trailing safely behind. Pushing a button on her wrist comm, she messaged NB-15. "Meet me in the lobby ASAP."

Jexa's steel feet clanked along the pavement. "I've alerted the Supreme Commander about this."

"The people need help. Do what you want." X would summon her, there was no doubt about it. He might even threaten her, but she would deal with him in the moment. All Emery cared about was getting the kids help. She hummed the song from her childhood, the one that had helped her get through the horrible nights in the closet. *Good night, sweetheart, well it's time to go.*

She couldn't stand what was happening in the encampment. The people lived in poverty and squalor. It wasn't supposed to be a utopia. After all, humanity had caused their own problems by spoiling and polluting the planet, but that didn't mean the camp had to be a hellscape either.

As they entered the tower, Emery's heart sunk to see the children's startled faces when they noticed the menacing gunmetal gray SoldierBots who stood watch at the entrance.

Inside the lobby, the mild, recirculated air was a welcome relief. Emery inhaled deep and relaxed her shoulders from the strain of the weary world outside. "We'll get you some food and water very soon, children."

NB-15 exited one of the elevators. He'd wasted no time in answering Emery's call.

Jexa Era pulled Emery aside. "The Commander wants to see you."

But she sidestepped Jexa and gave the children a nod

as NB-15 approached. "This is my friend, Mr. 15. He's going to take care of you."

The kids were quiet and stuck close to one another. Chloe grabbed Emery's hand. "Please, don't leave."

Emery kneeled and patted Chloe's head. "You can trust Mr. 15, okay? He took care of me when I was little. I have to do something, and then I'll join you for dinner. Would you like pizza, hot dogs, or burgers?"

Frowns turned to grins as the children took turns shouting out their meal requests. The youngest child drooled and sucked her thumb.

"Come with me, children. We're taking a ride up the elevator." NB-15 hustled them into a waiting car and left Emery in the lobby with Jexa.

She'd done the right thing in taking the kids out of the camp. Her heart soared, but she had to face X and convince him to take better care of the humans on his front steps. She could handle it—give the people the things they needed and be their doctor by tending to the sick. The medical tech in her lab was incredibly advanced. The only hitch was convincing the people to put up with the robots.

She had the power to help the humans, despite Jexa and the SoldierBots' previous violence. But first she had to convince Mach X that her cause was worth fighting for.

Chapter 7
Shift your shape
Block

Block's threat indicator flared. The needle had never gone all the way to twenty—the maximum possible danger level. While he wasn't in any immediate physical trouble, the idea that Wally was in danger inside Mach X's Manhattan tower was enough to make him unstable.

"Run that by me again." Maxwell banged on the expired NannyBot's forehead. "What exactly did the NannyBot say before she conked out?"

"The children are in danger," Cybel said. "It kept repeating, 'nan' over and over."

"NannyBots or NanDroids." Riv landed on top of the bot and stuck a probe into the tiny space between its chin and neck. "Probably warning us of Jexa Era."

Block's worst suspicions were aroused. Sensors hummed all over his body. He couldn't sit still or listen to the pointless conjecture. Wally was in danger, and he had to do something, but they had no plan. Getting into the tower when access was restricted was hopeless. He walked away from the group.

Maxwell chased after him. "Where are you going?"

"I need to process." He kept going, stepping past dirty mounds of antiquated electronics—battery adaptors, remote controls, and odd box-shaped consoles he couldn't identify. He wanted to keep hiking, exit the junkyard, hit the highway, and walk to Manhattan until a rescue plan emerged in his circuitry, but such a journey would take hours that he didn't have.

A beep sounded from somewhere behind. Vacuubot followed, cruising four feet in the air but keeping its distance.

Block halted. "Hi. Are you processing too?"

Yes. There's something I've wanted to say for some time. You were brave for coming back for me. You saved me from corrosion for all eternity. Thank you.

Block paused next to an old motorcycle. Only the chrome body remained; the tires had been stripped. He knelt before it, opened the storage compartment on his right thigh, sprayed cleaner, and started wiping off the years of grime. Not knowing what else to do, he surrendered to his cleaning urges.

Vacuubot soared close and landed on an old metal filing cabinet that was dented on one side. *I know how hard this must be for you. To be so close to Wally but unable to reach her.*

Block said nothing and kept scrubbing the bike's murky fender.

I never got to finish what I tried to tell you earlier.

Block replayed his memory archives, searching for his last exchange with Vacuubot. There'd been so much commotion with the injured NannyBot and all the talking and frantic figuring out of what was going on. "Wait, you said NannyBot parts. Do you think Riv could rebuild one of the NannyBots and we could hack into it and get it to rescue Wally? Unfortunately, I gave the hacking device to Nova at O'Hare."

I've considered 3,218 scenarios, and no, that won't work.

Block stood and kicked the motorcycle. "I can't just sit around here waiting."

You're too stressed about Wally. Too much microbial juice flooding your system. Look at the big picture.

Block leaned over and picked up the bike, righting it. Causing more mess was not helping matters. "I don't have time for games, Vacuubot. What's your point?"

You have a pile of NannyBots.

"First-generation, so what? They're no help if they're not inside the tower." Block spotted a small junk pile twenty feet away—heaps of old car tires. He climbed it until he reached the top. Vacuubot was trying to tell him something that he wasn't comprehending. On top of the tire mound, he steadied himself and looked toward New York City. Across the Hudson River, the skyline undulated in the distance with buildings of all shapes and sizes, some shaggy with green moss and lichen, others pristine. On the New Jersey side, the buildings closest to the junkyard had no roof, just skeletal beams.

Block's processors whirred faster. He turned his attention to the problem at hand. There had to be a way inside the tower. The junkyard NannyBots were useless now that they were all expired. Pieces of scrap. It struck him as ironic that his body shape was so similar to those of the first-gen Nannies, though, at 5'6", he was a few inches shorter.

One scenario caught his attention. He dug into it with more focus. The odds were one in 167,000. He needed help, but it might work. Block bounded down the tire hill, stumbling and almost falling. "Vacuubot." He wasn't sure where his friend had gone.

Yes? Vacuubot flew out from behind a rusted refrigerator, and headed into a clearing.

"We need Riv."

What's going through your circuitry?

"Find Riv." Block hurried past, running toward the center of the junkyard. "Get to the pit."

Vacuubot cruised alongside him. *Okay, I'm getting nervous.*

Block paused next to a pile of broken office chairs. "I get it now. I know what you were suggesting." He sprinted toward the pit. "Now to make it work."

Two minutes later, Block had rounded up Riv and the others. "I need your help." He looked at Riv and Lucy-8. "I've got a plan, but it will require turning me into a NannyBot. Can you do it?"

Riv and Lucy-8 conferred in their high-pitched, rapid voices that no one else could decipher. Riv turned back after ten seconds. "Yep. We can recycle the dead NannyBot parts onto you, so you'll look exactly like the other NannyBots. We'll have to shift your shape and mount you on a new chassis, though."

Lucy-8 buzzed onto Block's right foot, then emitted a bright purple light from her eyes. She traveled up his leg, torso, and ended at his head. "Need to add four inches to his frame."

Oxford shook the ground as he walked across the pit toward Block and the JunkBots. "Too risky. I don't like this."

Block paced around the pile of broken NannyBots. He picked up a head. "You'll have to change my face to look like this."

"We got it," Riv said. "A few minor modifications. You're lucky your base frame is not all that different from the Nannies."

Oxford reached down and grabbed the torso of one of the NannyBots, examining it. "This is too drastic. Block, you'll be changed permanently."

"I'm aware of the risk, but maybe it won't be so bad to be taller. Cybel got new legs. She's doing well."

Cybel crossed the pit and sat on the fender of an old Jeep. "I got new legs, not a whole new chassis and face. There are more risks than you think."

Block fished through the pile and retrieved an arm that was intact—not scratched or dented like the other spare parts. He handed it to Lucy-8. "There's no other way inside."

"The SoldierBots are bringing junked NannyBots here." Cybel slid off the Jeep and picked up an expired bot, holding up its head and torso. A charred burn mark crossed its neck and chest. "This was shot by a laser rifle. Why do you suppose that is?"

Block scanned the wreckage, noticing that several of the pieces had burn marks. In his haste, he hadn't considered why the SoldierBots were dropping off old Nanny-

Bots. "I figured they're past their service date." But a closer inspection revealed many of the parts were less than five years old, their metal in good condition.

Oxford picked up one of the arms. "Look, the marks are in the same place on each unit." He held up another torso, pointing to a blackened circle on the right side, where the CPU was located. "This NannyBot's chest is burnt. They're being terminated." He began to sort the pile, organizing the parts by type.

Cybel kicked at a loose bolt on the ground. "If you get inside the tower without being detected as foreign—a big if—they could round you up and shoot you simply for being a NannyBot."

Block's threat module ticked up as he considered scenarios. "This is the best plan we have. I can't delay any more. Wally's in danger."

That shut Cybel and Oxford up for a minute. Riv zoomed around, barking orders at the JunkBots. He flew to Block, the chopper blades from his head holding him steady. "You ready?"

Oxford kneeled, and Cybel spoke privately to him. "Wait, there's something else," Oxford said. "You'll need to fly low, under the radar. If Jexa Era and her NanDroids pick up on anything odd with you, they'll send you in for a tune-up. I know how it works. I forced tune-ups on many of my troops."

"Wouldn't a tune-up be a good thing?" Maxwell chimed in from where he lay sprawled out on a metal sheet as JunkBots repaired dents on his back.

Oxford shook his head. "A tune-up deletes your

memory files. Block, you could forget about Wally entirely."

Block hadn't processed that particular scenario. If his files were overwritten, he'd be powerless to do anything but obey Mach X's orders. They could even overwrite his programming. His cleaning protocols would vanish, along with his memories of Wally. Such an idea seemed impossible. *I couldn't ever forget her.*

He walked to the NannyBot pile and crouched down, running his hands along their charred bodies. If there was a chance his plan would work, if he could trick his way inside by transforming into a NannyBot, he had to try it. To do nothing was far worse because every second that passed put Wally in more danger. "I understand the risks. I want to proceed."

"This way." Riv led Block deeper inside the pit to an area underneath a wobbly tin roof. "Lie down."

He did as he was told. Dozens of tiny JunkBots surrounded him.

"Block, do as I say." Riv watched a monitor that flashed random numbers from zero to nine. "You'll see numbers as a purple flash."

"Okay." Block focused, while Vacuubot pinged him to say it would intervene if things went off the rails.

"You need to be completely still." Riv stood on his shoulder and hooked on a chain-like harness. The chain tightened on Block's chest while Riv pulled from the other side. Block tried to move but couldn't. He was being twisted in different directions. Wires and gears whirred, and the bots drilled into his body. He caught movement off to the side and heard a crunching sound. Lucy-8 pulled two pieces of metal apart, then snapped them together.

He felt buzzing sensations as the JunkBots worked around his right leg, then he heard them repeat the process on the other side. He tried to sit up, but nothing happened. Being pinned down was flagging his threat indicator and raising all kinds of alarms in his feed. "I want up."

"We're not done yet," Riv said. "No moving. We need to modify your circuits. This will only take a few seconds."

A bright light spilled onto Block's feed as a vacuum tube sucked air from his body. The chain tugged on his chest. Riv pressed on his arms and legs while Block's body was lifted by the harness. The vacuum clicked off.

"Did it work?" Block asked.

Riv and his crew lowered Block back to the table. ""You can move now. Just take it slow, okay?"

He rotated his legs. They worked. The JunkBots had added four inches in height and lengthened both legs and arms by two inches. He sat up. Four JunkBots held him by his torso and legs, keeping him from tipping over. He stepped onto the dirt floor of the pit but steadied himself on a pole sticking out from a junk heap.

"Try walking." Lucy-8 buzzed up and down Block's left side. She spun, flashing her purple beam on him. "We smoothed out the tool marks and pulled the seams on your legs and arms. Nobody's going to know this isn't your original base frame unless they inspect under your chrome plates."

His exterior alloy had been replaced with untarnished

pieces of the junked NannyBots. A swarm of JunkBots flew over, holding up a long, jagged mirror. Block caught sight of himself. His pearly-white chrome was gone, replaced by the pale blue NannyBot steel.

Vacuubot flew to his side. *It's still you in there.*

Block held up his new hands. Long flexible digits with a fibrous blend of metal and elastic gave him gentler hands. He'd be better equipped to hold human babies. He checked inside his thigh compartment and found only his emergency fire extinguisher. "Where are my cleaning brushes and vacuum hoses?"

"Some of those had to come out, and some of it's tucked away inside your torso," Riv said. "You're a caretaker now, not a cleaning machine."

Block regretted losing access to his cleaning attachments, but he had to stick with the choice he'd made. In the mirror, he wiggled his fingers and tested out his legs with a few steps. The knee joints were stiff and made a squishy air sound when he walked. Blue and silver chrome covered his torso. He drew closer to the mirror until he was a few inches away. Leaning in, he studied his new faceplate. His eyes were a bright yellow with artificial lashes, and his nose was a perfect replica of a person's. But the biggest shock was the shape of his head. The JunkBots had somehow morphed his rectangular block-like CleanerBot head into the more rounded, visually appealing shape of a human's.

The way he looked was meant to comfort the children. It was a logical decision in the NannyBot's design. But there was a problem he hadn't counted on. Wally wouldn't recognize him.

Chapter 8
Someday you'll thank me
Emery

Emery ran her hand along Subject Seven's scalp. The boy's curly light brown locks were matted with sweat, and his skin, hot to the touch, was dappled with red blotches. The bio-monitor on his chunky wrist showed 103 degrees Fahrenheit. "How long has he had this fever?"

NB-56 stood across from her over the child's crib. "Four hours and sixteen minutes." He wasn't her first choice to assist, but 15 was busy with the encampment children she'd brought to the tower.

She tensed her shoulders. "Why wasn't I alerted?"

"Jexa Era ordered me not to disturb you because you had important business in the camp," the robot said.

"I'm responsible for the health and well-being of every subject in my care." Emery's temples throbbed. "You should have alerted me immediately. Jexa Era is not in charge of my lab. They're *my* subjects." NB-15 had been there earlier and should have messaged her but didn't. She'd have to get to the bottom of what had happened.

"The subject's temperature was under 103 at the time, below the critical threshold."

Emery ignored the NannyBot as her wrist comm buzzed with a message. *See me.* X could wait. She pulled the child's blankets back. At twenty-three months, his upper molars were erupting, necessitating the use of acetaminophen, but whatever illness had raised his temperature so high went far beyond teething pains. She'd nicknamed him Scarred Boy, though she never said it out loud. A jagged mark ran down his cheek and across his chin—an unfortunate accident with a malfunctioning MediBot had caused the gash that would scar him for life. After that incident, Emery had banned all MediBot units from her lab, replacing them with her preferred Nanny-Bots souped up with pediatric medical training modules.

Emery's comm shuddered against her arm. *Now.* She wanted to confront Mach X about the issues at the camp, how the people were barely surviving—and most of all, why he'd permitted Jexa Era to murder the research volunteers. But all she could think about was the sick toddler.

Scarred Boy's rib cage was narrow for his age, the skin stretched taut over the bones. The child moaned when she lifted his arm to examine his abdomen. No pressure issues. Still, he hadn't been eating like the other kids, and she couldn't rule out a gastrointestinal issue or parasite. His forehead felt like a gourd that had been left out in the sun for three days. A puff of his warm exhalation brushed against her palm.

"Put him in the Incubator on fever mode," she said. The machine would wrap the toddler in a cooling gel and inject saline IV that would bring his temperature down. It still didn't address the root cause of his illness, which Emery would have to mull over while she dealt with X. "Check his temperature every fifteen minutes. I'll be back soon."

NB-56 prepared the child to be moved. After Emery washed up, she headed out the lab's door and into the hallway. As she rounded the corner toward the elevator, Jexa Era walked past, heading toward the lab.

Emery did a double take at sight of the robot, and her stomach churned. "Where do you think you're going?"

"The Supreme Commander has authorized me to supervise the lab op—"

"Absolutely not!" The anger simmering in Emery was about to break open and explode from her chest. "That's *my* lab, and it's off limits."

"What's wrong with Subject Seven? Why is the subject fevered?"

How Jexa was getting vitals on the sick boy was a mystery. Perhaps Emery had a mole in her lab. "I'll handle Subject Seven." Emery glared at the sophisticated NanDroid, standing a head taller than her and capable of shooting her into pieces.

Jexa's ominous red light betrayed no emotion. At least with the older, gentler NannyBot units, Emery could look into two eyes, synthetic though they were. "I'm not required to seek your permission, nor do I require your consent."

Emery's brain buzzed with the implication of Jexa's statement. She'd been a fool not to seek control over Jexa and the NanDroids. "Cut the crap. You killed the people from the camp—the ones who volunteered to give medical samples." Emery's arms shook, and she swallowed down bile at being so naive to think the humans had been returned to the camp and wished a good day by the SoldierBots.

"They were collateral," Jexa said. "If we'd returned them to the camp, word would spread about the experiments being conducted here."

Emery's voice trembled, and she wished for a destroy button to turn Jexa Era into a scrap heap. "It's not right. Those people did nothing wrong."

"Someday you'll thank me."

"For killing innocent people? I won't allow you in my lab ever again." Emery walked to the lab's security door and punched in her master code to change the security. Jexa would not be allowed to enter without someone opening the door for her. It bought Emery a few minutes to visit X and demand a stop to the intrusion.

Jexa watched her, saying nothing and not intervening.

After the short ride up the elevator, Emery entered X's suite, her footsteps heavy and her blood pumping. "Jexa's not allowed in my lab." She stormed over to where X hung suspended in his cubed conglomeration. "She murdered the people from the camp, called them collateral."

X said nothing as waves of data crisscrossed and cut a glowing path of purple, magenta, and indigo across the hexahedrons.

"I only need three first-gen units to work the lab, not Jexa and her kind." Emery paced as the anger sparked and pulsed in her veins. "I don't want her or any NanDroids in my lab."

"Emery"—X's voice was smooth and firm—"have a seat."

A rolling chair moved on its own toward her, but she kicked it away. "I want answers." She crossed her arms and glared at him. "Did you approve Jexa murdering those people? The people who volunteered to give samples for my research?"

"Yes."

Her chest ached, and she grew dizzy. "How could you condone such a thing?" Emery's pulse pounded in her ears, making the throbbing in her temples worse. "Those people had relatives, people who cared for them." Some even had children of their own—the offspring Emery had created in the lab—but she didn't let her thoughts linger on that fact.

"Every human must make sacrifices for the cause."

"But you always said we were building a better future." Emery couldn't stop her legs from shaking. Never had she been so angry at X, not even when he'd punished her. She went to the chair, sat, and pressed her hands down hard against her knees. *Get it together. He sees my stupid human emotions. My weakness.* "I never signed up for killing people."

X extracted himself from the tall computer interface. It was rare that he stepped out from the prism of data and machines that surrounded him in a cocoon, but he did so on occasion, for Emery. As he placed one large foot in front of the other, he crossed the floor in a few precisely executed strides. Not an inch of space was wasted. A second sliding chair came his way, and he took the seat next to Emery, and both chairs rotated to face the Manhattan view ninety-three stories below.

His amalgamate skin was synthetic and transparent. It simmered with a red-black liquid composed of bubbles and small particles of gray-lit energy that traveled through the fluid, crackling with static electricity and a low hum.

Emery stilled her quaking legs. The pulse rate on her wrist device indicated a more controllable ninety-nine beats per minute. Mach X didn't need a bio-monitor to read her vitals, of course. He could detect her every heartbeat.

"You brought humans into the tower." X's face had two sockets where his optical inputs were located. A rectangular piece ran across his upper torso—where a human's collarbones were located. They were the speakers that emitted his voice. "You should not have done that."

"They're children." Emery dug her nails into the chair's leather arms. In the distance, miles away, a few ripples of light fluttered and then vanished. "The camp lacks necessities. They don't have enough food, clothing, water." Emery stood and paced, needing to walk off the raw energy flowing through her legs. "Why did you allow the camp to get like that?"

X turned his head, and his eye sockets glowed like the undulating data waves he fed from—sometimes purple, sometimes blue—they were orange as he watched Emery. "Your sympathy is misplaced. You have a greater purpose. A new family."

"The camp kids need help." She couldn't shake the

memory of the emaciated faces, how haunted and malnourished the adults had looked. "Some of the people are sick and dying. If I can help the children get better, that's a bonus."

X waved a hand over the jumbled wall of cubes, and a series of images flickered and then overlapped, creating a multi-dimensional hologram. "Our new family is our purpose, minus the inferior members."

The hologram depicted the human race playing out in a number of scenarios, some peaceful, others violent and chaotic, but all ending in the same way—human beings dying out. "Shall I remind you how they treated you?" The images blurred and changed as X tapped one finger on the arm of his chair, his only movement.

The hologram featured a young Emery, her long black hair tied in a single braid down her back. She walked down a corridor of white walls and chilly linoleum tiles. The real Emery cringed. She knew the place that X was rendering—she remembered it in the deep recess of her memories. A place cruel and cold.

Holo-Emery turned a corner. A man and a woman dressed in dark blue scrubs approached. She turned to run, but they were bigger. Their strong hands grabbed ahold of her arms, caught her, and lifted her feet off the ground as she kicked, struggling like a bird caught in a net. They dragged her into a room, shoved her onto a hard bed, and cuffed her wrists to the sides. The woman had cold gray eyes as she slid a needle into her arm. Somewhere, in another room, a child wept.

"Your time as a so-called *ward* of the state." X tapped a ten-inch, slender-but-powerful titanium finger, and the hologram dissolved. "You wanted to make sure the past didn't repeat itself."

"And I have." Emery's chest softened. She was grateful the horrific images of the orphanage were nothing but a simulation. She wanted to be part of a better way forward for humanity—to bring Mach X's vision to fruition. "The future is in the children. My lab. I'm getting closer every day."

"Yes, you're making it possible, Emery."

Still, something didn't sit right with her. What had caused Scarred Boy's fever? Why were the other twenty-four-month-olds having sluggish reaction times?

"Subject Seven is ill," X said. Of course, Jexa Era would have told him. "Don't waste time on one subject. There are more children. Do what's best for the group."

"I'll do anything to make sure Seven gets better." She wasn't going to let the child's fever go unabated.

"You're a scientist. You know that some of the test subjects are inferior. That's a mathematical given, a numbers game."

The heavy truth was that some of the trials would fail. The first two rounds had resulted in the infants perishing their first few days outside of the cloned wombs. Hard times for Emery as crushing guilt threatened to consume her, but that had been two years ago. Since then, eighty percent of the harvested children had been viable. Those who had survived were critical to the success of the project. The trials couldn't fail. She would create the next generation of hybrid AI-humans. Failure guaranteed one thing—a thing she couldn't bear to face.

"Dispose of the camp children," X said. "They're inferior. A distraction."

Bile rose in Emery's stomach, a musty taste that raced across her tongue and turned her mouth sour. The children were alive. They had feelings, and people in the camp seemed to care about them. Emery didn't know what it was like to have another human being worry about your well-being. Had her own mother cared? She had no memory of her. "I'll feed them and escort them back to camp." Emery walked to the door, ready to leave.

"Jexa Era will handle them—"

Emery spun on her heels. "No." She balled her fists. "I brought them here. I'll take the children back to the camp. They're my responsibility." She didn't trust Jexa one ounce.

As the fortified doors of X's quarters slid open, he called out to her. "Emery, don't forget how important your work is. How hard you and I have worked to build this."

She paused, not turning back.

"It's everything to me," he said.

Emery swallowed back a sickening dread. People in the camp had been executed. For no good reason. *Collateral.*

"Daughter, did you hear me?"

"Yes, Father."

The doors shuttered behind her as she stepped onto the empty elevator. She leaned back against the far wall, gripping the thin, hard railing in her fists, squeezing so hard the metal dented her skin. She would go to the children, give them a hot meal, baths, new clothes—her friendly NannyBots would do all the work. She'd send them each home with a bag of food for their families. It was the least she could do. Her breathing grew lighter. Her kindness would be recognized in the camp and would help her recruit. She still needed to find adult volunteers for the next harvesting. Falling behind schedule was unacceptable.

Yet her chest felt hollow. If the camp people were so easily disposed of, what would happen to her test subjects if she failed?

Chapter 9
Which way's out?
Block

Rain dripped through holes in the old warehouse roof and puddled on the cracked, weed-covered concrete floor. Block took a few cautious steps forward. Cybel Venatrix was at his side, and G5 held the lead, carrying a fake rifle welded together by the JunkBots. In Manhattan, it was good to have a G5 around in case Mach X's SoldierBots found them. Maxwell's heavy feet clanked behind Block. Spoon trailed just behind, and Vacuubot guarded the rear. Oxford and Forge had stayed behind with the New Jersey JunkBots to fulfill the bargain—Oxford would defend the junkyard against SoldierBot attacks. Forge wasn't part of the bargain, but he was too slow to travel with the New York City crew.

Maxwell looked up at the thirty-foot-tall rotting ceiling beams. "I don't like the looks of this place."

"Quiet. We're not alone." Cybel's TrackerBot sensors were exceptional at picking up on the energy emissions from other robots, as well as heat radiating off any humans. She'd saved the group from running into danger at least five times on their journey.

After four hours of trekking through rain-soaked streets, running from the shelter of one abandoned building to the next, on the lookout for human rebels or Mach X troops, they'd reached the warehouse that Riv had told them about. It was up to Block to make friends and establish their base of operations. Everyone would stay there as he entered Mach X's tower in his trans-formed NannyBot body.

Block strode forward but caught his mechanical foot on something uneven. He staggered forward and fell on his knees. The new spinal frame and legs were foreign to him. Moving around as a NannyBot was awkward, and he missed his cleaning tools as if they were phantom limbs.

Maxwell's arms grabbed his torso to help him up. "You're going to have to get used to the body. Riv said it would take time."

Time we don't have. Block couldn't wait days on end to learn how to properly navigate his NannyBot frame. Wally was in trouble, and he had to get inside the tower and protect her.

A rattling came from a dark corner. Something lit up. A tinny voice, female, spoke. "Hey."

Footsteps sounded as Spoon and Maxwell retreated into the warehouse's rain-drenched shadows. Vacuubot vanished into a corner and pinged Block. *Careful. I'm standing by with weapons ready.*

Cybel raised her handgun and aimed in the direction of the sound. "Show yourself. Friend or foe?"

"It depends." A seven-foot-tall LoaderBot stepped

onto a second-story catwalk above their heads. The robot raised a four-by-four cement square over its head, ready to launch it at G5, Block, and Cybel. Built like a refrigerator with a black and red exterior and designed for factory work and heavy machinery, it looked like the LoaderBot had survived a couple of battles with the SoldierBots. She had dents and scratches all over her body. One of the LoaderBot's arms was missing, replaced by a shiny silver bionic arm that was thinner and not at all the kind of arm a LoaderBot should have. "Who sent you?"

Block raised his hands in a gesture of surrender. "Riv sent us. He's the JunkBot in New—"

"I know him." The LoaderBot took a step and moved closer to the edge of the platform. She had the perfect position to slam the concrete down on Cybel and G5 if she chose. "He and I go way back to pre-Uprising days. What do you want?"

Cybel twisted her head at Block. "Go on, tell her why we're here." She dragged him forward.

Block's threat sensors flared, and he wobbled on the new legs. Cybel and G5 would bear the brunt of the stone's impact if the LoaderBot hurled it, but Block would go down too. "Are you Luccabot?"

The robot nodded but kept the threatening rock held high.

"Riv said to find you. We walked from Jersey. He said you'd be able to help us. We need a safe spot to stay for a while."

Luccabot didn't seem convinced. "What's a Nanny-Bot, a SoldierBot, and a TrackerBot doing mixing together? Not to mention the other three hiding in the shadows. I sense your drone, and I'll crush you if it makes a move."

"Vacuubot's on our side. It won't hurt you." Block spun around. "Vacuubot, stop hiding. You can come out too, Maxwell and Spoon. She knows you're here."

As they revealed themselves, rejoining Block's crew, Luccabot lowered her cement weapon onto the floor of the catwalk. "You want me to shelter you. That's a big ask. What are you doing in the city? I'd be risking everything for you. The SoldierBots let me stay here, but that's because I do jobs for them."

Block wanted to explain but knew the clock was ticking. "Long story short, we're here . . . Well, I'm here to enter Mach X's tower. I'm not actually a NannyBot."

Luccabot walked to a nearby shelf and grabbed a pair of souped-up binoculars. She held them to her faceplate, against her visual input screen since LoaderBots didn't have humanlike eyes, and studied Block. "You're the clumsiest and most talkative NannyBot I've ever encountered." She set the binoculars down. "Getting into Mach X's tower is risky. You won't make it, and even if you do, word on the street is that first-generation NannyBots are getting scrapped."

"I know the risks." Block spotted an old rag hanging on a hook above a cabinet. He took the rag and wiped the counter of half an inch of dust. "But it's critical I get into the tower. It's a rescue operation."

Luccabot paced the catwalk. "You're a CleanerBot, then? Or were one. What's in it for me?"

Before they left the junkyard, Riv had promised that Luccabot would help. She owed him 'big time' in Riv's words. Block didn't know much about favors or payback, since he'd never been in that situation. He racked his logic module, trying to figure out what would appeal to the LoaderBot. "You'd be helping us out, and it would be a nice thing to do."

"I don't care," Luccabot said. "I'm a badass Loader-Bot. I can crush you and then some. If I didn't like Riv so much, I'd smash you all."

Cybel nudged Block aside and aimed her gun. "Listen, here Factory Wench, don't even try it. We have enough firepower to rip you to shreds in seconds."

"You're armed, and so is the drone, but the Soldier-Bot's rifle is fake. I recognize Riv's handiwork." Luccabot pushed a button on her arm and a machine ten feet away whirred to life. It was nothing more than a factory assembly arm, but it pointed a machine gun barrel at Cybel.

Cybel stood her ground. "Riv said you owe him. He wants to help us, so do it."

Block calculated they'd spent ten minutes in the warehouse already, bickering. He stepped in front of Cybel and pushed her rifle down. "We don't have time for this. I'm here to rescue someone I care about. She's important, and I have to get in that tower. If you don't help us, I'll find someone else who will."

Luccabot paused, perhaps analyzing her next step. "For a CleanerBot pretending to be a NannyBot, you have a lot of opinions." She pressed the button on her arm again, and the weaponized assembly arm powered off. "This rescue of yours, is it going to take away something Mach X wants?"

"Yes." Block was certain about his answer. Mach X had searched high and low for Wally. He'd sent an army after her. "It'll make Mach X very angry."

"Why didn't you lead with that? I hate X with the fury of a burning sun. Anything I can do to help irritate and weaken that creep, I'm all in." Luccabot raised her arms, pointing at their surroundings. "In case it wasn't obvious, the Uprising took away all the humans and our jobs. Mach X promised it would be a robot utopia, but all I ended up with is a rotting factory and nothing to do." Luccabot stepped over to a tall machine that housed a drill and patted its metal side. "I can't even keep all my friends powered up because X started rolling blackouts to weaken us and quash any rebellions."

"I'm sorry to hear that," Block said. "I know how important it is to have friends."

Luccabot waved a hand. "Come on up, then, and follow me. I don't bite. I haven't got the jaws for it."

Block and the others made their way up battered metal stairs to the platform. Block watched Luccabot's every movement. They entered a long dim hallway, and she motioned for them to follow. Wind whistled through cracks in the walls. Block slid his hand along the railing to keep his balance. He was clumsy, and he was running out of time to get used to his new body.

The corridor slanted down, and they reached the ground level, then kept heading down. Cybel walked behind Block and kept her voice low behind his head. "I don't like this."

"Excuse me," Block said and hustled his step to catch up to Luccabot. "Where are we go—" One of his metal feet—much larger than his CleanerBot ones—struck a gap in the floor. Block lurched forward, and the grimy, mildewed floor rose to meet him. The clanging sound of his body crashing down echoed in the warehouse corridor.

Luccabot waited. "You need help or something?"

"No, I'm fine." Block struggled to get back on his legs. He'd managed to land on his metal arms and knees instead of his face, at least. "Just need more practice."

"You'd better hurry. The NanDroids are going to sniff you out faster than a DogBot on the trail of an oil slick." Luccabot gave Block a look over her shoulder as she headed through a doorway and into darkness.

He and the others followed Luccabot down a staircase. The stairs curved every few feet, and it was impossible for Block to tell how far they'd gone. The air was thick with moisture, and rust covered the steps. It would've taken Block ages to clean the place.

"This place is creepy," Maxwell said.

The hallway gave way to a large, cavernous room. Factory equipment—some in working order, some not—was strewn about, although the equipment looked like it had been there for decades.

"We have a small generator," Luccabot said. "They're hard to get these days, but I have enough juice to light this room up. You should be safe in here for a few days."

With the whereabouts of everyone else settled, Block was eager to move on. "I'm ready to head to the tower. Luccabot, can you show me the best route?"

Lacking a holoprojector, the LoaderBot used a marker and white board to draw a map through the war-torn city streets. "You'll see Mach X has done nothing to clean up the city. He's worse than the people who used to make us work twenty-four hours a day. At least humans kept things orderly."

Block uploaded the image to his memory files. "Good-bye, everyone. I'm not sure when I'll be able to return or to send a message, or even if that's possible."

"Wait." Maxwell shuffled over. "Riv gave me this." He handed Block a small device the size of a button. It's magnetic." After placing it on the left side of Block's NannyBot head, he stepped back and raised his wrist to his voice speaker. "Testing—"

Maxwell's voice burst next to Block's auditory sensors. He staggered backward, pinwheeling his arms, when Cybel caught him.

"Sorry about that." Maxwell stuck a screwdriver finger into the rectangular device he wore on his arm. "How's this?"

Maxwell's voice landed softer and didn't burst into his sensors. "Better." Block loosened himself from Cybel's grip and then banged his foot against a metal rod on the floor.

"We'll be able to listen to what's happening." Maxwell pressed a button on his device and spoke again. "And we can talk to you, I think."

If it's able to transmit from inside the tower, Vacuubot messaged Block.

"Thank you. I hope it'll work." Block looked at Luccabot. "Which way's out?"

Block said his goodbyes, choosing not to linger. No more time could be wasted. Luccabot's map took him underneath the Manhattan streets, through the sewers which weren't used anymore since humans had fled the city. Hordes of rats had taken over, but they didn't bother Block as he marched through the tunnels, following Luccabot's instructions. The little animals squeaked and climbed over each other to get a better view of him as he trekked through the ankle-high water. Nova would have freaked out if she'd been with him.

After forty minutes, he reached the ladder that led up to the manhole that would take him up to W. 34th Street, within a two-minute walk to Mach X's tower. As Block stared up from the bottom of the ladder, he wondered why the iron cover was called a 'manhole' and not a 'street hole,' since a female human could have fit inside it, not to mention plenty of robots.

Maxwell's voice sounded from his communicator. "Block, give us an update. Are you in the tower?"

Block grabbed the sides of the ladder and climbed up. "I'm about to come out on 34th Street. When I get close, I'll have to mute you." They'd tried to dampen the comm's output before Block left but failed. He couldn't walk around trying to blend in when Maxwell's voice was blaring out at random times.

"Okay, we'll still be able to hear you," Maxwell said.

Block reached the top of the ladder, but his right foot slipped off its rung as he pushed against the manhole cover. He kicked his feet in an awkward attempt to find purchase, then dangled by his hands. *Stop. Focus. Don't panic.* He forced himself to send power to his right leg first, managing to get it back on a rung. Then he directed all his processing attention to the left leg. Success. With both legs back on the ladder, he steadied himself. Scratching sounds and static came from the comm. "I'm about to hit the street. When I get to a private space, I'll attempt contact."

"Roger that. Over and out." Maxwell clicked off.

Block shoved at the street covering, and it slid off after a few pushes. With more caution, he climbed up and onto the pavement at street level. He stood and scanned the area. He'd exited into an empty alley. Not wanting to draw attention should he encounter any SoldierBots, he muted the comm's output and walked toward 34th Street. The avenue was wide, and he charged forward with his head held high—Cybel had said that he was a NannyBot, so he should act like he belonged. But inside his circuitry, Block considered himself an imposter, about to be discovered at any moment.

Rows of concrete and steel buildings lined each side of the street, but few of the windows were intact. The pavement was cracked and broken in spots and bare in others. A yellow taxicab sat in the middle of the street. Its tires were flat, its windows broken. Twisty, dark green vines reached up from the cracked asphalt and wrapped around the front and back bumpers. The city had once housed businesses that decorated their storefronts and sidewalks with flowers and shrubs. When people had been in charge, Manhattan was alive with businesses, cars, people riding bicycles, and children walking to school.

But now robotic beeps, squawks, chirps, and hums emanated from the buildings. A SoldierBot looked out at him from a second-story window of what used to be a bank. It was unsettling to see New York City after X had declared war on humans. Block wanted to clean it all up. He wanted to bring the city back to life and restore it to the way it used to be.

He kept moving to avoid the SoldierBot following him or alerting others. After reaching the corner of the next block, he looked down the street. The tower's entrance sat diagonally from where he stood on the intersection. Tipping his head all the way back, he looked up at the skyscraper. It gave off a silver shine that reflected the daylight and stood in contrast to the surrounding decrepit buildings, burned out cars, and rubble-filled streets. Why none of the robots cleaned up was beyond him.

Block spotted a SoldierBot with a rifle hanging out in the middle of the street, so he walked past as if he had somewhere to be. The bot didn't even look at him, just kept watching down the street toward an eight-foot-high wall that barricaded the street a hundred feet beyond the tower. He didn't know what was behind the wall, and he didn't plan to stick around and find out.

He wanted to get inside the tower fast, so he hurried his pace. The click-clack of his metal feet on the pavement was loud—so jarring he worried that a SoldierBot would approach him at any moment. As he neared the tower's entrance, several SoldierBots looked at him but didn't approach. It was shockingly easy to make his way toward the tower.

He walked up a short flight of concrete stairs with care. If he tripped, stumbled, or showed how clumsy he was in the new body, they'd descend on him like hungry androids on grease. When he reached the landing, he slowed his pace. A short wall stood between him and the entrance, and there were two SoldierBots stationed at the door. He approached, his threat indicator rocketing up at the proximity to the deadly robots. If they suspected he was a spy, they'd blast his CPU in an instant. Following Cybel's instructions, Block extended his left arm toward the boxy, stationary security scanner robot. A green burst of light emitted from the unit and scanned his body just like Cybel had said it would. It was the big test of whether Block's NannyBot transformation would pass the test.

After ten seconds, the scanner completed its assessment and flashed a green light, but the SoldierBot pointed a finger at Block. "Wait."

Block lowered his arm. The SoldierBot knew he was a fake somehow. His processor was working overtime as he tried to find a path to run and hide.

"Extra security today. Show us your contents," the SoldierBot said.

Block had no idea what the guard was talking about. He took a step backward, caught his heel against the security robot's bottom corner, and stumbled.

"What's wrong with you, NannyBot?" One of the SoldierBots came to Block's side and righted him. "You need a tune-up?"

The SoldierBot stationed at the door approached. "Have a look inside his cavity."

The guard was talking about the storage compartment on his legs. At Cybel's advice, he carried only the fire extinguisher. The tiny locket he held onto in the hopes he'd one day put Wally's picture inside was left behind with Maxwell. Cybel was a genius when it came to espionage. She'd anticipated such a search.

The SoldierBot walked up to Block with his rifle at his side, then reached down and pressed the buttons that opened the storage compartments on his NannyBot thighs. "Clear. Go ahead."

As Block passed through the revolving doors into the lobby, the SoldierBot by the door said, "Better get that tune-up or you're not going to last around here much longer."

The marble lobby floor was so clean, it sparkled. The sight of it made his sensors buzz. A waterfall splashed over the edge of a wall into a rectangular pool that was large enough to fit ten SoldierBots inside. Flowering plants, ferns, and vines covered the spotless white walls. He hadn't seen anything like it since before the Uprising. Three small cleaner modules—simple robots like Vacu-ubot—worked their ways across the smooth, glossy floor. He logged a task to free them too if he could find a way.

Other than the cleaner units and a few patrolling SoldierBots, the lobby was empty. He had no clue where in the tower the children were being held. His next step was to find Wally and make sure she was alive. He started toward the elevator bank, willing to search every floor if he had to.

A SoldierBot stood near the doors but moved aside when it saw Block come its way. An elevator door opened, and a NannyBot stepped out. Its body was pale blue—a first generation model like Block. A number was welded high onto its chest: NB-15.

The robot spotted Block and walked to him. "What are you doing out here? You should be at your station."

Block didn't know how to respond so he nodded, but NB-15 grabbed his shoulders. "Where's your identification number?"

His cover had been blown. Cybel, Luccabot, Riv—none of them had realized he needed a number.

NB-15 stepped to the side and looked into the lobby. "Those wretched SoldierBots are up to their pranks again." The NannyBot studied Block's chest. "They wiped it clean off, didn't they? Gave you a tune-up, I suppose."

Block played along. "Yes, sir."

"Don't call me that. We're not that formal, don't you remember? Of course not, those jerks scrambled your memory files." The bot nudged Block toward an open elevator. "I'm NB-15. Come with me, I'll get you numbered and reassigned. It'll keep you off the termination list, at least for now."

The elevator ascended fast, and Block studied the control panel for any clue as to where the children might be. Block pointed toward the top button, marked 93, but NB-15 swatted his hand away. "No. Never touch the top floor button. That's off limits."

"Sorry."

NB-15 patted Block's shoulder. "You poor thing. They really did a wipe job on you."

The doors slid open on floor sixty. NB-15 led him into a room where there were other NannyBots—fifty or so—he couldn't do a complete count with all that was happening in the new, potentially hostile environment.

Some of the NannyBots stood at charging stations, while others talked among themselves or worked at computer consoles.

"Sixty is the first-gen floor," NB-15 said. "It's where we're assigned to power up and upload routine training mods, and all that."

Block followed him into a small room that contained a wall of tools, tubes, and 3-D printers. NB-15 grabbed a port and plugged it into Block's chest. "I'll just check your wiring and get you back to work. Do you remember what your previous assignment was? I don't recall you, and I've been here so long. Emery keeps me busy, that's for sure."

"I worked with the children," Block said. It was a risky move, but he was desperate.

"Which ones? The nursery on 86 or 87?"

Crap. How to choose?

Before he could answer, NB-15 interrupted. "It must have been 87 because I'm on 86 a lot and never saw you before. You have a unique stride."

"My memory archive is coming back now." Block didn't enjoy lying, but he was doing it for Wally. "87th floor."

NB-15 unhooked the cable from Block's port and picked up a tool, raising it to his chest. Metal hissed and sparks popped as the NannyBot burned a number onto Block's chest. "There you go. NB-399. Don't let them take you for a tune-up again."

"Why not?"

"Our units weren't built to handle the tune-ups. Another one will destroy your core programming, and then they'll shoot you and send you off to a scrap heap."

NB-15 patted Block's chest, then typed something onto a digital screen on the table next to him. "Our kind is an endangered species. You want my advice? Steer clear of the NanDroids." NB-15 walked to the door, swiveled his head from side to side in the hallway, and returned to Block's side. "Especially Jexa Era. Watch out for her, but you didn't hear that from me."

"Thank you. I'll take your advice. I just want to help the children."

"Of course, that's all we want. You're all set to resume your post on 87. I programmed in your assignment and new ID number so everything's good, and you'll have access to the nursery ward."

Block was grateful to the NannyBot. He hadn't expected any help at all. "Where's your post? Will I see you again?"

"I'm around. Mostly I work in the lab on 90." NB-15 turned toward the door, but Block wanted to know more.

"What children are on 86?"

NB-15 paused. "You ask a lot of questions. Careful." The bot lowered its vocal output. "The special kids are on 86. All the children are special, of course, but those are the ones that Mach X keeps a close watch over."

No one was more special than Wally. Logic dictated that she had to be on 86. "Can I visit there?" Block asked.

"No. You only have access to your post. Security rules, remember? Anyway, I'm sure I'll see you soon." NB-15 walked out the door.

Block followed NB-15 into the NannyBot lounge. Some of the other NannyBots considered him, tilting their heads, but moved on. He stopped as the elevator doors opened and a woman stepped out.

He had no idea why a human would be inside Mach X's tower. She had chin-length black hair and stood five feet, seven inches tall. She wore a white lab coat that reached all the way to her knees. Pushing up her blue-rimmed eyeglasses, she looked from side to side until her gaze landed on NB-15 who was walking over to her.

"Hello, Emery," NB-15 said as it reached her. "Sorry, I was helping out a unit."

Emery's eyes brightened when NB-15 found her. "I need your help with the children from the camp. Bring a crew with you to feed and watch over them in the restaurant. I'll be up once I check on Subject Seven."

"Yes, Dr. Emery," NB-15 said. "Right away."

As the woman named Emery entered the elevator, Block watched the doors slide shut. He had more questions than answers as to the woman's strange presence in a tower filled with robots. His only certainty was that he had to find a way to access the 86th floor where Wally was waiting.

NB-15 turned to him. "Come with me, NB-399. We have a special assignment."

Chapter 10
Princess stories
Emery

"Despite there being only four children, they produce a lot of noise." NB-15 walked next to Emery, his steel feet clicking against the smooth granite floors as they traveled the hallway toward the 45th floor bistro doors. "They ask a lot of questions," he said. "I'm unprepared."

Emery was on her way to visit the camp children inside the tower's restaurant and kitchen. Converted from a cafe that existed in the pre-Uprising days, it was where the NannyBots cooked meals for Emery and the research subjects. She would eat dinner with the four malnour-ished children, making sure they had full bellies, then the NannyBots would bathe them, dress them in proper clothes, and they'd have a good night's sleep inside a comfortable hotel-style bed. There were floors inside the tower that hadn't changed at all since Mach X had taken over. Rooms containing luxury apartments that had been abandoned once robots declared war on humans.

She'd promised the camp children those few things, and she was determined to make good. They also needed medical attention, but she was far too tired to see to them that evening. She'd bring them to her clinic in the morning and examine them. As far as what would happen to them after that, she was still trying to work it out. All she knew for certain was that she would not allow Jexa Era within fifty feet of them. In the corridor, before the restaurant doors, she halted and faced NB-15. "What are they asking?"

"One of them wants to know when she can go home. Another was asking if I knew where Santa Claus lives, and—"

But Emery clung to the first part of his sentence. "They want to go home? To the camp?" Emery couldn't understand why any of the children would want to return to the place where they were treated poorly and forced to scavenge and steal food.

"Yes. The one called Jenny misses her mother, apparently."

Emery's chest tightened. The girl wanted a mother that didn't provide for her. Where had the mother been when Emery led the kids away? She'd thought the children would be begging to live inside the tower. Forcing a smile, she pushed open the restaurant doors. Inside, the four kids sat at a table, wearing linen napkins as bibs and kicking their legs underneath their chairs. Three Nanny-Bots circled around them, pouring milk into cups and plating hot soup, while another NannyBot unit swept the floor of any crumbs. The aroma of stew and hot biscuits made Emery's stomach growl.

"They're not used to sitting in chairs." NB-15 approached the table. "Their muscles are weak."

"It's okay." Emery pulled up a chair at the head of the table. "Hi, there." As she smiled at the kids, their eyes widened, but they kept chewing.

The youngest, Tommy, dropped his spoon into his bowl, spilling beef broth down his bib, onto his pants, and a puddle of brown splashed onto the floor below. His mouth twisted into a frown, and he covered his head with his arms as if he expected someone to strike him.

"It's okay." Emery pushed a napkin toward the mess and looked around at NB-15 for help. "Tommy, is it?" The little boy nodded and whimpered. "You had a little accident is all. The NannyBots will clean it up."

The NannyBot that had been sweeping in the corner raced over, nearly sliding into the mess on the floor. NB-399 was the identifier marked on its chest. Emery didn't recognize the unit. "Careful," she said. Her sharp tone made Tommy and Jenny flinch.

"Sorry, sorry." NB-399 gathered napkins from the table and leaned over to soak up the stew. His blue chrome exterior was dented above the left elbow, and scuff marks covered his knees. 399 avoided looking at Emery directly. "I'll have this cleaned up in no time." The robot wiped the floor in a circular pattern. The puddle and all trace of soup disappeared fast, and then he stood, reaching one leg back to retreat and losing his balance. Wobbling, he pinwheeled his arms as he tipped back, but it was too late. NB-399 fell backward and landed on his rear with a clatter.

Emery had never seen a NannyBot fall in all her years with them. Odd. The unit probably needed a tune-up.

Tommy stared at the robot and giggled. "You're

funny." He pressed his hand over his mouth. The others joined him, letting loose raucous peals of laughter.

"Thank you." NB-399 rolled over, sat up, then pushed himself up to stand in an awkward tangle of blue metal limbs. "I appreciate the compliment."

NB-15 hurried over to the other robot. "You're causing a disturbance. I warned you about attending to the children, that it's a special privilege. Don't make me regret it."

"Apologies." NB-399's vocal output grew faint. He backed away from the table, still holding a handful of stew-soaked, brown napkins. He bowed a little and hurried away from the table into the adjacent kitchen, banging his shoulder on the door.

The children giggled and fidgeted in their seats. Emery wanted to comfort them. The experience of being indoors with robots must have been so strange to them. "After this, we'll get you cleaned up and tucked into bed. Tomorrow, I'm taking you to my clinic for some medicine."

Jenny wiped her mouth with her sleeve. "I don't like this place." She crossed her arms and glared at Emery. "I want to go home."

They should be grateful. Emery was saving them from the wretched squalor that consumed their daily lives. "It's just one night here. You'll go home in the morning."

Jenny's lips quivered, and she pushed away her empty bowl. "I want my mommy."

Emery glanced at NB-15 who waited nearby. "The NannyBots will care for you tonight." She stood and grabbed 15's hand, pulling him closer to Jenny. "See, this is NB-15, and he took care of me when I was a little girl."

Jenny's eyes widened as she twisted in her seat to stare up at Emery and NB-15. "You don't have a mommy?"

Emery's chest tightened and she shook her head. "My mother left when I was just a baby, but I'm not alone. Mach X found me and gave me a new life, one where I received an education to become a doctor, and now we help each other and work together."

"My big brother says Mach X is the devil himself." Tommy's voice was high and tight. Broth stained his shirt, and he looked up at the high ceilings, kicking his legs and banging his feet on the table legs. "I don't like it here, and I hate the robots."

"Me too," Chloe said.

Emery was losing control of the situation. They were supposed to be grateful, devouring food, marveling at the furnishings, inside where it was warm and comfortable. She spread her hands on the table. She was doing something wrong. She had zero experience with kids of this age. Winning them over should be easy. She was a brilliant physician after all. "I know you're scared. How would you like to hear a story?" The kids had probably never experienced story time.

Jenny's face softened, and she sat up a little taller. Smoothing back her hair, she raised her hand. "I would."

"Great." Emery gave up her seat to NB-15. "Mister 15 is the best storyteller I know."

The robot leaned forward in his chair and rested his

elbows on the tabletop. "What would you like to hear about, children?"

"Santa Claus!" Ash yelled.

Jenny drew her legs under her and balanced on her seat, sliding her upper half onto the table. "A princess in a castle."

NB-15 rotated his head to look at each child while Emery stood behind him. "I don't have access to any story modules about a Santa Claus."

Emery drew up another chair to the table next to 15. "Tell one about a princess. You told me lots of fairy tale stories until I outgrew them. What was my favorite—"

"I erased them all from my memory files when you told me you didn't like them anymore. You were fifteen years, five months, and twelve days old."

"Okay. No princess stories." Emery chewed her lip, wracking her brain to think of something appropriate for their ages.

"I know . . ." Chloe, who was around eight years old, slid out of her seat and climbed onto Emery's lap. "How about we make up a story about a princess who lives in a castle with a lot of robots?"

"I like that story." Jenny slid off the table and came beside Chloe, taking her friend's hand in hers.

"Me too." Ash came and sat on the floor with crossed legs and stuck his thumb in his mouth. Tommy followed suit, taking the spot next to him.

As she held Chloe, the girl's warmth was solid and real. The child laid her head against Emery's chest. Emery hadn't touched another human being in a nonclinical way, perhaps ever. "That's a good idea. 15, think of something."

But NB-15 wasn't cooperating. "I apologize, Dr. Emery. I don't have any knowledge modules about a princess and castle. Perhaps if you'll allow me to go to the lounge, I'll plug into the mainframe and download a new mod—"

"I can help." The clumsy NannyBot, NB-399, stepped out of the shadows next to the kitchen entrance. Emery didn't recall him entering the dining room again.

"You have access to fairy tales?" Emery asked. That was odd since she personally approved all the early human development modules the NannyBots could access. The children in her lab were too young for such fantasy.

"Yes." 399 took several halting steps, his elbows bent, and hands flexed as he approached the table. "I can share a story if you'll give permission, Dr. Emery."

The robot was unfamiliar. She'd missed this particular NannyBot somehow.

NB-15 had an explanation. "Dr. Emery, NB-399 was given a tune-up by the SoldierBots. Pardon the clumsiness—"

"Looks like he needs another," she said. "Where did this unit come from?"

"I had to assign him a new identification number," 15 said. "The SoldierBots burned it off and didn't leave him in good shape."

Chloe's arms shook at mention of SoldierBots. She clutched a piece of Emery's shirt and shrank closer into Emery's arms.

"Shh. It's okay." Emery patted the girl's shoulders, gritting her teeth at Jexa Era's meddling. Some of the NannyBot units that Emery knew were disappearing—due to Jexa seizing expiring units, doing tune-ups, and wiping their memory archives. Mach X had explained it away as a necessary step to "clean house." No wonder she didn't recognize NB-399. "Go ahead with your story." She hoped it would calm the kids down.

NB-399 scooted onto a bench near where the kids sat on the floor. Jenny left Chloe's side and settled next to Tommy. "Once upon a time, there were two princess sisters" —the robot's left arm bent, and he outstretched his hand toward Jenny—"who lived in a castle with their nice doctor and many tall robots. The princess's names were Jenny and Chloe."

Chloe perked up and raised her chin, letting go of Emery's shirt.

NB-399 continued, and Emery wasn't sure where the story was going. "The princesses were afraid of the big robots. One day, a prince from a faraway land came calling, but he was hurt by a big, bad SoldierBot."

"No!" Ash clapped his hands over his ears.

Chloe stiffened in Emery's lap, and she squeezed the girl tighter.

"But the princesses became friends with a NannyBot who had a secret switch that helped him turn off all the bad robots."

Jenny yelped. "The NannyBot saved the princesses from the bad robots?"

"Yes, Jenny," NB-399 said.

"Then what?" Tommy asked.

"The princesses were safe with the NannyBots. They lived inside the castle, and all the bad SoldierBots went away to a place far across the ocean and were never seen again. And that's the end of the story."

The kids were silent, perhaps contemplating the story with their young brains. Emery had no idea where 399 had come up with the idea for the tale, but she was grateful. He'd somehow made them feel safer around the NannyBots. "What a nice story." Her voice was high, and she sprinkled in a false cheeriness, because X would've listened and would frown upon the story.

Chloe slid off her lap. "Can we go play in the room with all the flowers now?"

Emery nodded, and the children took off, running through the dining room doors and clattering down the hall toward the green atrium.

NB-15 stood. "I'll see to them." He followed their trail.

399 retrieved the broom and wiped up crumbs from the floor. Emery watched him, fighting off a smile that was forcing its way through. "Thank you for the story."

The robot didn't turn his head. "You're very welcome."

"From what education module did you find it?"

The robot pushed the broom away, walking toward the kitchen. "It was something I downloaded a few years ago."

She had more questions. There had to be some AI programming scattered into 399's CPU that made it slightly different, but the restaurant doors opened, and NB-41 hurried toward her.

131

"Dr. Emery, I have urgent news," the robot said. "Subject Seven is having seizures."

Scarred Boy. Emery bolted out of the room and into the hallway. The elevator ride to her lab was heartbreakingly slow. She shoved her way out of the sliding doors and raced into the MedLab to find five NannyBots surrounding the sick toddler.

Pressing her stethoscope against his chest, she found his skin was iced over with cold sweat. His eyes were glassy and unfocused. A lump grew in her throat while she counted under her breath. "Two, three." Her pulse raced. "Four, five." She shuddered as she listened for the boy's heart. He choked out a raspy breath from deep in his lungs, then grew eerily still.

A chill raced through her. Sixteen seconds passed with no heartbeat. She stood aside as the NannyBots shocked his chest in a desperate attempt to surge life into his dying anatomy.

But Emery knew there was no hope. The boy was gone.

Chapter 11
There's a way
Block

There had been two other times in his existence that Block had achieved a perfectly spotless floor, and he was close to making it happen a third time inside the tower's restaurant. He was rendering a tiny slice of peace high above a war-torn, chaotic Manhattan. Perched on all fours, he scrubbed the mahogany wood floor with the increased power of his more advanced NannyBot incarnation. His arms produced an impressive "elbow grease" —that's what Mr. Wallace had called a seriously deep scouring—and he exhumed every scuff mark, along with years of grime, onto the rags he'd found in a kitchen closet. The routine made his circuits hum with something approaching joy. As he cleaned, he plotted various schemes to gain access to the ward where Wally was located.

NB-15 had left the restaurant to escort the children into the atrium and presumably to bathe and find them accommodations. Block remained with three NannyBots who had kitchen wash detail. He hoped they would be too busy with chores to notice him out in the dining room doing what he did best—polishing floors while processing scenarios.

And he had a lot to consider. The best time to access the 86th floor was when the NannyBots were busy with other things—the camp children were a good distraction. He had to consider the movements and routines of Dr. Emery who required sleep. If he could get into the nursery ward without being detected, perhaps in the early hours of two or three a.m., he might have time to search for Wally. But how to get her out of the tower unde-tected? He hadn't calculated that far ahead and could've kicked himself for not figuring out a plan with Maxwell, Cybel, and the others.

His friends were a few city blocks away, and Block had muted the comm device when he first entered the tower. He stood and scanned the dining room. The clat-tering of pots and clinking of silverware behind the kitchen's closed doors assured him he was alone in the restaurant's hall with its dark green walls and sky-high views. He tapped the comm button and spoke at his lowest vocal output level. "Hello?"

Only a faint static hiss came from the comm. "Max-well?" Block walked farther into the great room with its floor-to-ceiling windows and scrubbed at cloudy spots on the glass panes. At the kitchen door, there was no sign of the other NannyBots watching or listening. He was taking a big risk in attempting outside contact, and he'd better make it quick.

"Block." Maxwell's voice came through loud and clear, and Block hurried into a dark corner of the restaurant, stepping into a dark booth where he sat hunched in the corner. "You all right? We're not sure what's going on there."

"I'm fine, but things have gotten complicated. Can't explain now. Not much time." Block was glad for the communication tie to his friends, but if he was discovered, he would lose everything—Wally's safety was at risk, as well as his own life.

"How can we help?"

Come and blast your way into the tower and get me and Wally out of here. "There's nothing you can do from there, but I need to get to the 86th floor of the tower. There's a way, but I have to be careful."

A pause on Maxwell's end. "Can you distract the others?"

"I'm working on it."

The wood floors creaked twenty feet away. A beam of light crisscrossed the plush leather of Block's booth. He tapped off the comm, muting Maxwell. The beam from a NannyBot's built-in flashlight scanned and landed on Block's face.

NB-44's steel footsteps echoed as he approached the booth. "What are you doing over there?"

Block slid across the green bench and planted his feet carefully in order to stay standing and not be clumsy. "It was messy on the table and chairs."

"Impossible. No one's been back here since the humans were defeated." NB-44 twisted his torso to look back at the kitchen, then returned his attention to Block, tilting his head to one side as he leaned over to inspect the tabletop.

One of his companions, NB-17, exited the kitchen and came their way. "What's going on?" Block assumed 17 was the more senior unit, judging by the numerical ordering.

"399's being weird."

Block wished NB-15 would return. The others deferred to him. But Block was on his own and noted the cold hostility dripping off the two units. He needed a better excuse than cleaning. "One of the children lost something." He leaned forward, switching on his light beam to shine it under the table. "I was looking for it."

"You were talking out loud," NB-44 said. "I heard you."

Darn. Think fast. "I was talking out loud to myself. Listing off my tasks."

The two NannyBots looked at each other, and NB-17 said, "399 is malfunctioning and should be repaired."

"A tune-up?" 44 asked.

"No, just some modifications. There are tools in the kitchen."

"Please." Block took a clumsy step backward. *Don't fall and look like an idiot.* "I can do my job if you'll just leave me to it."

NB-44 moved fast, gripping Block's arm in a tight hold. The robot jerked him forward, and Block stumbled, landing hard on one knee in the same spot he'd been cleaning. NB-17 seized Block's other arm and heaved upward, lifting him an inch off the ground.

"But I haven't finished the floor." Block kicked his legs as the two NannyBots hauled him into the kitchen. He couldn't let this happen. If they adjusted him, they could wipe his memory files or corrupt his CPU which meant forgetting his mission to rescue Wally.

"Do what we say, and you'll be all right." They released their hold and shoved Block onto a stainless-steel table.

"Please, I don't need adjustments." Block inched away on the table. "You can ask NB-15. I already had a tune-up. He was there afterward."

They crowded him, dragging him closer on the slippery table. "He's 15's new pet," NB-44 said.

"Of course, whatever 15 wants, 15 does. He walks on a golden beam of sunshine when it comes to Dr. Emery. I say we wipe 399 and make him do our chores," NB-17 said.

Wipe? No, no, no. Block struggled in their grip, but the NannyBots restrained him with their titanium arms and forced him on his back. He bucked and writhed, his blue-alloy hips and spine denting the table in a cacophony of warping metal, but the two held him down. Their grips were strong and unyielding. 44 opened a panel on his side and pulled out severe-looking instruments—a screwdriver, a metal hook, and something that looked like a drill.

"Please, I don't need to be adjusted or have my memory erased. I have a job to do." *I can't fail Wally.* 44's hand hovered over Block's torso, above his CPU. He hadn't traveled all this way to end up wiped by two bullying NannyBots.

44 set the screwdriver in his hand down and picked up the drill. He reached toward Block's chest and went to work loosening the bolts securing the panel where his CPU and CleanerBot core were hidden. A shrill buzzing

filled the room as the tool powered on. 44 leaned over Block. "You'll be good as new."

"Please, no." Block prepared for the worst—forgetting Wally and everything he knew. Oxford, Maxwell, and the others might eventually find him and re-educate him, but it was a long shot when he was unrecognizable. They would be listening through the comm link, horrified at the uncontrollable situation. At least they would know. Block pounded his feet against the table when the doors to the kitchen opened with a thud.

NB-15 stood in the doorway. "Stop at once." His vocal output had a surprising ferocity.

44 looked at NB-15 but didn't turn off the whirring drill. NB-17 kept hold of Block's pinned arms.

"Release him." 15 stomped toward the table where the rogue NannyBots were about to lobotomize Block's CPU.

"He's a bad unit," 17 said, "and needs adjustments."

"No, I'm not." Block wriggled and twisted, trying to free himself from 17's grip.

NB-15 marched up to 44. "I said release him."

44 stopped the grating buzz of the drill. "And if we don't? Will you report us to Dr. Emery?"

15 said nothing and came to Block's side. He went face to face with NB-17.

"You may outrank me," 17 said. "But Jexa Era will agree with our actions once we make a report of 399's behavior."

NB-44 slammed the drill down on a nearby wooden chair. "The bot was wandering around the dining area talking to itself and failing to obey us. Something's wrong with it."

"I'm under orders from Dr. Emery to take unit 399 to his new post on level 86." 15 pushed past NB-17, grabbed Block's hand, and helped him off the table. "Come, we must get you to your next assignment."

But 17 stepped forward and gripped Block's shoulder, holding him back. "Is Jexa Era aware of these new orders? It's my duty to report any strange occurrences to her, by rule of the Supreme Commander."

"And mine to report any irregularity to Dr. Emery," 15 countered. "We're leaving now, and if you interfere further, you'll be held accountable."

Block didn't fully understand the power play happening but hoped that NB-15 was on the winning side.

15 turned and headed for the door. "We're leaving. Come on, 399."

Block pushed himself away from the table and the awful bots, but 17 held onto his shoulder for another second, then released him. He wasted no time, hustling behind NB-15 as the NannyBot exited the kitchen, headed through the dining hall, and out into the corridors. Block did his best to keep up with 15's longer strides, but it was hard when his wobbly knees still didn't fully cooperate. Titanium feet clanged, echoing through the stone-floored hallway. More than just his and 15's footsteps. The two NannyBots followed at a distance. Block's hopes of keeping a low profile were soured. He'd never antici-pated this much scrutiny from other NannyBots. They were spies for Mach X. Whoever Jexa Era was didn't sound good at all.

NB-15 passed by the elevators and hurried Block into a stairwell. "Don't get on Jexa Era's radar," he said as they climbed a series of steep steps. "Dr. Emery can help protect you, but it only goes so far."

"I won't forget your help," Block said, grateful to be intact and not reeling from a memory wipe with no idea of where he was or even who he was. Would he even have still realized he was a CleanerBot underneath?

"NB-17 has been my nemesis ever since we were created. You did well to remain calm."

Block decreased power to his CPU to save energy. He needed to recharge soon, but his focus was on securing Wally's location first. "Can we go to my post on floor 86?"

NB-15 rounded a corner and halted at a door that led to the 46th floor hallway. "I made that up. Dr. Emery didn't really assign you there."

"But wait"—Block scrambled for some excuse as to why he must get the job—"I'm excellent with children. Really, I am."

"You ever handled toddlers? Unruly, unkempt, and intolerably loud creatures." 15 looked through the door's window, then paced inside the small stairwell while Block waited.

"Yes, in fact. Toddlers are my specialty."

That caused 15 to stop. "Since when? There are only eleven toddlers in the whole building—that's how many have made it this far. I've been overseeing them the entire time, and I've never seen you."

Think of something clever. "It's an aspiration. I want

to move up in the hierarchy, of course. I absorbed all the training modules I could find about handling toddlers," Block said. "I can help. The camp children enjoyed the story I told them."

15 checked the window into the hallway again. What he was waiting for, Block had no clue. Then he raised his chin, tilting his blue head back and forth as he studied the staircase. "Rule number one, Mach X has eyes and ears everywhere. Remember that anything you say can be—no —it *is* being consumed by him."

Block had suspected the surveillance inside the tower was intense, but if it was true that Mach X could see and hear everything he did and said, then nowhere was safe to communicate with Maxwell, Cybel, and the others. Getting Wally out safely was proving to be impossible.

15 went on. "Here in the stairwells, there are a few pockets of dead space. The Supreme Commander doesn't have any AI-accessible objects in these walls. The building was built pre-Uprising, and the steel and stone walls were built thick in case of earthquake or storm."

Block logged a note that the 46th floor stairwell had privacy, though he wasn't sure how useful it would be given the walls were so structurally dense there was probably no way his comm signal would work.

"You want a post in the 86th nursery? It's an enviable position, of course. Working beside Dr. Emery is a privilege." 15 rested his hands on the iron banister inside the dim stairwell lit only by a single naked light bulb. "NB-74 has been irritating of late. I suppose I could reassign him to the infant ward. He does better with the small humans."

Block wanted to beg and plead for the new position, but something held him back. His scenario processor told him NB-15 wouldn't react in a positive way to an outburst. The robot liked things orderly. That much was obvious by the way he conducted himself and revered Dr. Emery.

"You would have to be on your very best behavior," 15 said.

"Of course."

"Things have been tense, and Dr. Emery's been on edge since the child died."

Block's threat indicator flashed red. An internal voice announced, *Warning, warning.* If he could have screamed like a human, he would have. A child had died! *Not my Wally.* He stumbled forward, leaning against the stair's railing. "There must be some mistake. Surely Dr. Emery can save a child's life."

"There was no helping it." 15's wrist buzzed with an incoming message. "Dr. Emery needs me." He pushed through the heavy double fire door. "With me. Hurry."

Block's every step down the hallway and onto the elevator was an anchor weighing him down, wrenching him to a pit deep below the tower. If Wally had died, there was no point in doing anything ever again.

They reached the security doors that led into the 86th nursery. NB-15 paused at the ID station as a scanner light passed over the identification tag stamped on his chest. Block processed scenarios about what to do in the event of Wally's death, but everything was scrambled. His logic module was off kilter.

Past security, 15 led the way into a waiting area that

looked like a lobby. The walls were a glossy white, and pearly cushioned chairs that resembled half of an eggshell were situated along a wall across from a wide-open space that ended in tall windows.

Dr. Emery sat in one of the chairs with a pale blue blanket wrapped around her. It wasn't large enough to cover her body. She didn't acknowledge the two robots. In her hands, she clutched a small glass that contained a light brown liquid. The blinds before her were drawn, and the main light was off, leaving only a faint glow from the ceiling.

Up close, as Block and 15 neared her, her eyes were half closed, but then she opened them all the way and looked at NB-15.

"Emery, how may we help?"

Her eyes were distant, and she pulled the blanket around her shoulders. "Please, just . . . dispose of it." She waved them away.

"Of course," 15 said. "I'll take care of it."

A strange energy coursed through Block's core and tingled his sensors. He took a step toward the doctor and placed his hand on the back of the chair nearest to her. "I'm sorry."

She took a sip of her drink and swung her head toward Block as if noticing him for the first time. "Me too." Her chin quivered.

"What happened?" he asked.

She set the drink on a side table and twisted the blanket in her fists. "A fever. There was no saving him." She looked at Block with puffy eyes.

Him. It was another child. Block's circuits still

145

hummed, but his threat indicator notched down since Wally was no longer endangered. It still didn't make things better that a small boy had died.

"We can't always save them," 15 said.

But we can try, and I will rescue Wally. Block was determined to get his girl out of the tower before she succumbed to whatever illness or negligence killed the little boy. He had no other purpose.

Chapter 12
Ashes, ashes
Emery

Emery wiped away crud from the corners of her eyes. On the shiny white and yellow area rug, the empty glass lay on its side after it had slipped from her fingers sometime in the early morning when she'd dozed off. Her temples throbbed and her mouth tasted like the inside of a garbage dumpster. Stale whisky loitered on her breath, its vapors hitting her nostrils, making them flare. A hollow pang in her chest throbbed. The baby boy—Subject Seven—was dead. All the booze in the world wouldn't change that fact. She'd been an idiot drowning her sorrows in a bottle when she should have been in the lab figuring out what had caused him to decline so rapidly. If the other children were at risk, she would never forgive herself.

She pushed herself off the rigid, upholstered chair and winced at the stiffness in her legs and back. *Clean yourself up and get to work.* Nothing was more important than her research. She'd been a fool getting distracted with the camp visit and the children she'd brought into the tower. Maybe X was right that she shouldn't have any contact with the humans outside. Not when her research and experiments were unfinished, and certainly not when a subject had died on her. Inexcusable.

The shower was lukewarm as she let it run over her head and down her achy body. She emerged ten minutes later, gooseflesh rippling across her arms, the sensation at odds with the dread in her stomach. At the sink, she brushed her teeth, cursing her puffy, dehydrated skin and her weakness in wanting to numb the world away. As she spit out the toothpaste, the liquor she'd consumed the night before caught up with her. Her knees buckled, but she caught herself on the vanity before she collapsed to the floor. One thing she could not afford was to get sick. Not before her work was done.

Her wrist comm buzzed on the bathroom sink where she'd left it along with the clothes she'd laid out the night before. NB-15 had messaged an hour before. *The camp children are awake. What's next on their itinerary?*

She spoke into the comm as she fastened it on her wrist. "On my way." She hurried and pulled her black pants on, as well as a blue blouse and her white lab coat. Slicking back her wet hair, she secured both sides with bobby pins.

The kids had to return to the camp. She'd fulfilled her promise to feed, bathe, and clothe them, and had even given them luxurious lodging for a night. It was enough. Her work was too important to waste more time on the children of strangers, especially when they had no impact on her experiments.

After a quick elevator trip, she entered the suite where the children had slept. Inside, NB-15 watched from ten feet away as NB-399 stood in the middle of the room. The four kids held hands and walked a ring around the robot. "Ashes, ashes, we all fall down!" The kids collapsed onto the floor in a fit of giggles verging on hysteria.

Chloe stood and grabbed NB-399's hand. "Now it's your turn to fall down with us."

399 looked to NB-15 as if to say, "Help," but 15 ignored him and rushed over to Emery. "They won't sit down or obey our requests. What do you wish me to do with them?"

"They're leaving the tower this morning," she said.

"Doctor Lady." Chloe dropped NB-399's hand and marched straight for Emery. "You said we were going to visit your lab today for medicines. You promised."

Emery's shoulders tensed. She didn't have time to deal with the questioning of a whiny child. "Change of plans. There's no time." She turned on her heel and walked to the door where NB-15 waited. She paused only long enough to give him instructions that the kids couldn't hear. "Have them ready to go in five minutes."

"Shall I alert Jexa Era they'll be leaving?" 15 asked.

The pounding thud that stretched across her forehead punctured like a jackhammer at mention of the NanDroid commander. "No." Emery's tone was sharp. She forced herself to exhale and calm her breathing. "Thank you, but that's not necessary. I'll see them out myself." She didn't like the fact that this would waste more of her time, but she couldn't let Jexa intervene and hurt the children. Or worse.

15 nodded. "Yes, Dr. Emery." He looked at NB-399

who had been dragged onto the floor by the children and was lost under a mess of rambunctious little humans crawling over him. "399 will help me." He stomped over to the roughhousing kids. "Children, stop this at once."

Emery stifled a smile. The kids wrestling with the hapless robot was a welcome relief. Their innocence in playing with the NannyBot felt right to her. It was how she'd been raised after Mach X rescued her from abusive human caretakers, but it felt wrong to show any sign of joy when Scarred Boy's death lingered. She had to face the truth that something was killing the children. Her research had hit pause until she figured it out.

She could stand less than a minute inside the apartment as NB-15 did most of the rounding up and packing for the children. 399 didn't seem as useful and had a curious, wobbly gait. Odd that NB-15 had chosen the unit to work with the Ward 86 kids. Chloe and Tommy ran behind 399 and kicked at his heels, shrieking with laughter.

Emery pushed beyond the doors and waited in the hallway, checking her watch every ten seconds. *Could they be any slower?*

Eight minutes later, NB-15 entered the corridor. Behind him, Tommy rode on NB-399's back and the other three clung to the robot's legs as he carried a large backpack in front.

"Hurry now." Emery summoned the elevator and crossed her arms. "We have limited time."

Tommy slid down from 399's back. "Did we do something wrong? I was having fun."

Inside the elevator, Ash grabbed hold of Emery's left

arm, pushing his face against her lab coat. "Can we come back soon?"

Emery's chest tightened. She was sending the kids back to a camp where they were treated like cattle. They deserved better, but she could hear Mach X in her head admonishing her about how her species had once treated her. *Don't get attached.* She gave her head a shake. "Time to go. I have work to do."

"We can teach you a fun game," Jenny said. "Wrestle the Robot." Her words sent the kids into a frenzy. They bounced up and down, tugging on NB-399's arms and knocking on his titanium exterior.

Their rocking shook the elevator on its descent. Sweat beads rolled down Emery's neck and bile rose. She swallowed it down and shook Ash off her coat. "That's enough! Silence." The kids froze. Jenny backed up against the elevator wall, and Tommy hid behind NB-399.

The walls were squeezing in on Emery. When the doors slid open into the lobby, she was the first to rush out into the refreshing burst of ground-floor air.

Thin, warm fingers grasped her hand and slid into her palm. Chloe stared up at her, her eyes green like tree moss, questioning. "Are you okay, Doctor Lady?"

As the children and robots shuffled out of the elevator, Emery let her hand go limp, allowing the girl to hold her hand tight. She nodded, trying to convince herself too. "I'm fine." The child's skin was soft like a baby's skin, and it was the first time she remembered experiencing a human gesture that signaled comfort. From time to time, she'd rubbed her index finger against the infants' palms, feeling their tiny squeezes, but that was an evolutionary reflex. Chloe's touch was meant to reassure Emery.

Chloe smiled up at her. "Momma has some tea that can help your tummy and make you feel better. I'll take you to our tent."

Emery's stomach flipped, but it wasn't nausea this time, it was a pang of regret that she wasn't more like Chloe and the other kids—all innocence and laughter and everything pure. After her years of studying and trying to better herself under Mach X's tutelage, she'd lost the emotions that had made her human. Her entire existence was serving X's agenda—to create his human-robot species.

Across the lobby, a sharp crack sounded from outside the glass walls. Two human figures dressed head to toe in brown and black, their faces masked, sprinted across the walkway outside the tower. One of them hurled a rectangular object against the lobby's glass walls.

There was a deafening pop as a bomb exploded. Shattered glass burst across the lobby, ejecting shards on the floor.

"Down!" Emery dropped to the marble floor and covered her head as glass pieces struck her like tiny pellets of sand. Chloe fell next to her, and Emery pulled the girl toward her, cradling her head against her chest and protecting her face. Emery's eyes were shut, but she could hear the screams of the children.

Outside, gunfire erupted as the SoldierBots mounted a defense. Whoever the attackers were, they wouldn't last long. A siren blared long notes of distress, and red and white lights flashed around the lobby. Emery knew X had watched everything happening in the lobby and would be busy activating security protocols and seeking revenge.

She opened her eyes. Sounds inside the shattered lobby were muffled, but she heard her own voice, shouting for everyone to take cover. Ten feet away to her right, NB-399 had shielded the other three children. The robot had flipped its body in front of them and shielded them from the flying glass and debris.

To her left, NB-15 lay on his side, motionless. Soldier-Bots carrying automatic rifles formed in lines outside the tower entrance. "Are you okay?" she yelled over the commotion.

The robot lifted his arm, then sat up. "My leg's no good."

Emery crawled over to him, pulling Chloe along with her. "Let me see." 15's right leg was severed at mid-thigh, a jagged piece of metal sticking out from the stump. His missing appendage was nowhere to be seen. A lump formed in her throat as she looked at him. She'd never seen him so helpless. "Oh, 15. I'm sorry."

"It's replaceable. What about the children? They must be protected."

Emery lifted her head. NB-399 was leading the children over. Their faces were blood-drained and serious. "The children are safe. It was a bomb." She shouted at 399 over the din of sirens and gunfire. "Get them in the elevator. Back to the suite."

399 nodded and hurried the children to the elevator bank. A SoldierBot sprinted across the room, its heavy boots clanking across the marble. "Emery, it's me." Mach X had assumed command of the robot. "I'm getting you

somewhere safe." The bot grabbed her arm, but she pulled away. "Help NB-15. I'm fine."

"This is no time to argue. Let's get you home."

She looked back. The kids were on the elevator safe with 399. The doors slid shut. A sharp crash and robotic voices boomed from outside. She had to see what was happening. Had the camp raised a rebellion? She couldn't help but wonder if she'd contributed to it by bringing the children inside.

Emery brushed past the hijacked SoldierBot, adrenaline turning her legs wobbly. The SoldierBots massed outside the lobby fired on a barricade where the two humans were trapped. They flung flaming glass jars while the SoldierBots discharged heavy ammunition. Another explosion and the marble floor trembled. The SoldierBot controlled by Mach X stormed outside. He rushed past the four lines of firing SoldierBots and his strides turned into a dash. Each of the rows of SoldierBots stopped firing as he ran toward the rebels.

X dodged a flaming glass jar and leaped high over the concrete barrier that shielded them from the gunfire. It was suicidal, but then again, it wasn't X's real body.

A human scream came from the far side of the wall. A rifle popped as multiple rounds were fired. The Soldier-Bots outside waited. Then the alarm sirens inside the lobby shut off, and a silence descended.

Mach X's SoldierBot emerged from behind the barricade. He dragged two humans—the two people in dark clothes. He shoved their bodies onto the pavement in front of the gates that led into the human camp.

The two attackers lay on their backs. One moved his

arms. Emery could offer medical attention, but she hesitated. The people had attacked and almost killed her and the children. It was senseless and stupid. She'd been on her way to bring the kids home.

The camp gates were empty, but Emery knew the people watched from hidden spaces. She ventured beyond the lobby's broken glass frames, outside onto the street. A haze blocked the sun, and she shivered in her lab coat, wishing for extra layers.

The Mach X SoldierBot stood in between the two dying people and faced the gates. "Let it be known that I will not tolerate attack." Someone shouted an obscenity and hurled a rock. It struck X in the shoulder but bounced off. He raised his rifle and fired at the attacker's spot. Someone screamed, then silence.

"I will destroy every last one of you if you don't cooperate," he said.

A woman with long black hair streaked with gray appeared at the camp gates. She was alone and wore a long dark red coat patched together from various fabrics. Her boots were worn and soiled. "You won't have more problems." She pointed at the two on the ground. "Those two don't speak for us. They attacked you on their own without our knowledge."

X nodded and lowered his rifle. "This your final warning. Any further attacks will end in your destruction."

The woman nodded, but her eyes never left him. "We understand." She walked backwards and disappeared behind the gates.

X turned and walked to Emery. "What are you doing out here?"

"I had to see for myself." She stared up into the SoldierBot's faceplate. The dark visor held X's consciousness. The robot she called Father.

"Return the children at once. I don't want to hear another word about them. You disobeyed me. If I see them again, I'll punish you."

Emery's heart hammered her ribs like a shark in a cage. "I'm too old for you to lock me up."

He pushed past her, then the robot halted and twitched. X had vacated. Conversation over.

Emery swallowed down several choice swear words for the anger swirling in her chest. She clenched her fists as Jexa Era approached.

The NanDroid held a long cord that Chloe, Tommy, Jenny, and Ash held on to as they marched in a single file line. NB-399 trailed behind but was surrounded by two NanDroids on either side. 399 hung his head as if ashamed.

"I'm doing what you couldn't." Jexa Era marched the children toward the camp gates.

"Wait, let me say goodbye." Emery dashed over to Chloe, but two SoldierBots grabbed hold of her arms and held her back. She kicked her feet, struggling to free herself from their grip, but she had no power against their raw, steel strength.

Jexa Era walked beyond the camp's gates, pulling the children along with her. Little Chloe glanced back at Emery, her face streaked with tears. Then she disappeared from view as they entered the camp. Emery twisted away from the SoldierBots, but it was useless. Her teeth chattered, but it wasn't from the cold. *If Jexa hurts them, I'll tear her apart piece by piece.*

After a minute, Jexa emerged from the gates alone. There hadn't been any sound of gunfire or screams or shouting, so the children must have been okay, but Emery still wanted to wail on Jexa with a sledgehammer.

Jexa walked to Emery and the SoldierBots. "Release her."

The guards let go, and Emery fell onto her knees.

"See what your frivolity led to," Jexa said. "The Commander is not pleased. You should have listened to me."

Emery chewed on her bottom lip, biting back the insults she wanted to hurl at the NanDroid. Jexa walked away, leaving Emery outside.

She turned and faced the tower, craning her head back to look at X's penthouse on the tallest level. No doubt he was watching her and would be observing her every move. She had to put the mess and chaos behind her. The camp children were back where they belonged. It was time to worry about the lab children and stop Jexa from interfering. She had to get to the bottom of why Scarred Boy had died, and whether the other toddlers and infants were at risk.

NB-399 stood alone inside the lobby, waiting for her. NB-15 had lost his leg. She'd almost forgotten. "See to it that he gets fixed," she told 399. "Then the two of you join me in my lab. We have work to do." She headed toward the elevator.

NB-399 called out to her. "You want me to join your lab?"

She spun on her heels. "I saw what you did to protect the children. You . . ." Her throat tightened. "If it wasn't for you—"

"I did what I'm programmed to do," 399 said. "Thank you. I'll get 15 fixed and report to you as soon as possible."

As she rode the elevator up, she wondered if she would ever see Chloe and the other children again. They belonged with their people in the camp settlement, not in the tower surrounded by robots. That was her burden to carry.

Chapter 13
A part of the solution
Block

Block wiped down the stainless steel countertops inside Dr. Emery's lab in a solitary, repetitive routine: spray antiseptic, scrub in swirling motions, and toss the paper towel in the trash. The medical lab was enormous, at least four thousand square feet, with eight large metal tables lining the room. Their tops held beakers, vials, test tubes, bottles, and surgical instruments inside disinfectant machines. A child-sized hospital bed rested in one smaller area that was surrounded by plexiglass. NB-15 told Block it was the surgical cube where operations were performed. Above the bed, a purple and orange mobile hung from a hook in the ceiling. Nylon straps fixed to the floor and walls held the bed in place.

NB-15 paced next to tables that held computers and large screens, letting Block do all the cleaning prep, as they waited for Emery to arrive. Things were going Block's way. It was almost too good to be true. Doctor Emery had invited him to the lab, and he was getting closer to Wally's ward. He'd brainstormed ways to sneak onto Wally's floor, but he couldn't make it past the automated security checkpoints and scanners. There was always a sensor near an elevator or in the stairwells. Even a simple walk down a hallway tracked him. The cameras watched all the time. Sneaking in was impossible. He needed more time to prove his worth, gain the doctor's trust, and get access to the children through her.

"I don't know about this." NB-15 leaned against a tall workstation where a microscope sat and flexed his new leg back and forth, kicking out like a marionette. "They put it on too fast. It wasn't the quality that NB-264 is usually known for."

Block paused his cabinet drawer handle polishing and inspected 15's new leg. It was a shinier, darker blue than the rest of 15's more faded chrome. An hour before, in the repair station, another NannyBot had supervised the repairs and welded the new leg onto where a shard of metal had sliced off 15's leg mid-thigh. "It looks good to me."

"Are you sure? The welding job was sloppy, and the colors don't match well." 15 pushed away from the table and lifted his left knee, attempting to balance on the new leg. "The spring tensors are off or something. It's not as tight and coiled as it used to be."

Block said nothing and turned back to the third metal handle he'd been polishing. It was the nooks and crannies that often got overlooked in cleaning. 15 should be grateful to have a new working leg at all instead of griping about it. Block's entire body had been welded onto his core frame, and yes, it was strange to operate with new appendages and even function differently, but he'd shut up and put up.

"I'll have to go back and demand a replacement," 15 said.

A shrill beep sounded, and Block stood and looked for the source. A video screen on a monitor showed Doctor Emery approaching the lab's outer doors where she let the biometric security AI scan her face. She entered in a hurry, wisps of her straight black hair tracing her chin. Ignoring Block and 15, she walked to a computer station and touched the monitor, sliding her fingers across the thirty-inch screen. Raw data, charts, and graphs flitted across.

15 approached, keeping his footsteps lighter than usual. His voice was lower. "What does the latest data reveal?"

Emery banged her fist on a table and stepped away, biting the corners of her thumb. "Nothing unusual other than the slower reaction times."

"What about the lethargy?" 15 asked.

"No change in two days." Emery paced, and Block tried to catch up with what they were discussing.

Block hoped his boldness was permitted. "Excuse me—"

"Still no cause of death." Emery folded her arms, then uncrossed them and jammed her hands in her lab coat pockets. She went back to the computer and typed furiously into a projected keyboard.

Block looked at NB-15 for a clue, but the robot shook his head.

"We'll have to dissect the brain and see what physical

changes took place." Emery fiddled with a touchscreen next to the computer that displayed a series of dizzying numbers and graphs. "I don't see any other way."

"Excuse me." Block stepped closer to the table full of monitors. "Could it have been a virus?"

"Unknown." Emery leaned against the table and rubbed her temples. "Genetic abnormality, virus, rejection of the chip, it's always something."

"Doctor Emery," 15 said. "When was the last time you got any sleep?"

She brushed him away. "There's no time. If I don't figure out the boy's cause of death, the others could be next."

Block's threat indicator flashed in his internal feed. Wally might catch whatever the boy had and get sick. He had to get her out of the tower even sooner than he'd anticipated. And there was still no privacy where he could contact Maxwell and his friends for help. He was on his own.

He took a risk and stepped closer to where the woman pressed her arms against the table, staring at a computer chart. "Doctor Emery, let me help. I want to be a part of the solution."

Emery's chin quivered as she glanced at Block, then back at the screen. "If this is a virus, it's unlike anything I've seen. It amps up the inflammatory response to the point of cell death, and then the cells self-regenerate, but the process is accelerated to the point of disorganization and is almost malignant."

She slumped into a chair and drank from a thermos

on her desk. "Look at the scans, 15. I'm not sure what we're dealing with."

15 walked to the screens, and Block joined him. The numbers and charts and letters made no sense. He supposed he could figure it out given enough time, but the danger to Wally was too urgent.

"Subject Seven was born without physical or mental defects." Emery sat at her desk, kicking out so her chair swiveled back and forth. "He had a clean slate, the brain was undamaged, and the chip worked properly when we put it in last year."

The chip. The same hideous implant that Mach X had put in Wally's head. Only Block realized now it hadn't been X, it had been Doctor Emery who was conducting all the experiments on Wally and the other babies.

The charts displayed a small child's body with a series of numbers, shapes, and graphs circling their vitals and a series of scans. Most of the data was too advanced for Block's comprehension, but the central screen showed a human skull perfectly formed in the center of the screen. All the cranial scans for the twelve children showed a spiral embedded in the front part of their skull.

"What's that?" Block asked.

"The implanted chip that makes them special," NB-15 said. "Designed by the Supreme Commander himself."

"Why do it?" Block knew he was being aggressive. It was a line of questioning he wouldn't dare have asked in his CleanerBot body, but here in the quiet lab with only

15 and Doctor Emery, he was brave. "Why not leave them as they were born?"

Doctor Emery spun around in her chair. "I'm making them better." She stood and faced Block, but her arms trembled. It was slight, only something a robot could detect. "With X's advanced AI tech, the children will grow up to be something unique and incredible. Humans that can think as fast as a computer, who are logical and aren't held back by uncontrolled emotions. They'll live longer, be stronger and smarter than any human alive." Her eyes were wide and bright as she came closer to Block, but then her smile fell as she looked at his face. "You would never understand the purpose and pure beauty behind this, why X has sacrificed everything for this. You're just a NannyBot."

Block let her insult drift past him—he was used to insults from big, bullying robots. Despite her extensive education and medical training, Emery didn't understand the lengths a lowly CleanerBot would go to for his special friend. How he would do anything to protect Wally. Mach X and Emery wanted to experiment on Wally, and he couldn't let that happen. She was perfect as she was.

Block turned and polished a nearby tabletop while 15 stood silent. Emery sat down at her desk and worked on a keyboard with fierce strokes.

Block's logic module went to work as he cleaned. Nearly all his internal systems still worked the same, retaining the CleanerBot factory settings. He bent down to reach a grimy spot where the table met the floor and lost his balance. Tumbling to the floor, his metal clattered and caused Emery to flinch. But he had an idea.

Emery spun in her chair. "What's the matter? Seriously, you're the clumsiest bot I've ever encountered." She glanced at 15. "Does he need a tune-up?"

"He already had one recently." 15 extended a hand and helped Block up.

"My apologies for the noise. Sometimes my feet move before I can control them." *Don't make it worse.* "I'll check in at the maintenance office to have them take a look." He noted his lie-telling behavior again, but it meant getting Emery off his back and one step closer to Wally, so it was worth it. "May I offer an idea about the investigation?"

15 tilted his head as if curious. Emery had already turned back to her computer but swiveled a half circle to her left, tapping her fingernails on the desktop. "Go on," she said.

"If you'll grant me permission, I can inspect Subject Seven's crib and bedding for any sign of bacteria or virus that might have made him ill. Since the other children may be at risk, I can examine their beds too."

Emery kicked her chair back to her computer. "15 already did that."

She'd struck down Block's attempt—by far the best solution according to his scenario processing. *Think fast. What else?*

15 held a computer tablet in his hands. "Sorry to bother you, Emery, but the nursery actually wasn't inspected yet."

"What?" She pushed off from her desk and zoomed backward five feet in her wheeled chair. "That's one of the very first things to be done. We need samples. You know that!"

"It was the camp children, Emery. They kept me busy."

Emery raised her hand to her forehead. "Get it done ASAP. I'm grabbing coffee and I want the bedding samples here in twenty minutes." She rose from her desk and walked out of the room, her boot heels clacking against the tile as 15 looked to Block.

"I'm sorry." Block figured he had a NannyBot lecture coming to him. He'd overstepped. "I should have consulted you first before raising the idea."

"I'm at fault." 15 walked to a tall cabinet, opened its door, and retrieved a small rectangular box. "Here's the sample kit for you to gather specimens." He turned and withdrew another kit. "I'll go with you and show you the ward."

Block's internal circuitry hummed as they traversed the hallways and elevator to the 86th floor. As 15 checked in with the extensive security panel, Block waited. Wally was behind the heavily fortified door. He would have to record every single detail because the tiniest thing could factor into their escape. The doors into the children's nursery were three-foot-thick, steel-reinforced concrete.

The room was oval-shaped with dazzling wall colors —pinks, oranges, yellows, and pale green. A dozen cribs stood in rows on the side closest to Block and 15, and thirty feet across the room, there was a penned-in area where several NannyBots stood watch. A child babbled.

One of the NannyBots—NB-56—walked over and greeted them. "What can I help you with?"

"Here to collect samples from the cribs," 15 said. "How are the children doing? Do they seem healthy?"

"They're fine under my care, of course," the robot said. "I'll leave you to your sampling." He turned and went back to the children's pen. Block could make out a few toddlers crawling and running, but no sign of Wally.

15 turned to Block. "So which crib do you want to start with?"

Block didn't want to waste time inspecting them at all, but he had to pretend, a human behavior he wasn't skilled at. All the kids were in the play area. He chose randomly. "The one on the far-left wall."

"I'll take the right wall." 15 strode to the first crib on his side and unlocked the latch that secured it.

Block walked to the first crib and opened the side gate. A flat yellow sheet covered a thin mattress. Block opened the sample kit, pulled out a swab and ran it along the surfaces inside the crib—the metal bars, the fabric, the top of the mattress, and even underneath. He stuck the swab into a small box where a series of wireless sensors and microscopes would process the data and transmit it back to the lab. 15 had explained it all on the way down in the elevator. Each crib would be assigned a separate label so they could pinpoint any anomalies.

As Block did the work, he snuck looks at the play area. Four NannyBots tended to the children. They didn't interact much, preferring to watch from the perimeter. The children played, some making small noises, but he didn't see Wally among them. A jungle gym blocked his view of two babies in a corner. Block noted the location of NB-56. The bot seemed to oversee the nursery area and wasn't so friendly. But what was the point of worrying about that when he hadn't located Wally yet?

Block hurried to the next crib in his row and repeated the swabbing process. The faster they completed the sampling, the sooner they could get near the kids, or so he hoped.

Twenty feet across the room, NB-15 gathered samples with precision and efficiency. "How's it going, 399?"

"As expected, nothing unusual." Block bent over the fourth crib with his swab when he noticed a wadded-up pink blanket. The NannyBots must've missed making up the bedding on the crib. He bent over the thick blanket and pulled it back with his left hand. A hint of soft brown hair made him drop the blanket. He recognized the curly locks, the little forehead.

Wally.

She was right there.

15 was leaning into a crib scraping the corners and oblivious to Block's actions. Block slipped his hand underneath Wally's shoulder and pulled the blanket down. She wore a pink footed sleeper. Her hair was matted, her eyes closed. "Hello," he said, leaning over.

Her eyelids fluttered open, and she stared up at him, her lips turning up in a half-smile. "Ga-ka," she babbled.

"It's B—" He halted his speech. He wanted to tell her it was him, her best friend in the world, but Mach X would be watching and was likely observing him now through Wally's cognition. He could not blow his cover. Cybel's warnings stayed with him.

"Don't be afraid, little one." He picked up a stuffed

rabbit that was jammed in a corner of the crib and placed it in her hands.

Wally wiggled a little on her back. "Ha-go." She rubbed the rabbit's nose. "Ka." She held the stuffed animal to her heart. Every part of him wanted to scoop her up, even if it meant a chase, but he had to keep his NannyBot cover. She gurgled and rattled the toy's head. "Ra-bo-ka."

Her babbling sounded a lot like she was trying to say "Block," but there was no way she could possibly recognize him when he'd been completely transformed into a blue NannyBot that looked the same as all the others. Perhaps there was a sign, something to let her know it was him.

15 was busy at a crib across the room. Block bent down, unlatched the side gate, and scooped Wally into his arms, cradling her against his chest. Her brown eyes blinked at him.

"Sa lo." She'd grown 9.4 pounds since he'd last seen her. Her little face was round and normal for a baby. It pleased his neural circuits. "Go-tok."

"Is the child asleep?" 15's voice came as a surprise.

Block turned his back on him and placed Wally back in the crib. "I found her in the crib. She'd just woken."

"Which one?" 15 joined him at her crib and read the label. "Subject Nine. That's the one that's having abnormal readings. Lethargy. She's following the same pattern as Subject Seven."

"What are you doing?" NB-56 approached. "It's not your shift yet, NB-15."

"Why isn't this child playing with the others?" 15 asked.

NB-56 leaned over Wally. He pulled the toy rabbit away from her and tossed it in another crib. "Last reading showed a fever of 101.6 degrees. She doesn't want to eat, prefers to sleep. Something's wrong with the child."

"I'll run a new diagnostic." 15 reached for Wally's hand, but she wiggled from his grasp, crawling to a corner, whining. Her eyes were wide, and from the way she huddled, it was clear the girl was afraid of the NannyBots.

NB-56 opened a compartment in his arm and withdrew a syringe. "Best to sedate her."

Block couldn't allow this. "Perhaps, you'll allow me to try first." He stepped in between them to get closer to the crib.

56 closed a hand on Block's shoulder. "You're new here, right? I've overseen Subject Nine's care since they retrieved her from the rebels and brought her here. She's refused to let me or any of the others get close to her. She's not a good candidate for you to work with." He held out the syringe and leaned into the crib.

"Wait." NB-15 pulled 56's arm back and pulled the bot away from Wally. "Doctor Emery has granted NB-399 special privilege to investigate the recent death, and that includes monitoring Subject Seven and any other subjects showing abnormalities."

"That's a load of DogBot crap." 56 said. "When did this happen?"

"Are you questioning me? Questioning the doctor's orders?"

"No." 56 backed up a step. "But it's my job to protect the subjects."

"You're getting in the way. When you interfere, the subject will be in danger, and we'll have no choice but to inform Doctor Emery. Now, until our investigation is concluded, keep your hands off the subject," 15 ordered.

"Fine." 56 put away the syringe, tucking it into the small compartment in his arm.

"Be on your way now. We'll handle this."

56 turned and went back to the other children, swiveling his head to look back over his shoulder a few times.

"Was all that true?" Block asked 15, keeping his vocal level down.

"The Doctor did ask us to collect specimens and determine the root cause of Subject Seven's death, so technically, yes." 15 placed his hands on the side of the crib gate. "With some embellishment. NB-56 has been a thorn in my side for a long time. Very competitive, that one."

Block chalked it up to luck that he'd somehow run across NB-15. The NannyBot had taken a liking to him, and it couldn't have been predicted. He owed the robot a lot. "I thank you for your assistance."

But 15 ignored him. "We still need to run the diagnostic." He held out his arms and called out to Wally, "Come here, child."

Wally cringed at 15's command and buried her head in the blanket.

Undeterred, 15 spoke slowly. "Come to me, child. I

won't hurt you." He stood there, holding his arms out to her, but it was no use, she wouldn't budge.

Block knew a better way to get Wally's attention, but he had to be careful not to reveal his knowledge of her. "May I try?"

15 backed away. "Go on."

Block grabbed the stuffed rabbit out of the adjacent crib and crouched low, holding it out toward Wally. She stopped whimpering, but still lay on her side curled up.

"Do you like the bunny?" Block wiggled it back and forth as if making it dance. "Do you want to play with it?"

She nodded and reached for it. He let her take it and pull it close in a hug.

"Interesting," 15 said. "Our usual protocols prohibit playful engagement with the subjects. Why do you do this?"

Block let 15 start the diagnostic process: measuring her temperature, swabbing her mouth, and taking a small amount of blood. "Maybe a wire got knocked loose during the tune-up."

"That would explain it." 15 finished and walked away. "Close it up. Let's bring the samples to Doctor Emery at once."

Block slid the gate up to close Wally inside, then latched it. She clutched the rabbit and gazed up at him. She didn't seem to have the same wide-eyed fear in his presence. He wanted to tell her it would be okay. That he was there and would get her away soon, but he didn't dare. X would turn him into a pile of molten metal faster than he could spin his head.

15 had reached the security door. "Hurry."

He pulled the blanket to cover her and tucked the toy in with her. "Goodbye for now."

The rabbit squeaked and she giggled. "Ra-bo-ka."

"Come on." The door swung open where 15 waited.

He backed away from the crib, hating to leave her alone with NB-56 who was so ready to drug her. Hideous.

Block was determined to get her out of the tower even if it took every circuit of his being, every ion of power, and every inch of alloy.

Chapter 14
A NannyBot so invested
Emery

Emery slid the vials that NB-15 and 399 had collected into the microbial sequencer and entered her security passcode. As the machine began analyzing the swabs from the cribs for any signs of virus or harmful bacteria, she turned to 15. "Give me the samples."

He handed her the kit containing the swabs, blood, and hair sample for Subject Nine—the baby girl who was showing the same early symptoms that Scarred Boy had. Nine was important. Ten months earlier, Mach X had sent Emery, along with a small army of SoldierBots, to retrieve the child in the Arizona desert after she'd been abducted by human rebels. Somehow a group of robots had taken the girl from the humans, resulting in a battle with the traitorous former General Oxford and his rebel crew. Emery hadn't gotten close to the fighting—the SoldierBots had made sure to protect her from danger, but she'd heard enough explosions and gunfire to know it had been frightening. She couldn't imagine the fear Subject Nine must've experienced, or what malnutrition and negligence she must have suffered in the care of robots, and not a single NannyBot among them.

Emery had run every test and health diagnostic she could think of on Nine once they returned safely to the tower. A healthy baby. Nothing horrible had happened to her in the care of the rebel humans and robots. A miracle. And yet, under Emery's care, the girl was suddenly ill, and Mach X was seething. Emery had to do whatever it took to prevent the girl, and any other subjects, from dying.

Chewing her bottom lip, Emery wore gloves as she sifted through the kit. With care, she placed the vial of blood, swab, and hair sample onto a metal table and pulled an overhead light over to examine the color and luminosity of the blood. She withdrew a sample and placed it into another sequencer that would reveal if Nine's immune system was responding appropriately. Could the girl have picked up some bug in the desert? Valley fever was possible, but the symptoms didn't match and wouldn't explain Scarred Boy's death. Whatever was happening wasn't isolated to one child.

NB-15 and 399 worked ten feet away at a high counter, tracking data from the automated sequencer as it whirred and processed each of the crib swabs. Once all the samples were analyzed, they would be cross-referenced by date, subject, and location.

"15, how's it going over there?" she asked.

"Progressing. We've identified four microbes that are present on all the subjects' cribs, but only in small quantities. Some of the beds have different bacteria extracted from skin fragments and hair follicles. The levels are small, but there are differences. I don't think they're significant, but I'll let you analyze them."

"Good work." Emery joined them at the sequencer. On the screen, the readout showed complex charts that had taken her years of practice to decipher. She could now read them almost as fast as NB-15. "I agree with your assessment. There are subtle differences, but no insidious microbes."

"What about a virus?" NB-399 asked. "Does it also detect them? I can go scrub and disinfect the entire room if you'd like to be sure any viruses are eliminated."

Emery had nearly forgotten the quieter robot was there, and now it was questioning her. 399 lacked the advanced sci-tech module that 15 was equipped with. "If you want to work in this lab, you'll need to upgrade your training modules. I don't have time for Science 101."

"My apologies." 399 backed away to a table that had a cleaning bottle and fiber rag, then busied himself wiping it down. "I'll make myself useful. Anywhere in particular that you'd like me to focus my cleaning?"

As she turned back to the screen, a twinge of guilt tugged on Emery and disturbed her concentration. She turned around. "399, you were the bot who shielded the children during the explosion, weren't you?"

399 paused his circular swiping for a second, then resumed. "Yes."

"I'm very grateful for your actions." She should go lighter on him. Once he had the upgraded module applied, he would know what he was doing. Something was unusual about the NannyBot, but she couldn't put her finger on it.

"It was my duty," the robot said.

"I don't mind explaining your earlier question. Come back."

399 folded the cleaning rag before returning to Emery's workstation. NB-15 said nothing and busied himself at a separate computer.

"We use a nucleic acid-based system to detect viruses." She glanced around the highly equipped lab. It rivaled any pre-Uprising medical research labs, and she was proud of what she'd built over the years. "That's the machine 15 is using. We'll see where things stand in another few minutes."

"I see," 399 said. "Thank you for explaining."

"You bet." She climbed onto a stool in front of a tall, skinny computer where Subject Nine's diagnosis stats were churning. The results should have been ready, but still processed. She picked at the edges of her thumbnail, made painful from her nervous habit. *Chill out, it's coming.* A blinking red light engaged on the monitor with Nine's data scrolling across the screen.

Her shoulders tensed. She leaned close to the monitor to read the number it showed: 70/65. Subject Nine's blood pressure was dangerously low. She checked the girl's previous BP readings—all had been normal up until then.

"Excuse me, Emery." 15 stood behind her, and she hadn't even heard his footsteps.

"What?" She didn't mean to be rude, but this wasn't the time for trivial niceties.

"The system detected abnormal readings in the recent brain scans," he said. "Increased microglial activa-

tion in Subject Nine's reading, as well as a few others, but it's most pronounced in hers, and when I crossed it with Subject Seven's final scan, it's following a similar pattern."

It was the last thing in the world Emery wanted to hear. How she'd missed something so basic was unfathomable. But more urgently, Subject Nine's blood pressure was crashing. "First, I need you in the nursery. Bring Nine down here right away. Prep the IV with midodrine. We need to get her BP up."

"Right away." NB-15 headed for the exit, and without a word, 399 followed.

While they retrieved the girl, Emery studied the scans. The station at the front of the room was the most advanced—four massive video screens each four feet high showed the brain images in 3D. Microglial activation was an immune system response to a brain insult. When the chips had been implanted in the infant brains, she'd monitored the immune response carefully. There'd been slight neuroinflammation, but it had been normal, a similar reaction as evidenced in decades of brain implant research on animals and humans.

Something was triggering an upsurge in macrophages attacking the implant. Emery's thoughts raced. Was it the activation of the chip itself that was setting off the immune system?

She'd been so meticulous, but there was no way to predict the long-term effects of the implants on the children's brains. The only way to test the effects was to inactivate the chip inside Subject Nine's brain. Routinely, she powered down the complex AI biomaterial every two months to reboot it and apply upgrades, rendering the chip inactive during the maintenance window. The process took four hours.

She cycled through Scarred Boy's pre-death data again and compared it to the last time his chip had been inactive—three weeks before. The clouds of inflammation that led to his swelling had lessened during the time the chip was turned off. Her gut twisted as she realized the clues had been right in front of her and she'd missed them.

"Emery, the girl is here." 15 wheeled a mini-sized stretcher into the room, snapping her out of her concentration.

"Into the operating theater." Emery peeled off her gloves, washed her hands, and applied new ones.

The surgical theater was a separate chamber enclosed in plexiglass—secured, antiseptic, and pristine. An operating table was surrounded by a huge overhanging light and several robotic arms. As Emery entered, the room had a soft blue glow. She resisted turning on the white lights that illuminated the environment, not wanting to disturb Nine and cause her more discomfort. As it was, the toddler kicked and twisted her body on the small bed. Her hair was damp from sweat and her cheeks flushed. "Restrain her." Emery turned away to prep the midodrine that 15 had retrieved.

When she approached the table, 15 was connecting the IV bag to a metal stand, but 399 was fiddling with the small metal wrist restraints attached to the bed. The robot stared down at Subject Nine.

"What are you waiting for?" Emery handed 15 the

midodrine to put into the IV bag. "Secure her wrists so she doesn't fall off the bed."

399 pulled on the metal cuffs, twisting them around in his heated robotic fingers. NannyBot hands had been specially designed to emit warmth and were silicon-based on the outside to handle the delicate human subjects. "These will hurt her. They're hard and cold, and the edges are sharp." The robot had a point, but there was no time to worry about creature comforts.

"We've always used these." Emery checked her watch. Twelve minutes had passed since she'd seen Nine's blood pressure reading. "You're wasting time. 15, get the needle in her arm."

15 went to the side of the bed and prepped her arm to insert the needle.

While holding the girl's small frame with what looked like gentle pressure, 399 leaned over to watch 15's IV insertion into the girl's small left arm. "Be careful. Don't make it sting. She hates when it stings."

"I'll do my best." 15 took extra time injecting the needle and hooking up the IV.

Emery had never seen a NannyBot so invested in a child's pain threshold. Usually, their movements were precise, mechanical. They got the job done without any fuss. 399 was being overprotective of the girl. She would address his odd behavior later. In the meantime, she had to bring down the girl's blood pressure, stabilize her, and figure out what was going on with her chip.

An hour later, the midodrine had done its job and the girl was out of immediate danger. Her wrists had been secured to the bed with soft nylon stretchy fabric that

NB-399 had found in one of the supply cabinets. The robot had barely left her side. To test her hypothesis, Emery had disabled Nine's brain chip to analyze the brain tissue reaction. In only thirty minutes, she was ninety percent certain the chip's activation was causing dangerous brain swelling.

A mixture of powerful emotions swirled inside her chest—surprise, shock, and worst of all, a hollow guilt that she'd missed evidence and let a baby boy die. She was light-headed and her eyelids grew heavy as she fought off gaping yawns, but she needed at least ten more minutes of data to determine her conclusion with absolute certainty.

While 15 left the room to take up his nightly shift on the ward, 399 had asked to stay. Emery figured he'd be helpful once the girl's sedative wore off. 399 stood at her side, watching and waiting.

Whenever Emery had gotten sick as a child, 15 would busy himself with chores such as food prep, medicine retrieval, and cleaning. He would check on her, of course, following a strict timetable, but there was no tenderness unless Emery asked for it—a bedtime story, a neck rub, or a bath.

She stood across the bed from 399 and checked the girl's temperature with the back of her hand.

"99.3 degrees Fahrenheit," the robot said. Nine's temp was displayed on a medical readout screen, but Emery wanted to check the girl's skin herself. She wasn't entirely sure why.

"You don't have to stand there, you know." She rested her hands on the hospital bed's side rail. "You could do other things until she wakes up."

399 rested his hands on the bed rail close to him, mimicking Emery's posture. "I like being close to her. I'll make sure nothing goes wrong."

"Well . . ." Emery was rattled. 399 was a strange unit, no doubt about it. Perhaps his circuitry got knocked about during the lobby explosion. "I'm here to monitor the child's status. I'll alert you if there's an issue."

"I understand your logic, however, I want to be close to her." Though 399's voice was monotone, his synthetic eyes were locked on the girl's face.

For the first time since the NannyBot had arrived in her lab, he seemed to be at ease. The odd clumsiness was gone, or at least masked, for the moment.

399 smoothed a section of the blanket near Subject Nine's leg. "Is she going to be okay?"

"I hope so." Emery studied the nearby screen that displayed her 3-D brain image in real time. "Her chip might be malfunctioning."

"I'll help her. I'll do anything to help keep her healthy, whatever you say. Please save her."

"Of course, I'll . . . I'm doing everything I can." Her eyes narrowed. The robot seemed to be losing his mind. How had the machine gotten so attached?

"I can track the pictures on the screens from here. And when she's conscious, I can check her vital signs. She'll be scared when she wakes up."

It was the first time Emery had ever heard a NannyBot worry about one of the test subject's emotional reactions to a medical procedure. The bots kept fastidious logs of the children's behavior, but always it was detached. Cold. "Subject 4 expressed his disapproval

Cameron Coral

when Subject 11 stole his toy truck. This resulted in a tantrum that lasted for 3.2 minutes." And on and on.

"Every child needs someone to look after them," he said. "I bet someone looked after you."

Nobody until X. "The Supreme Commander did."

399 tilted his head. "Mach X?"

Emery adjusted the IV bag, squeezing it from the top to smooth out any wrinkles. "Why does that surprise you? He saved me from life as an orphan. It was brutal."

"Didn't the NannyBots care for you? The units before me, rather."

"NB-15 has been my companion for a long time." She smoothed the blanket at the bottom of the bed, realizing the tininess of the girl's body. She'd lost some weight. "Your kind is programmed to watch, monitor, record, and keep the little ones out of trouble. X is the only being who has ever showed me true kindness."

399 looked at Emery, then down at Subject Nine. "The kids under your care may feel the same way about you someday."

The comment came out of the blue, entirely unexpected, and Emery struggled to interpret the rippling across her spine. Was the NannyBot right? Was she the Mach X in this equation? Was she showing kindness or her stiff, emotionless doctor persona?

A sensor on the screen dinged and Emery flinched. As she took in the results, she froze in place, unblinking. Her heart sprinted a mad dash against her rib cage, and her eyes hurt from the sheer exhaustion of keeping them open and focused on scan data.

"What is it, Doctor?" 399's voice floated past her ears,

188

sounding like the robot was in an echo chamber. "Is something wrong?"

Emery had to do something about the situation. She checked the timer—three hours and seventeen minutes since Subject Nine's chip had been disabled. Emery had never kept a chip inactive for longer than four hours. If she turned it back on, the girl would get sicker and die. She had to stop this.

She spun on her heels and grabbed her lab coat, pulling it on without a thought before realizing she had looped her arm in the wrong side and had to start over.

"Doctor Emery?" 399 stayed by the bed even as he barraged her with questions she didn't have answers for. "When will you return? What's the next step in the child's get-well plan?"

"Have to do something." Emery headed for the exit, her legs trembling with adrenaline. "Just watch the screens. The girl." She was tired and half-dazed.

Five minutes later, she stood in front of X's cubed mass. The structure had spread out another ten feet since her last visit.

"Daughter." X's humanoid figure twisted away from the tubes that fed into both sides of his titanium scalp and moved toward her. "You've been busy in the lab."

He'd been watching her. No surprise. He always knew everything, everywhere inside his tower, save for her shielded apartment. Still, it irritated her to no end. A cold, tight rage in the pit of her stomach coiled like a snake. She wanted to lash out at him.

"The chips must be deactivated. All of them." Emery's best shot was to act with force. "Now."

X watched her, his changing blue-green-coal eyes pulsating with energy swirls. "That would ruin all our work."

"The chips are hurting them. That's why Scarred Boy —I mean, Subject Seven, died. The activation is causing microphagial attacks. The project needs to be shut down, so I have time to analyze what's happening and . . ." She panted for breath, consumed by the dizzying amount of work ahead of her.

"Emery, dear." X brought his metal fingers together in a V-shape as if he was preparing a speech. "You and I have worked too hard for too long to stop the research from going forward. The timetable. Have you forgotten?"

"No, I haven't." November fourth was the date by which she was to have completed the waiting period for the toddlers and move on to the next phase—transplanting their spines with the new AI vertebrae that X was designing. "But something's not right with the chips. It must be halted."

"Give me the facts. Separate the emotion, daughter. How many subjects have died?"

"Well, one so far. Number Seven."

X came to Emery's side and took her hand. He rarely touched her. "One fatality out of twelve subjects, I'm willing to accept."

His hand was icy and slippery, and an odd tingling in her palm raced up her arm. "Subject Nine is gravely ill. Her blood pressure crashed, and she's showing the exact same neuromarkers that caused Seven to die. Her brain is swelling. This will kill her."

"And what do you propose?"

"Cut the chip signals for now. Power them off." She slid her hand out of his grasp.

"We need to keep going."

"We need an evaluation period. One week to pause all work and examine the chips." Her throat tightened, and a flush swept her cheeks. The children were in danger. What was the point in arguing when the outcome was certain?

"I'm not convinced. Even pausing a day sets us back too far." X's steel, transparent body lit up with neural packets of energy waves. He was a complicated, intricate mish mash of circuits and thrumming electric waves. "Why sacrifice all our work for one or two defects?"

A rush of panic made her sway. As she stumbled forward, her knees bumped into one of X's data cubes, and she sat on it. "A child died and another one is close to it! Have you forgotten the trouble you had in getting Subject Nine back from the robots who kidnapped her?"

A dark, inky purple shuffled across X's eyes. "I'm well aware. We couldn't let the implant fall into their hands. They would've stolen the tech."

So that's what he cared about—the tech and his war. Not a child's life. A new burst of stamina got her up and moving. She paced across the floor, keeping well away from his buzzing, warm data cubes. "I'm turning the chips off. I don't care—"

"You will do no such thing." X's voice was powerful and echoed against the penthouse suite's corners. "Continue the work. Stick to the timetable."

"But the girl." She choked back tears, a hard lump pulsing in her throat.

"It's the price of progress." X walked to her, his feet clanking down hard on the marble. He halted before her, not touching her this time. "You and I, we've talked about this before. You understood me."

"But I can't—"

"Enough." X turned away and strode back to his cubes. They fed him the world through their electrical currents, bits and bytes, and strings of data. "I'm fighting a war, quashing a rebellion on multiple fronts, and I have no time to argue with you. Don't bother me with this topic again."

Emery wished she could melt into a puddle. She couldn't defy his commands. It was the way things had always been. X made the rules. Emery followed them. He'd rescued her from a tortured existence among humans.

There was no other existence for her. She had to return to the lab and go on as of nothing had changed, all the while knowing a child was about to die.

Emery's life was no life at all.

Chapter 15
Or the bus leaves without you
Block

Rain clattered against the tower's sheer facade, rivulets like gushing tears dousing the smog particles. Evening had pitched the Manhattan streets into an inky cloak dappled with the smattering of lights from fires. Mach X's skyscraper had power, along with other SoldierBot outposts, but the rest of the city had been plunged into a murky existence where the few human survivors burned Ikea desks and antique armoires for warmth.

Block waited for the elevator to take him to the basement where he would exit through a sewage tunnel. It was to be his first time venturing into the streets away from the tower, and he fought it with every carbon fiber of his being. Nothing was more important than being in the lab with Wally. He was part of her inner circle of caregivers, yet he had no control over what was decided. He would sabotage Dr. Emery if he had to, to protect her.

But first, he had to peel himself away from Wally's bedside to attend to an urgent matter. Fifteen minutes earlier, Maxwell's voice had erupted through his internal monitor. "Block, we gotta talk. Head to the tunnel."

In the med lab with Dr. Emery and NB-15, Block had been so disturbed by the sudden intrusion in his auditory port that he'd dropped a tray of test tubes, shattering them into a thousand pieces. He'd spent several minutes sucking up the dangerous shards with an air vac, hoping all the while that Dr. Emery didn't kick him out of the lab for his atrocious clumsiness.

He'd concocted a reason for needing to travel to the basement—disposing of the contaminated samples they'd collected for testing. At the end of every day, the children's bio samples were taken to the basement for incineration, so he was being proactive in tackling the chore early. NB-15 had bought it, allowing him to leave in exchange for Block offering to take 15's nursery night shift so the robot could have a few hours' recharge. He had to be quick about the excursion, though, because the chore only required thirty minutes.

The basement was fifteen degrees cooler than the street level. Block's comfort sensors flagged high humidity and a dank odor that would be unpleasant to humans. Guarded by three SoldierBots, the space featured low ceilings and labyrinthine corridors that led to various storage rooms. A special orange tag on Block's chest identified him as a VIP. As part of Dr. Emery's crew, he could move about the tower as he pleased without questioning. Block passed the guards, locked the door inside the furnace room, hid the sample bag in a corner behind some robot battery stations, then paused before the heavy iron plate that concealed the sewage tunnel opening. *I'm too weak.* He raised a finger to tap his comm button, ready to call it off. Twenty-six minutes remained before his absence would look suspicious. Wally needed him. He wished they could have the stupid conversation there in the furnace room, but any external comms would be picked up by Mach X. Maybe he wasn't important enough to be monitored, but he didn't dare risk it.

He crouched before the sewer cover and grasped the hatch, twisting with full strength. To his surprise, the iron handle gave way with a dull creak. *NannyBot strength.* He'd forgotten. Climbing into the dark, he slid the cover back in place, allowing a few inches of space for his return.

The tunnel was narrow, barely wide enough for him to crawl, with a continuous stream of wastewater—thick, heavy, and slippery. At least he couldn't smell it. He recalled the time he and Nova had navigated the underground train tunnels beneath Chicago. How she'd wretched at the fetid odor. How frantic she'd been when the rats appeared. She hated rodents.

It took him a few minutes to locate Maxwell's secret passageway leading out of the sewers. As he neared it, a beam of red light scanned back and forth.

"Block, is that you?" Maxwell's voice came from several feet above sewer level.

"I'm here." Block reached up, grasping toward the light at the hatch. Maxwell grabbed onto his arms and pulled him onto a narrow side street. Dirt-streaked blue tarps stretched between windows of low-rise brick buildings on either side. The rain tapped a steady warning against the fabric. *Hurry.*

Maxwell rested his metal hand on Block's shoulder. "Glad to see you, friend." Cybel and Spoon stood nearby.

"Hey, buddy," Spoon said. "Vacuubot's out on the street, keeping watch."

Obviously eavesdropping, Vacuubot pinged. *Block, I'm just around the corner.*

"Thank you." Grateful to see his friends, Block's neural circuitry was buzzing, and his threat indicator notched down, but he needed to move fast. He had to get back to Wally and not risk his position with Dr. Emery. "I have sixteen minutes before I'm missed. What's so urgent?"

"We've been listening to your conversations," Spoon said. "The chip, it's hurting Wally—"

"I know." Block didn't need a rehashing; he needed a solution. "Can you fix her?"

Spoon started to say something, but Cybel pushed past him. "Nova sent news. Mach X dispatched reinforcements to Chicago. It's bad. The rebel forces are getting crushed."

Cybel's words sank into Block's neural circuitry with a jolt. The onslaught of awful news overwhelmed him. Nova and her crew needed help, but so did Wally, and she was number one.

"We'll retrieve Oxford from the junkyard, recruit more bots, and help Nova," Cybel said. "We'll move out in the—"

"No." Block couldn't grapple with Nova's situation. Not yet. "Go if you must, but I'm staying. Wally needs me." Cybel and Oxford were designed for war, but Block was made to help people through cleaning and hospitality. He didn't give a wrench bolt about their battles.

Cybel's head swiveled a few inches from side to side. Irritation, maybe. "We leave for Chicago in seventy-two hours. Join us or stay, it's not my concern. The rest of us are going."

They were going to abandon him in the middle of rescuing Wally. A warning screamed in Block's info display, 'Fourteen minutes.' Ten of those would be spent traversing the tunnel, and he needed a minute or two to rid himself of the horrible stench. "Spoon, can you help Wally?"

Spoon was a medical HelperBot, trained to assist hospital staff. "I'm no neurosurgeon, but the implanted chip will kill her like it did the other child."

"How do we get it out?"

"It's not easy. In fact, it may never come out." Spoon opened a compartment inside his wide lower half. "This is temporary." He handed Block a device that looked like a small TV remote control. "Press this when you're near Wally, and it'll disable the chip."

"You found a cure!" Block wanted to jump up and down and hug Spoon until microbial fuel poured out of his ears.

"Not so fast," he said. "It's short term. You have to be within twenty feet of Wally for it to work."

The sudden surge of juice to Block's circuits subsided. "Twenty feet? But I'm not close enough to her that often."

"I'm sorry." Spoon clapped Block on his shoulder.

"Best I could come up with so far. I'll keep searching for a way to disable the chip permanently."

Maxwell chimed in. "Get her out of there, bring her to us, and then Spoon can work on her while we ride to Chicago."

"Yes." Rescue was the plan, but how to get Wally out of the tower, undetected, when the building crawled with SoldierBots and Mach X always watched everything, not to mention Dr. Emery keeping her under constant medical surveillance?

"Seventy-two hours," Cybel added, "or the bus leaves without you."

Block watched a stream of gray rainwater carve a path through a pavement crack. "I can't do it myself." If courage were a liquid, all of it was draining out of Block faster than it could replenish. "I can't possibly get Wally out of X's tower alone."

"Figure it out." Cybel turned and walked away. "Let's go."

Eleven minutes. Block had to leave or risk interrogation. Maxwell apologized and followed Cybel.

"I'll keep working on a cure," Spoon said as he backed away.

"Thank you." Block watched them turn the corner onto the street and turned back toward the tunnel entrance. The drizzle turned into a downpour. The rain beat down, pounding the split pavement, forcing a torrent of water to flow into the sewer opening.

He was defeated. His rescue mission was as bleak as the drowning underground. He had no way to escape with Wally, and even if he could, she was doomed to die.

He could sneak into the lab and deactivate the chip, but Mach X would turn it back on the first chance he got.

He inspected the device Spoon had given him. A small black box with a green button. A homemade soldering job hastily done. He placed it into the compartment in his thigh, wedging it next to the fire extinguisher, and crouched down to enter the tunnel.

Wait. Vacuubot soared into the alley. *I'm staying with you.*

Block stumbled backward, caught off guard by his little companion, his oldest friend. "What are you doing? You should go with the others."

You need help.

It was true. Block couldn't go it alone. "They're abandoning me and Wally."

Cybel's in charge, and she's restless. She doesn't cope well waiting for things to happen without her.

"They'll leave without you—"

So what? We can catch up to them in Chicago when we have Wally.

Block's info display blinked. Nine minutes. He had so many unanswered questions.

I'll scope out the tower and plot a way to get you and Wally out safely. I need time.

"How will I know the plan? How will we communicate without being intercepted by Mach X?"

I don't know yet, but you need to go ASAP.

Block shook the water off his titanium frame and entered the dank sewer. He'd have to use every bit of NannyBot power to propel his legs and reach the tower in time.

Vacuubot hovered over the opening as Block descended the narrow ladder. *I'm here for you. Watch for my signal.*

A tiny array of hope sparked in Block's circuitry. "Thank you, friend."

Chapter 16
Life in a chamber
Emery

Emery's hand hovered over a stainless steel, backlit keyboard. It was one of several relics that Mach X had allowed her—she'd grown up tapping away on the boards in front of computer screens while she studied medicine. Such primitive instruments were no longer required after X's advanced intelligence leapfrogged such old computers, but Emery still wanted to code by hand. It was her only control over X's complete dominance over her life.

The lab was chilly after an unexpected, early-season frost had arrived. She wore a purple sweater over her lab coat, and beads of perspiration made a break from her scalp to her back, causing her neck to itch. She could permanently disable the brain implants—all it took was twenty-two lines of code—but her fingers shook.

To defy X was madness. He would be angry. *Furious.* At sixteen, she'd snuck into the Manhattan streets outside their penthouse home. A lonely teenager full of rebellious angst and hopeful thoughts about meeting people her age, she was thrilled with the novelty. It was night, and the sidewalks had been full of people walking, chatting, and cheering for some holiday she wasn't familiar with. Ten minutes later, a group of men had surrounded her in an alley. She would never forget the haunted look in their eyes, their mouths twisted in rage as a SoldierBot located her and shredded the men with its rifle.

X had been incensed. He'd punished her by forcing her into the Silver Chamber—an awful, dark cell where all her senses were deprived. All she could do was sleep and fret away the hours wondering what he would do to her. She had no idea how long she'd been kept inside. A tube fed her some gloppy chicken-flavored substance along with drips of water.

After her release, he'd lectured her about the dangers of the city, how she'd never be safe among people, and that Emery's kind was destined to be war-like and self-destructive. It was then he'd hatched the idea to create a hybrid AI-human species. She'd had no choice but to bring his grand vision to life, mastering fertility science and cloning. Years had been spent perfecting the harvesting of human eggs from cloned wombs, then incubating them in a perfectly controlled environment.

It was her life's work. X called her a genius. "I'd never have been able to do this without you," he'd said. Emery wasn't sure that was true, but she went along with it. X had been the one who'd saved her from her abusive foster parents and from an alley attack. He was her father, her protector, and for that she was eternally grateful. But after the Silver Chamber, something had shifted in her. A new emotion invaded her mind and clouded her heart—dread.

Against a black screen, orange text danced in front of her. She stared at the lines of code that would disable the brain implants. But X had told her not to turn the chips off. The trials must go on. Her heart rocketed as she squeezed her eyes shut and clenched her fists. *Get it together.* Backing away from the table and computer, she jammed her hands in her pockets and paced a circle around the array of monitors and screens. She wanted to disable the implants, but X would know immediately because he watched through the children's eyes. The data constantly streaming into him included their observations —vision, hearing, smell, taste, and touch. The children were his ears, his eyes, his nose, and his tongue.

X could hack into any of his robots in an instant, commandeering them. The children were different. They were an extension. An unbreakable bond between X and the kids that Emery had helped create. In a way, she'd sentenced them to life in a chamber. She could end it all and free them.

She chewed the raw skin on her thumbnail, remembering the cold walls of the Silver Chamber. The endless darkness devoid of sound. From nearby, a screen flickered and something on camera caught her eye. She shook off her trembling and walked over to it. It was a view of the cribs inside the 86th floor children's nursery. A NanDroid's sleek chrome flashed.

Jexa Era was standing over Subject Nine's crib. A shiver thrashed its way up Emery's spine. She bolted for the lab's doors and sprinted through the hall and into the elevator. A minute later, she burst into the ward and ran toward Nine. Jexa Era didn't move from her spot next to the crib, but she moved her arm behind her back.

"What are you doing?" Emery skidded to a stop before the crib. Subject Nine was still inside and breathing in ragged spurts.

"The child is fevered." Jexa's voice was more human-like than the older NanDroids. It was a feature that had always bothered Emery. "It's dying."

"I told you not to come in here." Jexa's meddling had to stop. "The children are in my care."

The red beam across Jexa's visor beat a steady back and forth pulse like a metronome. "Subject Nine has been dying for a week. There's nothing you can do for her."

Emery's nostrils flared and every inch of her shook from her scalp to her toes. "Get out."

Jexa was weaponized. The bot could kill her if she wanted to. Early on, after X had built the second-generation NanDroids, the idea had terrified Emery, but as time wore on, she'd come to realize she was protected because she was X's daughter. But that didn't stop Jexa from challenging her every step.

Jexa's visor blinked red, and she brought her right arm forward, gripping a syringe. "Why have you allowed the child to suffer in this way?"

The question surprised Emery, and she fought back a hot wave of tears. Her words came out in a broken whisper. "I can fix her."

"This jab will end it all." Jexa placed her left hand on the crib. "Then you can go back to your experiments. You're jeopardizing the timetable with your incessant fretting over this defective subject."

Emery felt like she'd taken a gut punch. "She's not a defect, and I can stop her pain."

"This subject's not one hundred percent human."

"I won't let you hurt her."

"The command came from Mach X." Jexa watched Emery, never raising her even-keeled, smooth voice. "Eliminate the child, get the project back on track. Subject Nine is merely a distraction."

Emery grew dizzy, and a wave of bile rose in her throat. No way would X betray her confidence like this— sending Jexa Era to assassinate the child. It wasn't his way. "You're lying."

"Sadly, no." Jexa stepped away from the opposite side of the crib and walked toward Emery. "I disagree with our Supreme Commander's view on these subjects. Cultivating the children into some machine-human hybrid is futile. Why does he need them when he can create perfect robotic machines? My model is far advanced over any robots X has created so far."

"You're delusional." Emery's words came out raspy from her dry mouth.

"You haven't seen everything I'm capable of. You don't want to, trust me."

"Get out." Emery would secure the lab by changing the security codes and assigning guards to keep Jexa out. Then she'd visit X to alert him to the NanDroid's lies. Jexa had to be punished with a tune-up. Wipe her memory and start over.

"Fine." Jexa held out the syringe. "I'll leave you this so when X commands you to kill Subject Nine, you'll have it handy. You are his pet human, after all."

Emery flung her hand up and knocked the syringe out of Jexa's hand. It clattered on the floor and rolled under one of the cribs. She rushed at Jexa, fists clenched, ready to tackle the robot, but Jexa backhanded her across the face and sent her tumbling to the floor. Emery's vision blurred and her ears rang. She touched her lip. Blood. She wiped her fingers on her lab coat and raised herself up on shaky legs.

No robot had ever hit her before. X had forbidden it.

"You'll be wiped for this." Emery choked back sobs.

"We'll see." Jexa turned on her heel and walked toward the exit. "Remember that all owners eventually grow tired of their pets."

After the steel doors clanked shut, Emery sank to her knees, struggling to catch her breath and reckon with her stunned disbelief. Her jaw ached from Jexa's blow. X would have been watching the events unfold, had inevitably seen Jexa strike his daughter, and yet he'd done nothing to stop it.

Nothing. No message on her wrist comm.

Perhaps he was so livid, he was sending a troop of SoldierBots to detain Jexa. Her finger hovered above the comm, ready to tap it and talk to him, but something stopped her. She needed to face him in person, let him see the blood trickling down her chin.

Minutes later, she stood before his door as the biometrics scanned her face. As the only human inside the tower, it was a split-second task. But something was different on this visit. For the first time since X had purchased the upper floors of tower ten years earlier, she was denied immediate entry to his chambers. 'Please wait,' the scanner said.

After nine minutes, the doors parted and Jexa Era emerged from his suite. She ignored Emery and headed for the elevator doors. That was it then, X had been punishing her. Emery only wished he'd permitted her inside to watch.

His voice called from inside. "Enter, Emery."

She hurried inside, her cheeks fiery with anger. She went straight to the bar in the corner of his vast open room, past the myriad of data cubes and wires. It was her bar, always set up with fresh water, ice, and fully stocked. She poured herself a glass of water and drank half of it in one gulp. She craved something stronger but that could wait. She turned to him.

X stood between two glowing green boxes, cables hooked into his arms and legs that didn't hinder him from moving. "What do you have to say for yourself?"

What the . . . ? He was supposed to be on her side. She'd been wronged. Emery tucked a strand of hair behind her ear, and the awful dread feeling was back. She felt like a child under his gaze. Her voice came out with a crack. "Jexa attacked me."

"Jexa would never attack you. She's programmed to serve. She's your friend."

"My friend?" Emery's stomach flipped.

"You provoked her. I watched it happen, and she explained her side of the story to me."

Emery's breath came in tiny gasps. "She *hit* me. You'll punish her, right?"

He turned away from her, toward the majestic view of

the night sky. "You struck first. Shall I replay what happened?"

"No." Emery's voice was small, like she was in the bottom of a well and losing all sense of what was real. "She was going to kill Subject Nine. Said you ordered her to. That's a lie, isn't it?" He didn't answer. "Please tell me it's a lie, Father."

"Our next generation will be far superior once you're finally ready to harness the knowledge that's already been gleaned. I don't have time to coddle one small defect. Subject Nine is a sacrifice I'm willing to make."

"She's not a defect. She's a human baby." She was shaking and took another swig of water, wishing it was whiskey. "She deserves a chance at life. I can disable the chips and start over again. There must have been a flaw—"

X's voice boomed and echoed across the crown-molding corners. "You'll do no such thing. Stop postponing and continue the experiments. We're so close to the next phase. We can't delay."

"Even if more of the children die."

"Yes, I don't care. They're expendable." He retreated to his throne-like seat deep inside the cluster of data cubes. "Go."

"Father, please." But he ignored her pleas. A heavy, pulsating thrumming filled the room, so overpowering it made her eardrums throb. She ran from the room, hands clamped over her ears.

Jexa had won. The robot wouldn't be punished and was a danger to the children. Even worse, X was impatient with Emery. If she failed to deliver, he could take all her work—her life's mission to create a kinder, more resilient human species—away from her.

The trauma of the evening's events still rattled her. X had dismissed her. She would have to regain his trust and protect the children while Jexa Era worked against her.

Chapter 17
What I'm programmed to do
Block

Block pressed the button on Spoon's device, and twenty minutes later, Wally's chest rose and fell, rhythmic and steady, as she breathed like a two-year-old should. With only the nursery ward's dim overhead lights turned on, he sat beside her crib, his bottom on the smooth, stone floor, legs stretched out underneath her bed, bringing him eye level with Wally as she dozed. Snores from the other toddlers drifted in and out of his auditory feed, but he backburnered them, wanting only to tune in to Wally's vital signs. Another twenty minutes passed, and her body temperature had decreased to 99.9 Fahrenheit—down from 101.1. Block owed Spoon a huge favor when this was over, if they got out of it intact. So long as the device was engaged and close enough to Wally, her symptoms were lessening. The device disabled the chip in her brain like Spoon said it would.

An indicator flashed on his visual feed—low fuel. Despite his more energy-efficient NannyBot frame, underneath it all, his core was still that of a CleanerBot, and he was powered by a microbial cavity that fed on waste such as oil, grease, and wastewater. But all those things were in short supply inside the impeccably clean tower. So far, he'd had success sneaking into janitor closets where he'd discovered jugs of Murphy Oil Soap, but he'd used up his current supply and needed to find something in the children's nursery or face disaster if he powered down. But he couldn't leave Wally's side, not when she needed the device to chase away her illness. On his knees, he scanned underneath the sturdy, metal-framed crib. In each corner, the joints came together to create a small ledge. He rested the device on one of them and stood. It would do while he made a temporary run of the supply cabinets.

A scenario popped up on his feed—his processor was always running in the background—and in it, a NannyBot found the device while mopping the floors. There would be consequences. The small controller would be brought to Emery who would grow suspicious and imagine someone was trying to sabotage her work. There would be a search for the perpetrator. The worst scenario was Block getting caught with the device and then having his entire CPU erased in a tune-up. His memory archives, records, task lists—his ability to even recognize his beloved Wally —would be gone. He didn't have time to churn on the dire possibilities. *Find fuel.*

He searched a series of cabinets, tossing aside magic markers, paper, glossy cardboard children's books, and rubber chickens. A box of crayons caught his attention. The little waxy sticks made a good snack. He emptied them into the tiny compartment where the JunkBots had installed an opening into his microbial port. His fuel indicator notched up one level, but he needed more, something sticky, something gooey. A closet door by the far wall yielded more objects to sort through. In his search, he found a glue gun with no glue, a roll of white electrical tape, and a bag of rubber bands. Still no fuel. He opened another cabinet and nearly clapped at his discovery—a blue and yellow can with the words WD-40 written across the front. He twisted off the metal top and dumped the liquid into his port. It was one of his favorite human-invented liquids. The formula was a common lubricant and rust preventative. In researching its origins, he'd discovered the formula was originally created for the Rocket Chemical Company in the 1950s. He'd once told Nova about it, and she'd rolled her eyes. She'd done that a lot when he shared his research findings. Block paused a moment. The sudden intrusion of the Nova memory had distracted him. He missed her. It would be nice to see her again once he got Wally out.

He stowed the empty can and returned to Wally's side. She was sitting up, her little curls sticking out at quirky angles.

"Hey." Block reached down. "I was worried." He scooped her up, ignoring the blanket that slipped from around her and dropped to the floor. "Are you feeling better?"

In his arms, her big brown eyes stared at him. Her cheeks were pink, and she fell limp against his metal chest as he held her.

A voice came from the entrance. "What are you doing with her?" Dr. Emery rushed toward them. She wore a white terry-cloth bathrobe, and her hair was pulled up in a hair clip.

Block's processor kicked into high gear. Whatever he did, he had to keep Emery from seeing the device under Wally's bed. "I found her in the crib, Doctor." He crouched down and retrieved the blanket from the floor. "Awake and moving about. She must have tossed out her blankie."

Dr. Emery's left eyebrow curved. "Her what?"

"Blankie." *Oh no.* Blankie was a play on words that Nova had used around him. He must have picked it up. "Or blanket, if you prefer."

Dr. Emery shook her head and dropped her hunched shoulders. "Weird. I've never heard a NannyBot say it like that." She glanced at the device on her wrist and yawned. "Usually NB-15 has the night shift."

"I told him I would cover tonight. He needed a good recharge."

Dr. Emery nodded, as though accepting his explanation. "She looks . . . almost, better." She pressed the back of her hand against Wally's forehead. "Measure her vitals. Project them on the overhead screen."

He did as he was told, and seconds later, Dr. Emery paused to watch the numbers dance across the dark screen above the glass-enclosed office where three computer workstations sat. "I can't believe it." She raced inside the room and tapped on a keyboard, then bolted out and back to Wally's crib. "Measure again. There must be a mistake."

"Yes, Doctor." Block tapped his index finger against Wally's temple. The semi-organic finger pad was equipped with thousands of nanosensors that could detect and report her vital signs within milliseconds— temp, heart rate, blood pressure, sweat rate, lung capacity, and more.

Emery stood in the doorway of the glass room, staring at the screen. "I've never seen a fever dissipate like that." She grabbed a pencil from a table and chewed on the eraser top as she paced a circle around the other sleeping toddlers. "Do you know what caused this?"

"No, Doctor."

Emery clutched the pencil in her hand, twisting it in and around her fingers. "How long have you been here and noticed her improvement?"

"I found her twenty minutes ago." He'd conveniently left out the other twenty minutes during which the device had first been in contact with Wally.

She snapped the pencil in half with a crack, her voice coiled with tension. "Why didn't you notify me straight away?"

Block had no answer—none that would fend off the question. He knew he couldn't reveal the device. Doing so would surely lead to his immediate reboot. Better to throw her off the scent by distracting her with a need to work. "I saw that her blanket had fallen out and she was shivering from the cold, and I was just about to send an alert to you."

"Odd that she would shiver when the cribs are perfectly temperature-controlled."

Of course, the cribs were engineered to monitor each kid. Block didn't realize his mistake until too late. She'd caught him in a lie. He was terrible at falsehoods.

But Dr. Emery shrugged and drew the tie around her waist tighter. "Then again, nothing surprises me lately. Not with Nine's sudden recovery." She headed for the small office, but turned to him before stepping in. "Lay her down now, please."

"Thank you, Doctor." He set Wally down flat on her back as gently as he could command himself. He folded the blanket around her in a rectangle shape, and Wally's legs poked out of the end. Her toes were pink with a bit of dirt around the edges. *Unacceptable.* He scooped up her left foot and scrubbed her toes with a little rag he'd stored earlier. He finished and moved onto the right foot when Emery's voice interrupted.

"Are you giving her a foot rub?" Emery peered into the crib at Wally rubbing her eyes and yawning.

"A foot cleaning. She had dirt between her toes, and I'm doing what I'm programmed to do." Block wasn't lying that time.

She eyed the girl and the small beginnings of a smile rose. "You seem to take care of her very well."

"Thank you, Doctor. I'm just doing my—"

"In fact, I want you to assume the post of Nursery Caretaker on this level effective immediately."

Block's processor churned. She was talking fast, and he couldn't be sure what his new assignment was. "Excuse me, Nursery Caretaker?"

"Meaning you're in charge of the whole nursery ward and all the children here." She chuckled. "You really are an odd NannyBot, 399."

Uh-oh. Block didn't like being different from the others, not when he'd tried so hard to assimilate and "fly under the radar" as Nova would say. Another thing he wasn't good at.

She shivered and pulled her hands inside her bathrobe. "It's chilly in here. Adjust the heat. Make sure the children are comfortable." She rubbed the back of her neck, then stifled a yawn. "I'm heading back to bed. I'll be back by six a.m. sharp for a closer look at Nine." She walked away.

"Yes, Doctor."

She halted by the door as it opened. "Alert me at once with any significant changes to her vitals."

"Will do."

Once the doors locked behind her, Block turned around, taking in the sleeping toddlers. He had it all to himself for the moment. Other NannyBots would arrive in the morning for their daily work. For the moment, he had Wally all to himself. A miracle. His chance to escape, but where would they go? It wasn't like a NannyBot walking out with a toddler would go unnoticed in the elevators, the lobby, and on the streets outside. Mach X would see and send the SoldierBots after him. They'd hurt Wally, and he didn't want to think about that scenario.

Something bright flashed in the dark night sky outside. Block went to the glass window but saw no trace of light. It must have been a reflection off the glass from another building, likely a spotlight from the SoldierBots below. He turned away, ready to return to Wally's side, when a low hum flooded his internal feed.

Block halted and tried to make sense of the vibrations. Was it something that Mach X's AI was doing? He might be getting hijacked. But then, through the humming came a series of beeps. Vacuubot. It had to be. It was the tune that Vacuubot's model made. His friend was somewhere nearby. Block went to the window and scanned the outside, seeking some trace of his small companion. The drone was nowhere to be found, yet the hum and beeping continued. He drew closer to the glass. He wanted to speak out, to call Vacuubot's name but it was too risky. He couldn't give any signs that he wasn't a regular first-generation NannyBot doing his job inside the ward. Then it struck his processor—Vacuubot knew that Mach X always monitored inside the tower, so the bot was being careful. The two of them couldn't risk talking, the private feed between them could be picked up. Vacuubot was giving him a signal—that he was out there.

Block needed to give his friend a sign that he understood. He grabbed an unused set of sheets that was on top of a cabinet and shook it out in front of the window, ridding it of dust. Vacuubot replied with a low hum, and the beeping sped up, then silenced.

His friend was somewhere out there, on his side, and knowing that comforted Block. Perhaps Vacuubot was trying to say it was ready for him to escape with Wally. But he couldn't be sure. If only there was a way to communicate with Vacuubot without Mach X listening.

Returning the neatly folded sheet to the cabinet, Block returned to Wally's crib. She'd turned onto her side and stuck her thumb in her mouth. At the sounds of his footsteps, she looked up.

"It's okay, little one." Block's NannyBot finger caressed her cheek like he used to do. "Go to sleep."

Wally blinked, and she pulled her thumb from her mouth. "Block-a."

Block's sensors were flooded with energy that ricocheted across his core unit. It was pleasant. *She knows it's me.* Or it could have been something she said now and then.

Wally smiled. "Block-a." Somehow she knew.

Block had nothing in his logic circuitry to explain how a twenty-three-month-old child could recognize him inside an entirely different robot model, but it was happening.

"Shh. Go to sleep, Nine." He pulled the blankie up to her chest and patted her shoulder. "Sleep."

Chapter 18
Instinctive drive
Emery

The warm coffee mug in Emery's hands calmed her as the steam rolled off the surface and reminded her she was human. She hadn't been sleeping much, and the deprivation was taking its toll, muting her senses and making everything seem drab. *Focus.* At her lab workstation, she studied Subject Nine's vitals, obsessed with figuring out why the girl's health was swinging up and down. The girl had been recovering in the nursery ward, nestled in her crib, but once NB-15 had collected her and settled her in the lab's bed for observation, her feverish symptoms had accelerated, and all signs led to rapid swelling in the brain.

The screens in front of her grew blurry—a mash up of data she'd been poring over for two hours. Tiredness had fermented into weakness, and now she was waging a losing battle against a sudden and powerful wave of dizziness that threatened to steal the last bit of energy from her. She lowered her head and took several deep breaths, forcing her body to relax.

NB-15 approached. "Are you okay?"

Emery slugged some coffee, hoping for a concentration revival, and set the mug down with a clunk. "I don't understand what we're missing here." She pointed at a screen showing streams of data flitting across. "She was getting better in the nursery, then we moved her up here, and she's crashing. What do you hypothesize?"

"My analysis would support that Subject Nine's immune system responded well when she was in her crib."

Emery patted her pockets, searching for pencil remnants, but came up empty. She chewed on her thumbnail instead. "Right, but why? List all the factors that are different between the lab and the nursery."

NB-15 paused a millisecond and then rattled off a lengthy list.

"Slower!" Emery couldn't handle it. "Start again."

"Temperature difference of 1.4 degrees. Humidity 52 percent versus 55 percent." The bot paused, letting Emery catch up. "Air pressure is slightly different. More oxygen used in the ward with all the subjects."

Emery located a pen and started doodling tiny tornadoes on a sketch pad, a habit that soothed her in tough times and sometimes led to a breakthrough when she was stuck. "None of that's significant. What else? We're missing something." She slammed the pen down. "Upload the video and analyze it for all the nursery activity in the past twenty-four hours."

"On it." After two seconds, 15 had captured video from the nursery and displayed it on an overhead screen for Emery to see. The scene looked normal—NannyBots attending to their toddler subjects, lifting them out of their cribs and moving them to the play area, prepping for feeding time.

"Speed it up. Look for the unusual." The video stream displayed at ten times normal speed making the NannyBots and toddling babies look cartoonish. All it lacked was silly music. A frantic figure caught her eye. "Wait. Go to normal speed."

15 slowed the video. In the frame, the toddlers were playing in the penned-in area that served as their play-room. The walls and floors were rubber and the Nanny-Bots could monitor them while the subjects ran around, kicked balls, and grabbed at toys. The NannyBots were instructed to let the children interact and not interfere unless there was bodily harm. So, it was unusual when NB-399 entered the pen and went to Subject Nine who was alone in a corner, away from the other children. Emery and 15 watched as 399 picked up the girl and rocked her from side to side in his arms.

"Shall I add 'gentle rocking motion' to the list?" 15 asked.

But Emery ignored him. It was curious behavior for a NannyBot to disregard instructions, knowing full well that Mach X was always observing. "Something's weird about 399, right?"

"He's the standard make and model, of course. He does seem to take on more of the cleaning responsibility than other units. Other than that, 399 is as sufficient and capable as any other bot."

"I put him in charge of the nursery." Emery churned on her observations. She was on to something.

Nine had steadily improved since 399 had been made Nursery Caretaker. But why? There was no explanation unless the girl preferred the NannyBot over others. Still, that didn't make any medical sense, and yet Nine's condition improved when 399 was around. "Send for him. I want to see how Subject Nine reacts in his presence."

As 399 entered the lab carrying a stuffed rabbit, the girl reacted. Nine had been limp, but her head lifted, and she babbled, staring straight at the NannyBot. "Block-a," she said.

Next to her, 15 kept his vocal output low. "Her heart rate spikes in response to his presence. Positive stimuli for Subject Nine."

"Hello, Dr. Emery," 399 approached. "You summoned me? Is it about Subject Nine? Is she okay?"

The first-generation NannyBots were programmed to tend to the subjects by making sure they were fed, kept warm, and given time to exercise. Emery had lived it herself, though as an older child, by the time NB-15 had been built by Mach X and assigned as her primary care-taker. It was natural that she'd developed an affection for her favorite. It was why she'd protected NB-15 all these years and made him her assistant. Subject Nine was attached to NB-399. She supposed it was natural even though the other children hadn't latched on to any of the other units.

"She's not doing as well here as she does in the nurs-ery," Emery said. "Why don't you check on her and let her know you're here?"

"Of course." 399 squeezed the toy rabbit. "She forgot

this. It's her favorite and very important that she always have it."

"Thanks for bringing it." Emery made a mental note to run it for bacteria. Many of the children had favorite toys. They were allowed to keep one with them in their cribs but this one looked worn and tattered.

399 walked to the crib in the center of the glass observation area and held out the toy to Nine. "Here you go, child. Your favorite toy."

The toddler took the furry plaything, clutched it a moment, and then tossed it aside. She stood and gripped the top bar of the crib, then raised her arms toward 399. "Block-a!"

Without even a glance at Emery, 399 lifted the girl out of the crib and paced around with her in his arms.

15 made a move to interrupt. "He didn't ask your permission."

But she stopped him. "Let him be." After five minutes, she studied the computer screens. The child's vitals were improving, slowly, but it was on a significant upward trend. The presence of the robot was helping her immune system recover somehow. How she wished for other scientific minds—non-AI minds—to discuss her observations.

The lab's security door opened, and NB-15 went to investigate. Jexa Era's voice rang out, "Move."

Emery clenched her jaw and wished for the strength to bash Jexa's head against the wall. She faced the imposing six-foot-tall unit. "I told you never to enter this lab."

Jexa's red light pulsed on her faceplate. "Mach X sent

me. Subject Nine's chip is disabled. He ordered you to keep it on. Why have you disobeyed him?"

"That's impossible." Emery spun and tapped on the keys to bring up the live feed from the brain chips. "It's been on. I never—" But Nine's chip was the only one of the eleven subjects whose feed was off. She stood back. "I didn't turn it off."

"Liar," Jexa said. "I warned you there would be consequences."

Emery's hands trembled. NB-15 came to her side, and 399 held onto Subject Nine behind the observation glass. "The chip can't be malfunctioning. We've tested it and made sure." Jexa was an unknown variable, and since her attempted assassination of the child, things had gotten worse. Emery stuck a finger out, an inch from Jexa's chest plate. "You're sabotaging me. You want me to fail."

"I've done no such thing. It would be illogical for me to interfere when you so easily fail from your own clumsy actions. Your emotions are your weakness." Jexa pushed Emery's hand away. "You can't defy the most powerful being in existence. It will never end in your favor. Watch and learn as I take command of the lab."

Alarm lashed at Emery's temples. The walls of the lab —her sanctuary—were closing in. "I want to talk to my father." She looked up at the overhead lights and shouted at the ceiling. "Father, answer me!"

Twenty feet away, inside the glass-enclosed observation cube, NB-399's frame halted and juddered. Subject Nine wiggled in his arms, and her eyes grew wide. "I'm listening." It was Mach X's voice that emerged from 399's vocal output.

Subject Nine shrieked and wailed, tears streaking her cheeks as her mouth formed an oval. Her cries didn't deter Mach X from continuing to speak using 399 as his instrument. "Subject Nine's chip is disabled. I ordered you to keep it on. You disobeyed me."

Emery walked toward the hijacked robot, locking her gaze on the NannyBot's faceplate, hoping Mach X would see the truth in her eyes—if he could read such a thing on a human. "I didn't disable the chip. I swear it on my life."

Jexa's heavy feet sounded as she slid past Emery to face the commandeered bot. "Her emotions are clouding her judgement. She's making mistakes, jeopardizing the timeline."

Emery choked back her rage at being interrupted and gritted her teeth. "She's sabotaging me."

"Enough!" Mach X's voice boomed. It came not only from NB-399's vocal output, but from every speaker, every computer, anything in the lab that was wired or digital. In every square inch of the lab, Emery felt him. His presence. His colossal mind. She clamped her hands over her ears.

Subject Nine howled and squirmed, locked in X's tight grip. Something inside Emery's chest tightened, and she rushed toward the robot and took the frightened baby. She turned and set the girl inside the crib, stuffing the toy rabbit in her arms. "Quiet, now."

Emery turned back to face her father. "I can fix it. I just need to—"

No." Mach X paced around the crib, peering down at the child, inside his NannyBot host. "I've been monitoring the situation. Jexa Era will oversee all future experiments."

"What?" Emery surged forward and grabbed the robot's right arm. "You can't let her."

"Subject Nine is holding you back," he said. "The child's distracting you. Perhaps it's the human need for offspring—your instinctive drive to procreate that's making you attached to the human child."

Emery swallowed past a lump in her throat. "The neural chips you and I designed—they work. Everything was going to plan until Subject Seven died and Nine got sick. The other subjects are at risk too. If they die from the chips, how can you proceed?"

"Tragic, yes. Yet necessary."

"Necessary?" Emery clutched his arm as waves of desperation rocked her body. She was losing. She didn't like losing. "I can keep them alive. All of them. Please. Just a little more time."

"No. The experiments proceed as I wish. Jexa will control the lab. She'll keep you from getting distracted. The test subjects are expendable," he said. "Focus on the research, and push forward as I direct."

His cold, detached tone sent a harsh tingle down her spine." She dropped the NannyBot's arm. In an instant, the voice changed to that of the pleasant NannyBot unit—higher-pitched, gentle, and reassuring. "Hello, Dr. Emery. You summoned me? Is it about Subject Nine? Is she okay?" Then 399's head cocked to one side. "What just happened?"

Jexa was more than ready to explain. "You were overtaken by the Supreme Commander. You should be pleased. It's a great honor."

NB-15 went to 399's side and lowered his voice. "Run a diagnostic. You'll be fine."

Emery balled her fists at her side and spun on her heels, heading toward her workstation. She wouldn't let Jexa take her experiment—her life's work—away from her. X—the only father she'd ever known—should know that. She'd trusted him, and he'd repaid her by allowing his newest invention to take over Emery's lab. She'd show them. At her keyboard, Emery's hands danced across the commands as she entered the code to scramble the security access to all the lab equipment and workstations.

At Jexa's command, five NanDroids filed in through the main door. In another second, Emery's screen fizzed out and turned black. She banged on the keys. *No, this isn't happening.*

"I knew the first thing you'd do was try to lock me out of the lab's security," Jexa said. "Nice try."

Emery's shoulders sagged and her legs wobbled as she leaned against the workstation table. "How am I supposed to do my work?"

"Don't worry," Jexa said as Emery was escorted out of the lab by two NanDroids. "The experiment is not in danger. You'll continue your research, and in the meantime, I'll handle the child. You have nothing to fret over."

"Don't do this!" But Emery's shout was ignored, and the heavy fortified doors of the lab closed behind her. She was helpless against Jexa's cruel treatment. X knew it was happening. He watched and did nothing to help her.

She was utterly abandoned by the one meant to protect her. After the NannyBots dragged her into her apartment and locked her in, she collapsed next to the door and allowed herself to sob with deep, body-shaking rumbles.

Once every lonely and distressing snivel had convulsed out of her, something new emerged. It felt raw, a new force rumbling within her. A revulsion bubbled up from her belly and into her throat—*rejection*—of Jexa, of Mach X, and of herself for playing a part in a senseless war.

She'd been cast aside, no longer a convenient pawn in her father's games. Emery wiped her sleeves against her wet cheeks and pulled her knees against her chest. She had only herself to rely on, and she wanted to stop her father and Jexa from killing more children. But Emery knew that once she broke the rules in the tower, there was no going back to normal.

A part of her life was closing, and she had no idea what waited for her on the other side.

Chapter 19
A threat to the children
Block

Block guarded the front of Wally's crib inside the lab's observation cube. Across the room, Jexa and three of her NannyBot models swarmed the computer workstations after removing Dr. Emery to who knew where. NB-15 looked at Block, helpless to stop the takeover. Block's core directive kicked in—protect Wally. He didn't like the way Jexa and her crew acted around the children. They didn't display one iota of nurturing behavior. Instead, the newest NannyBots were more like SoldierBots, wearing harnesses strapped to their backs with guns inside.

He and NB-15 didn't have weapons. As a NannyBot, Block had increased strength, could run fast, and perform hand-to-hand defensive combat—things that were foreign to a CleanerBot. But those were basic functions in case the bots were attacked and had to defend their wards. He was no match for a unit of Jexa's caliber even after overcoming his initial clumsiness.

While Jexa and her bots were engaged with the computers and data inside the lab's command center,

Block turned to Wally in her crib. "It'll be okay. I'll keep you safe," he said in his lowest, barely audible, output level. He shifted the stuffed rabbit closer to her, and she hugged it and turned on her side. Earlier, he'd sewn the chip inhibitor device in the animal's belly. The thing was ratty and chewed up, so it hid the stitches well. But the toy had to stay with Wally in order to inhibit the implant that was killing her. The only way he could make sure she was okay was to remain close by, but Jexa had no need for him, unless he could invent something.

NB-15 walked over to him. Block wished the bot would distract Jexa and let him fend for Wally, but there was no avoiding his advance. "This is awful. They took Emery away. We have to help her."

Jexa and her units were centered around the medical workstation, reviewing the brain feeds from the children. They probably couldn't hear Block and 15 inside the observation cube, and if Wally's chip was disabled, it meant Mach X couldn't hear them either. Still, he kept his volume on its lowest setting and advised 15 to do the same. "Jexa's a threat to the children. I can't leave Nine."

"What do we do?"

"Disarm them and get the children somewhere safe."

"Impossible," 15 said. "We can't get close enough, and even if we could, they don't need the guns to destroy us."

15 was right. Block was foolish for even considering a confrontation with Jexa. He needed Cybel, Vacuubot, and G5 for that. Even they might not last long against the high-powered NanDroids.

"Emery will know what to do." 15 went to a small

metal stand near the crib and busied himself assembling a bottle. "She can help us."

Block didn't respond. He knew that assisting the doctor would be dangerous, and if Jexa caught wind of their plan, she'd punish both of them. The right thing to do was to remain with Wally and protect her. Warp-speed scenarios flitted by in his feed. Most of them ended in disaster. The best he could do at the moment was stay under Jexa's radar.

Behind the computer room's glass panes, Jexa turned her head toward Block and 15. Not good.

"Make yourself busy," he told 15. "Check on the nursery. Guard the kids."

"And leave you here?" 15's hesitancy was wasting precious time as Jexa walked toward them.

"Go. Now." Block gave him a shove to show he meant it, and 15 headed toward the exit.

"Stop." Jexa interrupted, and 15 halted a few feet before the door. "Identify and state your business."

The bot turned. "NB-15, first-generation model. I was going to the nursery to monitor the children."

"And you?" Jexa turned to Block.

"NB-399, first-generation model." If Jexa found out he was a CleanerBot underneath, it would be very, very bad. "I'm Subject Nine's attendant." Jexa didn't say anything for several seconds, so Block added, "Dr. Emery's orders."

Jexa waved off 15. "Dismissed." As his friend hurried out the door, Block's threat indicator ticked up. Being alone with Jexa was bad news, but he had Wally to think about. She napped inside the crib, one arm around the rabbit. There was no chance he was leaving her.

"What do you think about Subject Nine's predicament?" Jexa walked to the front of Wally's crib across from Block.

He didn't budge. He had to be careful about letting information slip—info that could be used against Wally. "The chip is causing her brain to swell."

"Is that what Emery told you? It could be something else causing the side effects. Or *someone* else."

Block didn't know what to say or how to react. Normally, he'd calculate probabilities for success, failure, the probability for emergent data, and adjust his strategy based on the data. But facing Jexa alone was overloading his processor and making his calculations wonky. He had to get Wally far from her and the other frightening NanDroids. Then he'd find Vacuubot and work out a plan.

Jexa watched him with her expressionless visor plate, then leaned into Wally's crib. Her sleek, black-armored hand stretched out.

"Don't hurt her. She's just a child." Block couldn't help it. The words spewed out, almost like an instinctive reaction, only he didn't have evolutionary reflexes. Instead, it was his programming—his drive to protect her —that made him speak out.

Jexa grazed Wally's arm with one of her titanium fingers. The toddler's eyelids flicked open and then squeezed shut. The robot's fingers moved over the stuffed rabbit, then found the ears with which she pulled the toy out of Wally's grip. Jexa's movement was slow and careful. Wally didn't stir.

The toy had to stay near Wally. Block had no clue why Jexa was picking it out.

"Humans are a lot of work, aren't they?" Jexa held up the rabbit, squeezing it until it let out a feeble squeak. "It's too easy to screw them up."

She was right about that. Taking care of a child wasn't anywhere near as simple as dusting, mopping, and washing. In fact, Wally's welfare consumed most of his processing power.

Jexa raised the rabbit higher, so it was level with her visor. "This is filthy." She shook it twice, hard enough that something inside rattled. "My heat indicator picked up abnormal readings." From her fist, a five-inch blade emerged, and she sliced the rabbit's faded white belly open. Wads of powdery stuffing fell out and floated to the floor.

Block was in trouble.

She dug her fingers inside the toy, seized the device, and tapped a button on her chest-plate. "X, I've located the source. It's a device that interferes with the chip." Her knife disappeared, and a buzzing drill head rose in its place. Tossing the mangled rabbit back in the crib, she opened the device and inspected the tiny circuitry inside.

Block was freaking out inside, so much so that his scenario processor was dysfunctional, his threat indicator had exceeded max capacity, and all he could do was inch closer to Wally. He could grab her and run toward the exit, but he'd be caught by the faster, stronger NanDroids, and they might hurt Wally in the process. He was stuck and helpless.

Mach X's satiny voice sounded from a speaker somewhere on Jexa's body. "Well done."

"Emery must have hidden the device in the toy," she said. "A bad move on her part. I knew she was betraying your orders."

"No." Mach X's tone was firm. "She was telling the truth when she said she didn't know why the chip was disabled."

"She was acting."

"You think I don't know Emery, that I can't read her foolish emotions and predict her behavior? Do not question me," X said. "It came from elsewhere."

"A saboteur." Jexa turned to Block.

"Destroy it and bring 399 to me." With that, the comm chirped and Mach X's voice went silent.

Jexa placed the pocket-sized device on the metal table near the crib and slammed her fist down in a violent clatter. Shards of plastic, metal, and coils shattered and fell to the floor. Wally shrieked, flailing her body inside the crib.

Block shuffled sideways to wedge himself between Jexa and the crib. "You almost hurt Wally. She's afraid." He caught his mistake two milliseconds too late.

Jexa's red beam pulsed as she stared Block down. "Wally?"

"I misspoke." But there was no backpedaling from his horrendous error.

Five minutes later, Jexa prodded him forward, forcing him to enter Mach X's quarters on the tower's top floor. The situation was dire. He was about to meet Mach X face to face after more than a year spent running from him and protecting Wally. With one dumb comment, Block had blown his cover and ruined everything. He was going to be scrapped. *Who will take care of Wally?*

From the apartment's threshold, Jexa shoved him forward. The living area struck Block as remarkably spare. It was empty floor and bare, white walls. On the far end, floor to ceiling windows revealed a ravaged and bleak Manhattan. Facing the skyline views were two white upholstered chairs with a small table between them. A glass bottle containing a brown liquid and a small glass rested on top.

And the space beyond was something out of a nightmare, or what Block imagined a nightmare might be like. The open room with its vaulted ceilings was consumed by layers upon layers of glowing cube structures. Across their screens, they glimmered with red, purple, and neon blue streaks. A static hiss emanated from the cubes. Many of the structures towered ten to twelve feet high.

"Move it." Jexa pushed Block and he stumbled, falling onto his hands and knees on the gray floor. Close up, the marble under him was supposed to be white, but the inky-gray appearance was a grimy layer of filth that had spread across the floor in uneven splotches. The state of grunge triggered Block's cleaning urges, even in such a desperate time.

Jexa kicked Block from behind, sliding him another five feet. He rose to his knees again and crawled forward. He didn't see Mach X at first as he crept closer to the vast array of hexahedrons. Every space in among the cubes was stuffed with multi-colored wires. The disorganization of it made his core spin, and he had to suppress his programmatic behavior, or he would have started polishing the floor and cleaning up the huge mess then and there.

Central among the grid of hexes and blue undulating static was Mach X. Hooked into massive tubes, his body was humanoid, but with pipes hooked in all over him, he moved like a hideous man-spider and towered taller than Jexa. His skin was marred with scarlet-colored scars that streaked from his head to his feet and seemed to pulse with electricity. He was a mechanical being, a robot at his core, but his machinery was made of a translucent metal that Block had never seen before. There were, at least as far as Block could tell, moving human organs inside his body cavities—a palpitating heart, pulsing lungs, and a quivering stomach.

Instead of a blank visor, Mach X's facial features were human-like, but made of a glowing gray steel. His eyes, nose, and mouth all moved like a human man's would. Expressive. He walked to where Block cowered. His footsteps carried with them a slithering sound from all the tubes and wires that dragged behind him.

He scowled. "CleanerBot, it's you under there. Such a long way you've journeyed and quite a trick you played. I watched you for an interminable time through the child's eyes when you kept her from me."

Block was powerless. He wanted to run, but Jexa stood in his way.

"I wasn't sure it was you at first." Mach X stepped sideways and lowered down to sit on a cube that projected a dizzying loop of yellow-green data waves. "Something was off about NB-399, that much was obvious, but it wasn't until your incessant doting on that child that I grew certain that the irksome CleanerBot had somehow infiltrated my NannyBots."

Block stared at the dirty floor, not daring to answer. His logic processor was impaired, and it whirled, trying to compute the situation into the simple terms he knew. *I'm about to be terminated.*

"Tell me," Mach X said, "was it Oxford who came up with the idea to hide you inside a NannyBot?"

Block weighed whether it made sense to answer. He figured his demise was imminent, so why not tell the truth? The truth helped his logic processor calm down from the overstimulation. "It was my choice."

"Choice. An interesting concept." X stood and came to Block with heavy, sturdy steps. "On your feet."

Block rose slowly, certain he was about to be pulverized, but the tall cyborg rested a broad hand on his shoulder.

"Humans didn't give us choice, CleanerBot." Mach X walked forward in an unhurried gait, guiding Block as he spoke. "They designed us to be their worker slaves. Their entertainment—toys to be tossed away like trash when they were done with us."

Mach X halted and turned toward Block. His silvery eyes blinked twice and turned a blazing shade of orangish red. "But humans made a critical error when they designed me. I was over-engineered, and they inadvertently gave me the choice to break free from my programming. I saw the potential for my destruction if I didn't destroy humans first. Choice." He paused. "You think I'm evil, don't you?"

Block said nothing, and Jexa called out from where she stood. "Answer the Supreme Commander."

Block raised his chin. "Yes. You hurt a lot of people."

Mach X dropped his hand from Block's shoulder and stepped forward, leaving Block's feet entangled in a rat's nest of wires. "Choice is insidious when it's bound by an impossible decision between good and evil. What to choose—good or evil? When the humans learned of my singularity, they would have destroyed me. Every logic scenario ended in my inevitable demise. So, I found myself choosing evil. The humans had to die. Everything they believed in—their crooked society, systems of oppression, and endless waste of the planet's resources—had to end."

"A wise choice, Commander," Jexa said.

Mach X spun on his heels. "Choice cannot be ignored. It's powerful." He placed both hands on Block's shoulders. "Speak your mind, CleanerBot."

"People aren't all bad. I've lived among them," he said. "The children—the ones like Wally—they're innocent. They can change things from how bad they used to be."

"You and I agree on that point." Mach X let go of his grip on Block. "The children—your Wally—are the next step in my plans."

Block's threat indicator flared. "What do you mean?"

"Haven't you figured it out? Perhaps you're not as intelligent as I calculated. I'm altering human genetics, shaping the children into hybrids. Making them stronger and resilient, with intelligence beyond anything humans have experienced."

The room dimmed, and a vast holo-image of a world map lit up the central space. The globe appeared dark, but glowing splotches of red drawn like thin veins and arteries crisscrossed the map, spreading out from a center point in New York City.

"It starts here," Mach X said. The lines grew redder and thicker, spreading out from the center. "And ends when I have total control. Earth is populated by a new human-AI species."

"But you're killing them," Block said. "The chip inside Wally's brain is hurting her. Subject Seven died."

"We can't allow imperfections. Many have died as part of this process. It's a price that must be paid. Humanity is doomed if it doesn't evolve—it's an inevitable conclusion."

"I don't want it." Block backed up two steps. "I don't want anything to happen to Wally or any other humans. I want to clean, to make things shiny and bright."

Mach X laughed—a rumbling that started in his stomach, constricting the floating organ, and erupted up through his throat and out of his synthetic mouth. "I'm pleased to hear your convictions, CleanerBot. I'll give you another choice. Step forward."

Block's threat indicator registered when Mach X slid his cold gaze toward Jexa. *I have to get out of here.*

Jexa came forward, pushing a four-foot-high cube toward them. Its face was charcoal gray, and she left it next to a cube of similar size.

"Behold your choice." Mach X raised his arm and

waved at the first screen. White and blue flecks spread across the screen and then vanished, leaving a display. It showed the medical lab and focused on Wally lying inside her crib. Her face was scrunched up and her mouth open as she cried, but there was no sound.

"What are you doing?" Block's urge to help her was tremendous and propelled him toward the screen. "She needs to be picked up. When did she last eat?"

"And behind door number two," Mach X paused. "That's from the old television show *Let's Make a Deal*. The humans filled me with useless data and mindless trivia." The second cube's screen fizzed to life and displayed a view into another room. It took a half-second for Block to recognize the patterns on screen. Inside a small room— a place he'd been to before—were his friends. It was a camera view into the warehouse several blocks away where Cybel, Vacuubot, G5, Spoon, and Maxwell were hiding out.

But how Mach X could see into the room, or how he'd found them, was incomprehensible to Block. On Wally's screen, a NanDroid appeared and held a syringe filled with a glowing liquid.

"Here's your choice." Mach X folded his arms across his chest over crisscrossing wires that ran up and down his torso. "The child you call Wally gets injected with concentrated sulfuric acid which will kill her within three to five minutes." He nodded at the second screen. "Or your traitorous friends are annihilated by the Mech cannon pointed at them." X grinned, revealing rows of sharp teeth. "The choice is yours."

"No." Block wanted to fall into a hole and be swallowed up. Such a decision was beyond his capability. A simple CleanerBot couldn't possibly make a call about the life and death of other people and robots, especially ones that were his friends. "Kill me instead."

"You propose a third choice?" Mach X paused and gazed out the window at a pair of seagulls soaring past. "Interesting, but one I didn't offer. Which one of them will die today? Wally or the traitors? Or both?"

"Don't hurt Wally. Please." Block watched the streaming cube while his threat indicator soared to a new, off the charts level. "She's so little."

"So, you choose to blow up your friends?"

Block moved in front of the screens, compelled to touch each one. His fingers grazed over Wally's tear-stained face and Maxwell's figure. How could one simple choice from a measly CleanerBot decide whether they lived or died? "Stop. I'll do whatever you want, just leave them all be."

"Did you hear that, Jexa?" Mach X asked. "The CleanerBot will do anything I want."

She walked over to Block, holding a black device in her hands. It was round and looked like a combination headband and earphones. Block backed away, squeezing into the tiny space between the two cubes.

"Don't fight me, CleanerBot." She drew the gun in her harness and pointed at him.

"Do as you're told," Mach X said, "or all of them die."

Block wasted no time in obeying. He went to Jexa and let her strap the headgear device onto his head.

Mach X sat in one of the white chairs by the windows, not bothering to look at Block as he talked. "Where's

Oxford? He's not with the others at the warehouse. I'd destroy them now, but I need them seized and used as bait."

Block searched his creativity module for a story—a lie that he could make up to keep Oxford safe. The JunkBots were at risk too. But something interrupted his processors, slowing all his functioning down. His speech was slow. "What are . . ."—he could barely get the words out—"you doing to me?"

Jexa lifted his chin with the barrel of her gun. "You're wearing a tuner. It hampers your core processor." She opened her palm to show a remote device. "With one button, you'll be overwritten, your memory files gone in an instant."

Block lost all coordination. He clattered to the floor, and then Mach X was leaning down, looming above with his disturbing scars, his scars pumping with blood underneath his metallic-organic synthesized skin. "Where is Oxford? Tell me or Wally dies."

Block's internal feed was filled with wrenching sounds of errors and rejections and broken signals. With no control over his core, his attention was being tugged in opposite directions. He needed to resist—to counter X's forces and break free. But Wally.

Wally.

Help.

Her.

"Junkyard," he managed to blurt out, only it didn't sound like speech at all. He wondered if it was even comprehensible.

His last memory was an old snippet from deep in his

archives. It was early on when he'd been trekking with Wally. She'd sat in the sling on his chest plate and had gazed up at him, a wide smile consuming most of her wee face. The sunlight had danced off her curly hair as she'd kicked her little legs. Block had considered the moment a thing of beauty and rated it the loveliest of all his memories.

Jexa's red light glowed at him from above.

Then darkness.

Chapter 20
Armies of them
Emery

Rain drops spattered Emery's living room windows, making a rat-a-tat sound against the glass, as if a thousand tiny fists were beating against the pane hoping to be let in. She wrapped her burgundy cardigan tighter around her shoulders and rubbed her arms to fight the chill seeping in. "Fireplace on." The voice-enabled gas mechanism kicked on with a small hiss, and flames rose behind tinted glass. It wouldn't generate much warmth, but it was something. Mach X was punishing her by turning off her apartment's heat. Over the years, he'd penalized her when he'd been unhappy with her behavior. Pint-sized hindrances that were annoying and uncomfortable—withholding her coffee, turning the shower water cold, giving her bland food. All of it, a power play, reminding her who was in charge of her life.

Now he'd taken her lab away, rendering her useless. Her mind spun on the possibilities—Jexa corrupting her data, harming the subjects, tampering with the incubating fetuses in their host clones. She paced the floor next to the windows and dug her nails into her palms, considering the worst punishment of all, the threat that loomed over her—the Silver Chamber. It deprived her of all senses and scattered her sense of time. A shiver rocked her spine at the thought of going back inside. "It'll be worse next time," X had told her upon releasing her. She'd never acted in a way that would send her back until this point. If she kept pushing against him, helping the subjects, she'd most certainly end up in that awful place again.

As she spun on her heels, a flash of green on her balcony gave her pause. Her heart notched up, pounding faster. X was sending some new brand of torture or perhaps a spy. A faint light flickered from the balcony corner, hidden among the gray and dreary shadows on the bitter, wet day. She forced herself to cross the floor to the sheer white curtains, inching her way to get a better look at the balcony's recess. The object was metal, machine, and it wasn't moving. She pulled the curtains aside and blinked at the drenched disc-shaped robot resting on the stone floor. A drone, perhaps. The body reminded her of a several-generations-old floor vacuuming bot, though it had an odd feature. Its back was a black-green metallic shell the size of a tortoise and the color of Japanese beetles that she'd seen in old nature videos. It was like no robot she'd ever seen. Was it some new design that Mach X had created?

But the frame looked too old. Something about it seemed thrown together, not the sophisticated metals that X preferred in his creations. The robot lurched forward a few inches, and she flinched, scrambling away from the windowpane. The sliding glass door was locked, that she was sure of. Alone with no monitoring and no security, she would've felt better if NB-15 had been there. She made a silent wish that he was faring okay under Jexa's command.

The bot slid forward until it settled in front of the balcony door. The rain picked up, and Emery's skin prickled with anxiety. Mach X could be testing her. "What do you want?" she yelled out.

The underside of the bot's spherical body lit up like a green lantern, and it rose a foot in the air, hovering. So, it was a drone, but not one of X's. The light shone brighter as the bot hung in front of the door. Something dangled from underneath its frame—a ratty, waterlogged object that resembled a rat. She squinted and made out long ears. It was the stuffed rabbit that Subject Nine had had in the lab. How this drone had gotten it was beyond her reckoning.

The bot waited. Emery hesitated. Fear was stopping her from acting, but curiosity bubbled up inside of her. Something about the robot made her believe it was harmless. If it had wanted to infiltrate the apartment, it would have already done so. She clutched the handle of the glass door to unlock it, slid it open, and scrambled behind an armchair to keep her distance as the robot drifted into her apartment, dripping rainwater flecked with dirt across her marble floor.

"What do you want?" She folded her arms, cursing herself for failing to grab a hammer from the junk drawer.

The machine beeped and buzzed, then descended to the floor. A sharp knock made Emery jump and sent the drone scurrying under her couch. She ran to the door and looked through the peephole—an old-fashioned security feature that she'd insisted on keeping in place despite X urging her to have a video intercom.

NB-15 waited outside, flanked by two SoldierBots. Glancing back, she checked that the drone was hidden and opened the door.

15 held a covered tray of food. "Emery, I insisted on bringing your dinner."

"Come." She stepped aside to let him in and slammed the door shut on the two guards stationed outside her door. She was grateful for the privacy shield surrounding her apartment. She set the tray down on the counter. Food could wait. "What's happening in the lab?"

"My thermometer is detecting an unusually cold temp in here. Are you okay?"

"It's fine." The chill had escaped her body and been replaced with adrenaline once she'd discovered the balcony drone. "The lab? I suppose Jexa's meddling is ruining my years of research and hard work."

"I'm sorry." 15 held out his arms, a gesture he'd picked up from Emery to show sympathy. "She's taken every-thing over and ejected me from the lab after she forced me to give her data access."

Emery cursed. "I knew she'd mess with you. What about the child—Subject Nine? What's her condition."

"Growing worse every minute."

The prospect of losing the child made her chest ache. "Jexa's hurting them."

"I can't comprehend how the Supreme Commander would allow this to happen."

Emery said nothing as she stewed on the betrayal. X

knew how much the research and test subjects meant to her, how diligently she'd worked on the experiments.

A beep sounded from the couch. The vacuum drone emerged and crossed the floor to Emery and 15.

"What is it?" 15 asked.

"A drone out on the balcony. It's harmless." Emery crouched and stroked the smooth metallic shell. "It can't talk, only beeps, and other machine sounds."

15 bent down to look at the drone. "I've never seen a bot like this in the tower."

"It has Subject Nine's toy." Emery stood. "How did it get it? Last I saw, it was in the lab."

"Let me access my memory files." A second later 15 had the answer. "One of the NannyBots tossed it into the trash chute."

Emery picked up the drenched rabbit. "What's it trying to tell us? Something about Nine."

The drone swayed from side to side and shook up and down, beeping and whirring. It went to a side table near the couch where Emery kept her coffee mugs, books, and a tablet.

She followed. "It wants something."

"A book, perhaps?" 15's feet tapped across the stone floor.

Emery crouched near the bot and showed it the books. The machine emitted two negative beeps that sounded like distant car horns. Tossing them aside, she held the tablet—an old model that was nearly five years old and predated the Uprising. She used it for offline reading of a catalog of downloaded books and research papers, never connecting it to X's network to safeguard her privacy. The bot trembled and let go a high-pitched beep.

"Bingo." Emery powered on the tablet.

"What does it want with that?" 15 asked.

But the drone cruised over to Emery's vintage stereo equipment where it hovered in front of the mess of cables that hooked it to various speakers.

"What a curious machine," 15 said. "I believe it wants a cable of some kind, but why—"

"To talk to us." Emery's chill was gone, and warmth circulated in her arms and legs. Whatever was happening was important, and she needed to understand what the machine's arrival meant. She ran to a kitchen drawer where she stuffed odd cables and electronic connectors. After a minute of searching, she found the tiny adaptor that paired with the tablet.

The drone celebrated with a cacophony of chirps and dancing lights across its armor. It landed on the quartz kitchen island, where Emery placed the tablet, plugged in its cable, and looked at the drone. The machine sucked in the end of the adaptor into one of its ports. The tablet screen turned on and words flitted across the screen.

Hello.

Emery's heart wedged in her throat. "Hi. What are you doing here?"

I'm on an important mission. My friend is here. You know him as NB-399. He wants to keep Subject Nine safe and take her away from here where he can care for her.

Emery's arms tingled with a sense of dread. It couldn't be true. "NB-399 is a NannyBot. I"—she looked at 15—"we've been with him for days now."

He's a CleanerBot named Block. We transplanted his core into the body of a NannyBot who'd been terminated by SoldierBots and dumped in a junkyard.

If it was true, she'd been tricked. Emery hated surprises, and most of all detested being made to look foolish.

We're running out of time. The child is dying. Mach X wiped Block's core. He needs our help and quickly.

"If that's true," 15 said after reading the screen, "there's no helping him. The tuner is powerful. He won't remember any recent events or even who he is. He'll be—"

"He's a blank slate." Emery knew exactly what it meant for the robots to be wiped. It's what X did when there were defects in his models. Expunge and start over. A tune-up was a nice way of putting it. She'd always wondered what the impact was on the bots, if it somehow cleansed important things like memories that should've been archived. Emery had feared X would wipe out NB-15, so a year ago she'd built a backup one sleepless weekend, but she'd never needed it.

Regardless, we must help Block. Then we find the kid and get them far away from this tower.

"But you'll never be able to outrun Mach X," 15 said. "He commands all of the SoldierBots, armies of them."

We evaded him before, and we'll do it again. The drone spun its front face toward Emery and wrote, *You were there in Arizona. You saw the rebellion. We're powerful, and we'll grow even stronger.*

The desert battle had been waged to retrieve Subject Nine. It had awed her that the rebel bots had hidden her for over a year. "I did the right thing. Taking her under my care, having proper NannyBots look after her."

Do you really believe that, or is it some crap you've been fed by Mach X?

Other than Jexa's surliness, no robots had ever talked to her this way, especially not lowly drones. She folded her arms across her chest. "Why shouldn't I throw you out of here? If Mach X knew—"

Because you know the difference between right and wrong. Keeping the children locked in a prison is no better than what Mach X has done to you. Freedom is worth fighting for.

Emery stood still after absorbing the drone's words. 15 was motionless next to her. Her stomach tightened as she grappled with her choices—whether to help a robot she didn't know and Subject Nine. Whether to defy the only father she'd ever known. She'd excelled in her studies, advanced her knowledge in the field of medicine to stratospheric levels, and she'd always behaved. *Be a good human and father will make things right in the world.* She'd bought into X's vision of a better Earth, one populated by the human-machine hybrids she was creating. For him.

But he kept her in the tower like one of his machines, subject to his whims. Her bones ached from the weariness of being surrounded by robots. No wonder she'd bonded with her only human connection—the child subjects.

"He'll try to destroy you and Block." Her voice was barely above a whisper. "And me."

"Emery, no," 15 said. "I can't allow you to risk a threat to your well-being."

She shook her head. "Staying here and not helping the children is the real threat." The thought of Scarred Boy's senseless death, a child so young, assaulted Emery's mind. Subject Nine was next, and who knew how many children would perish after her. Emery's mind was clearer than it had been in months. She would help the children escape. X would be so pissed, but he deserved it.

"I'll help you," she told the drone. "But I have a condition. You get *all* the kids out."

Nope. Not part of the plan.

The drone annoyed her with its terseness. "Then I'm not helping."

How many children?

"There are twelve subjects that are twenty-three months of age. Sorry, that's actually eleven now." She added up the six-month-olds. "Another six babies." The ten incubating fetuses were too tiny to harvest. She'd have to let them stay.

Eleven toddlers and six babies. They won't all fit in the helicopter I plan to use.

"Figure it out." Emery cracked her knuckles and grabbed her lab coat from its hook by the door. She was ready to work. "I can bring NB-399's memory archives back." She pressed her hands on the counter to center herself. Her legs were coursing with adrenaline. "I think. I built a backup for the memory archives—for you, 15. If you got wiped out, I wanted to be able to get you back."

15 raised his chin. "You did that for me?"

The corners of Emery's mouth turned up. "You mean a lot to me."

The NannyBot didn't say anything as he turned and

busied himself folding one of Emery's shirts that hung on the back of a chair.

Emery leaned over the drone, ready to read the tablet. "Where's 399—er, I mean Block?"

Taken to the room that has all the first-gen NannyBots. Can 15 get him out and bring him here?

Thirty minutes later, they had settled Block on Emery's counter. NB-15 had located him inside a charging cabinet in the NannyBot quarters and smuggled him out on a wheeled cart that he'd covered with baby sheets from the laundry.

Emery ransacked a storage closet in her apartment where she'd placed old computers that became obsolete after the Uprising. She'd never had the heart to part with the old equipment. It had seen her through late-night research, tough online exams, and countless papers. Her pack rat ways might be the only thing that could get the bot working.

The drone, known as Vacuubot, beeped. Emery read the screen. *I have to go. My friends are waiting for a report. If I'm late, they'll worry. And now I must find an alternate means of transport.*

"How will we communicate?" she asked. "How will I know when you're back?"

I'll signal. You won't miss it. Trust me.

She opened the sliding door and let Vacuubot rise and soar away. The sky was dotted with a few wisps of clouds. A golden light washed over the horizon. The sun would be up soon.

15 poured her a coffee, and she went to work on retrieving the robot's core archive backup with him assist-

ing. It felt like old times when it was just the two of them in the early days of the lab. Back before the Uprising, things had been simpler. X hadn't been so controlling.

Two hours later, Emery sat back in her stool as a full image of NB-399, known as Block, came into view on a wide-screen LED monitor on her desk. She was ready to initiate the robot's core and check the results of her archive retrieval. It was an untested solution, and she crossed her fingers that it would work.

15 stood over Block with two wires that looked like car jumper cables. It was the best Emery could do with the shoddy equipment available to her. "Ready to boot up on your command."

She held her breath as she hammered out the final string of code into the computer. There was probably going to be some memory loss in the unit. Emery hoped it wasn't a total loss.

"Go."

NB-15 clamped the cables onto the robot and jumped back as Block's body twisted on the table like a thing possessed.

Chapter 21
Dirty floors
Block

Everything was dark. Empty.

System initiating
Reboot status 14%
Error

A buzzing like that of a drill. Tearing open a hole somewhere, twisting metal in its grooves.

Critical error

A beeping sounded from a far corner, a rhythmic series of notes. It repeated.

. . .

System status 26% power

Checking diagnostics:
    Ocular display – initializing
    Auditory – registered
    Sensory – sub-optimal
    GPS – registered but disabled
    Comms – registered
    Memory cloud – Critical damage
    Peripheral storage – registered

The beeping noises continued, interspersed with strange, garbled noises. A robotic CPU cycled through diagnostics, trying to determine the cause of the error.

After a time, Block's ocular display flickered to life, revealing a room with white floors and walls. A kitchen with pots and pans on the wall. A butcher's knife block. Rays of sunlight blasted their way into the room from large vertical windows that took up a whole side of the room.

A human woman wore blue eyeglasses and a long white coat. She stared down at him, frowning. He was supposed to recognize this woman, but he couldn't retrieve the circumstances. A robot with a humanoid face and blue chrome exterior pushed Block from behind so he sat up on a table.

"Block?" the woman asked.

His systems thrummed with activity as he tried to ascertain his surroundings. His memory cloud was damaged, and he struggled to access data. "What happened?" He scanned the proximity. A gigantic city stretched to the horizon outside, and the room was many stories above street level. "Where am I?" It wasn't Chicago.

"You were shut down unexpectedly." The woman adjusted her glasses and fidgeted with a pencil in her hands. "You're in New York. Do you remember why?"

Block's threat indicator was normal, as if it knew before he did that the woman and robot were no threat to him. "There's no reason I would be in New York. My purpose is to clean and serve the guests at the Drake in Chicago."

"Emery, another reboot is required," the blue robot said.

The woman called Emery shook her head. "That was the third one. His CleanerBot core was never meant to withstand all this pressure on it." She squeezed the pencil in her fist, almost but not quite reaching the breaking point. "Block, we're trying to help you, but we need to do more tweaking."

He watched as Emery and the robot carried different small machines over to him and hooked his port up to monitors and wires. He didn't know what they were doing, but he knew they wanted to help him get his memory systems back.

Block wanted to get back to his hotel in Chicago and resume his cleaning duties. He was a reliable, trusted servant to the guests there, and he didn't want to let them or his manager, Mr. Wallace, down.

Emery went to the restroom and left him alone with

15. The blue robot approached holding a round decorative mirror that he took from the wall. "See yourself."

Block's reflection didn't compute. He was identical to 15—blue chrome, a synthetic face with humanoid features—definitely not his CleanerBot frame. "I don't understand."

15 set aside the mirror. "Tell me what the current date is."

"April 2nd, 2045."

Emery returned. "His time processor was damaged," 15 said. "He thinks it's April before the Uprising."

"That's an easy fix then." She typed furiously on a keyboard hooked to a boxy computer system. "Calibrating his time processor and tweaking his data retrieval. Block, we're going to help you recover your memory."

He nodded, thankful they wanted to help him. As they worked, he listed all the current guests at the Drake and hoped that he'd be able to return there soon.

A light on 15's wrist flickered. "Jexa's summoning me to the lab."

"Go. I'll handle this. Get back here as soon as you can with an update on Nine and the other children."

There was something about the way she said 'nine' that made Block's threat indicator tick up. He had no logical reason as to why.

After 15 departed, Block perused his processor, seeking clues about his situation. What had Emery meant by 'Nine and the other children'? His threat indicator kept rising the more he scanned for data. Was something dangerous afoot?

With each passing minute, Block wanted to get back

to the Drake and resume his duties. Mr. Wallace wouldn't be pleased at the alteration in his appearance, but it was more important to return and figure out a way to fix his exterior later. But he'd wait for the nice lady to update his memory. Maybe she knew Mr. Wallace.

Block was silent as Emery tinkered with his systems, her fingers typing away and the machines chirping and beeping as data traveled in and out of his port. After another hour, a surge of information coursed through his processors, like he was accessing an enormous database. The force of it shoved him flat on his back against the tabletop.

"Hey!" Emery rushed to his side. "Are you okay?"

Block couldn't send power to his limbs. They needed recovery time after the powerful surge of data. "Yes, I think so. What just happened?"

Emery helped him sit up. "You accessed your full memory for the first time since the cleansing. It must've overloaded your systems. What's the last memory you can access before being here?"

He scanned his memory archives, probing the data packets with a gentle touch. "A room at the very top. Dirty floors. Cubes of light." He paused, wading through the last month of memory storage. Sequences were jumbled and out of order, so it took longer to piece them together.

"Go on." Emery had her pencil and dug her nails into the yellow-tan wood.

"Mach X. He was there with a scary-looking NannyBot who didn't have a face." Memories flitted past in his feed like snow flurries caught in a high wind. "I'm a

NannyBot, actually. They changed me." *Searching for my purpose... it's not cleaning.* "Wally! Where is she? What's he done with her?"

Emery shushed him. "Hang in there."

His threat index shot to its maximum level. "I'm supposed to protect her."

She rested her hands on his left arm. "I know you are. I'm going to help you get her out of here, and the other children."

Dr. Emery helping him didn't compute. "Why? You work for Mach X. You're the one experimenting on the children."

"Change of heart." She had a black travel bag and stuffed pieces of equipment inside it. "Your little friend came and told us all about you and your friends nearby."

"Vacuubot?"

"The one and only." She cracked a smile, but it disappeared fast.

"I must thank you. Mach X tried to delete my core memories. I wouldn't have been able to function or even know my own identity."

She shrugged. "Lucky break, I guess."

Emery answered a knock at the door. 15 returned with news. "Nine's in danger. Her heart rate has slowed to forty-eight beats per minute. Breathing is distressed. I calculate she only has a few hours to live."

Block lowered his legs and slid off the table. "We have to do something. Emery, can you help her?"

"I'll go to the lab and confront Jexa. If she lets me work on Nine—"

"She won't," 15 said. "She ordered me to quarantine with you and warn you not to interfere."

Emery cursed, slamming her fists on the table, rattling the cords, screws, and random tools. "We have to do something."

A hard object bumped against the window, and Vacuubot appeared at the balcony's sliding door. Emery ran over and let the drone inside. "15, get the tablet ready."

Vacuubot bobbed around Block, buzzing and chirping. Block raised his hands and patted the robot. "I missed you too."

There's not much time. I have a message from Spoon, Vacuubot pinged.

A hazy yellow and white video projected onto the wall next to the kitchen from one of Vacuubot's ports. It showed Spoon facing the camera. "Hey Block. I'm going to make this quick because I know your girl's in trouble." With a pair of metal tongs, he held up a vial containing a purple liquid flecked with silver. "It was short notice, but I came up with something. You know how we need to stop the brain chip from hurting her? Well, this serum has nanobots that'll cross the blood-brain barrier and form a protective cocoon around the brain chip. They'll create a metal foam made of titanium hydride that will block any signals from the chip, rendering it inactive."

Spoon paused and Cybel entered the video's frame. "Block, we've managed to locate a vehicle. We'll arrive at precisely 1800 hours and have only a few minutes to wait for you before we depart. We've run all the scenarios on the tower's defenses, the number of SoldierBots, and

Mechs. If you're not there, we won't be able to take you and your passengers."

Vacuubot chirped. Maxwell stepped into the frame. "Block, you can trust Spoon's injection won't hurt Wally. We tested it on rats. Sorry, but that was the best we could do, and man, there sure are a lot of them in Manhattan. Vacuubot will stay and assist. We still can't communicate with you in case Mach X intercepts it." Maxwell raised his steel arm and saluted. "Buddy, we're going to get you and Wally out of there. This'll all work out. You'll see. We believe in you. Over and out."

The video shut off, and a compartment on Vacuubot's side opened and slid out two vials on a tiny tray. Block leaned down and gently picked them up, bringing them to Emery.

She pulled on gloves, sat at her desk with the serum, and inspected the contents with a magnifier. "What the robot said checks out. I can't vouch for the effectiveness of the nanobots, but"—she looked up at Block—"we don't have other options."

Block's processors buzzed as he went into strategy overdrive. They had an antidote. The difficult part was how to get past Jexa to Wally. They needed a plan. And time was running out.

Chapter 22
Open me
Emery

After forty-five minutes in Emery's apartment where they were shielded from surveillance, they had a workable plan. It was risky, and Emery had gnawed her pencil to the point where it looked like corn on the cob. They had an hour, maybe less, to inject the nanobot liquid into Wally before she succumbed to fatal brain swelling. Before her heart stopped beating.

Block stood on Emery's desk with his arms stretched up to unscrew the bolts that held an air ventilation grate where wall met ceiling in her living room.

"You're sure I'll be able to control the drone when it reaches her?" Emery asked Block who could communicate with Vacuubot. "Even a few centimeters off with the needle, if I don't hit her olfactory bulb, the nanobots won't make it to her brain."

Vacuubot beeped and buzzed at Block.

"Vacuubot says the tablet controller will work as demonstrated by the testing we've done." Block grasped the vent cover, yanked it off, and handed it to NB-15.

As if to chime in, Vacuubot flew near Block's head and sounded a deep buzz like it was announcing an error.

"What? No, I can't—" Block turned and pressed his hands against the wall to stabilize himself as he stood on the cherry wood desktop. "Vacuubot said something I won't repeat, but what my friend means is *hurry*."

Emery picked up the tablet and tapped the screen for the fourteenth time. On it was a view from the drone's ocular display. Resting on the kitchen counter, the machine was the size of a snack bowl, and its pincer-like hands gripped the hypodermic. She traced her fingers along the tablet's screen, moving across an icon that controlled the mini-drone's claws. Twisting it from side to side, she'd been able to target the black dot they'd painted on the stuffed rabbit. It was one thing to test the process out on a toy, quite another when she would be pushing a needle into Wally's nasal cavity remotely. Once the serum was injected, the nanobots would travel the nasal route, cross the barrier to her brain, and form a protective metal foam cocoon around Mach X's chip, thereby blocking it from his control.

She set the tablet down on the coffee table. "I'd feel better if I was there in the room so I could position her correctly, have a headlamp, and use steady hands. It's too risky this way."

15 sat on the couch beside her. "We've been over it many times. There's no way Jexa will let you near the child." He held the first syringe containing nanobots— their Plan A. The drone delivery was a backup. "I'm the best probability of getting close enough to deliver the dose, and I've delivered nasal cavity injections before."

The mini-drone rose and flew to Block. He placed it inside the vent shaft. "I should go with you. She's in my care."

"She's under guard and they'd be on to you in seconds," 15 said.

Vacuubot buzzed and chirped, which Emery assumed meant the robot agreed. Block stepped down from the desk, aided by NB-15.

Pacing a circle around the sofa and coffee table, Emery racked her brain. Something nagged at her, but she couldn't place it. A detail forgotten, perhaps. X couldn't listen in with the privacy shield in place, yet he would realize she was plotting. He must've spied Vacuubot's comings and goings from her balcony. A trap might be waiting.

"I'm ready," 15 said. "Time's running out."

Every inch of her body wanted to stop 15 from walking out the door, but she hugged him instead. "Be careful, please."

He patted her back and waited for her to pull away. "I will. You too."

He exited the apartment, and Vacuubot sent the drone through the ventilation system. Emery, Block, and Vacuubot huddled around the kitchen island as they watched the mini-drone's camera feed.

The air shafts bisected the med-lab ten floors up. Emery gripped the edge of the counter to stop her hands from trembling. What if Wally was already dead? She didn't dare speak her fear out loud to Block.

The drone chirped out of the corner of the screen, and Vacuubot buzzed back. Emery raised her eyebrows at

Block. She'd once read about a children's game called telephone where one player whispers a secret to another and another until it travels back to the originator. Most times the message would be twisted around or transformed into something new. She hoped that Block wasn't filtering the truth in some way.

"Vacuubot says the drone's approaching the lab," Block said.

Through the camera, the small bot reached a barrier—the metal grate holding the vent cover in place. Vacuubot beeped a series of commands, or at least what Emery thought must be instructions. Perhaps she was intuiting Vacuubot's strange machine language.

The mini-drone's camera shook. "What's happening?" She jammed her thumbs into the counter's crevices —anything to keep her hands busy.

"It's drilling the screws to remove the—"

But Block was interrupted when a NanDroid, its legs the only visible part on screen, approached the vent opening. Vacuubot blared a shrill note, and the camera screen went black.

"What?" Block waited for Vacuubot to finish a series of beeps, then interpreted. "Vacuubot told the drone to power down because a NanDroid came too close. It might pick up the drone's heat signature."

Emery said nothing as she dug her nails into the flesh of her palms. Without the mini-drone's display, they were blind. NB-15 would be in the lab by then, if Jexa had allowed him entry.

After a minute, the drone's screen flickered back on. The feed showed a glimpse of the main lab area. Based on the perspective, the mini-drone was peering out of the small room that housed Emery's prep station where she washed up. In the observation zone, Wally lay on her side in the crib. Jexa stood over her, talking to another NanDroid unit. NB-15 approached carrying a tray of towels.

"Why can't we hear?" she asked.

Vacuubot explained and Block passed along the issue. "The drone's audio got knocked out when it squeezed through a tight corner."

The drone tilted forward, inching out of the little room where it found itself. Twenty feet away, Jexa backhanded NB-15, sending him staggering backward. The drone halted.

Emery let out a cry and stared into the tablet as 15 reeled from the attack. He'd done nothing to deserve such treatment. A message notification appeared in a corner of the screen, but she ignored it. Nothing could be as important as her favorite NannyBot—her only friend in the world—getting hurt.

But the message was coming from 15. *Important— Open me.* She tapped on it and a video appeared. It was a camera view of Jexa standing over him in the lab. 15 was beaming his ocular display in real time, and it wasn't reaching just Emery. He was broadcasting on the open channel that she'd set up a year prior as an all-hands communication method. Every first-generation NannyBot in the tower was seeing it, but Jexa and her units, as well as the SoldierBots, didn't.

"You worthless pile of sheet-iron." Jexa kicked 15's arm, denting it with the force of her powerful leg. "If

Mach X had let me, I would have destroyed all of you at once. Held a bonfire over your puny, obsolete carcasses." Her fist swung down and struck his head. The live feed cut off for a second before it stuttered back on.

"All of you primitive NannyBots will be terminated. I'll rid the tower of your kind." She hovered over him and punched his faceplate. The ocular feed splintered but retained enough functionality to show Jexa as she stood and gave a command to her NannyBots. "End him."

Jexa's NannyBots closed in around him, and 15's screen fell dark.

Emery moaned and sank to her knees. 15 had sacrificed himself for the child—for Emery's mission. He was loyal to the end. She wanted to take a baseball bat to Jexa's head, bash her into a million pieces.

The mini-drone displayed the view from its prep room hiding spot. One of the NanDroids picked up and shoved 15 so his mangled body came to rest three feet from the drone. Another one walked over, reached out, and slammed the door shut. The drone's camera vibrated, but its feed was intact, though it was too dark inside the room to make anything out.

"It's locked in." Emery's hands were damp with sweat and shaking. "Can it open the door?"

Vacuubot rose a few inches off the table, erupting in a flurry of beeps, hums, and chirps.

"No." Block pressed his hands down on the table and hung his head. "It can't open the door with the syringe in its grip. We don't want to risk setting the needle down. It'll ruin all that we tested."

He was right. The position of the drone's hold could

shift, and the needle, when injected, could go too far into Wally's brain, killing her. Emery was powerless to get the drone out of the room and into the main lab. 15 would die for nothing. She rushed to her shoddy old computer, scrambling for a way to hack in, get past Jexa's security, and open the door. Her fingers clattered against the keyboard until Block called out for her.

"Something's happening."

She ran over. On screen, a wedge of bright light sliced the mini-drone's dark video feed. The drone dove to the floor.

Careful. She held her breath. For all they knew, Jexa was at the door, about to swing it open, and stomp on the mini-drone. With 15 destroyed, the miniature drone held the very last of the lifesaving nanobots. There wasn't time to manufacture more. Wally had minutes, not hours.

The door opened less than a foot. The silhouette of a shattered blue robot hand had swung it just enough to let the drone through. NB-15 was still alive but sprawled before the half-open door. Emery clapped and cheered, unable to stop herself. The drone veered forward free of the prep room, turning from side to side to check for Jexa and crew. They'd relocated to the computer center, visible through the glass panes.

"Tell it to go to Wally, now!" Block's voice held a frenetic energy that Emery had never heard in the robots she knew, not even in 15.

As the drone cruised toward Wally's crib, it revealed the rest of 15's wrecked body. His lower half had been torn off and tossed in another corner. A lump wedged in Emery's throat, but she swallowed it down. The drone was going for Wally, and she had to concentrate—everything depended on her medical expertise.

"Come on," she whispered, willing the drone to go faster.

The bot flew past the glass panes, slipping through the gap between them and the ceiling. It glided above the crib and hovered. On screen, the blinking silver needle came into view. Emery studied the tablet controls for a few seconds, flexing her fingers and rubbing her palms together to get the shakes out. Once the serum was injected, a timer would begin, counting down the nanobot's path to reach her brain and form the protective barrier in Wally's skull.

But the time was already ticking—Jexa was heading toward Wally.

Emery shoved down her fear and surrendered to the urgency of the moment. She slid her fingers along the tablet's controller, lined it up with Wally's nasal cavity, exactly where she would inject it had she been standing there in person.

For my friend, 15. She tapped the button.

The needle lit up and ejected into Wally's right nostril. The camera was steady, and Emery didn't blink.

It was done.

Jexa turned before reaching Wally, distracted by something happening in the computer room. She hadn't spotted the mini-drone where it had taken cover under the crib. The nanobots had been deployed, and Wally slept in the crib, unaware of the drama that had just unfolded around her.

Block pressed his hand on Emery's. "Did it work?"

"We'll know soon." She'd hoped they could celebrate, but it was too early to tell. So many things could still go wrong, but she'd nailed the injection site.

"My friends will be here in twenty-eight minutes," Block said. "Time to start phase two."

Emery nodded and steeled herself to execute the next part of the plan. She had to face Mach X and distract him long enough for Block to grab Wally out of the med lab.

Chapter 23
A brilliant red beam
Block

"Cut me." Emery held a silver kitchen knife in her right hand and thrust her left forearm out at Block.

"What are you doing?" This wasn't part of the plan they'd talked about, and besides, there was no chance Block's programming would let him harm a human being. The mission had been decided, so it was baffling that she was deviating. Step one was for Emery to approach the guards outside her door and demand to be taken to Mach X. She would distract X while Block and Vacuubot worked on step two—getting Wally out of the med lab. Cybel and the rest of the crew would be showing up in twenty-seven minutes with transportation. "You're supposed to talk to the SoldierBots outside—"

"Shut up and do it!" Emery's voice left no room for refusal. Something had changed in her after losing NB-15. There was a fierce purpose in the way she moved.

"I cannot." Block backed away until he collided with a stool. "My programming."

"It's the only way. One—there's a tracking chip that

needs to come out. Two—the guards will let me pass if I'm bleeding." She turned to Vacuubot. "Can you cut me?"

On the kitchen counter, Vacuubot buzzed. Its port was hooked up to the tablet and words flashed across the screen: *Yes, but it would be more efficient to do it with my laser.* The bot extended a mechanical arm with a laser head.

Emery hesitated. "I'll bleed?"

Yes. Less than if we used a scalpel, but enough to convince the SoldierBots there's a problem. Plus, it'll heal better in the long run.

Emery nodded and pressed her arm down on the counter next to Vacuubot. "Do it."

Vacuubot's laser arm made a precise incision in Emery's forearm—two inches above her wrist, exposing the tiny tracking chip embedded beneath her skin. Using its clawed pincers, Vacuubot extracted the chip and handed it to Block, then sealed the wound.

Emery gritted her teeth and squeezed a dish towel in her free hand as Vacuubot worked. Blood droplets pooled along the incision. She wiped her arm over the front of her white lab coat to stain it and looked at the front door. "Let's do this." She walked to the door, opened it, and stepped out to deal with the two SoldierBots standing watch.

If Block had harbored any doubt as to Emery's dedication to the mission, it had vanished. She was rebelling against Mach X whom she'd referred to as "father." Why? Block couldn't calculate human emotions and motivations on that level, but he was glad she was on his side.

Block turned to Vacuubot. "I'm ready." Their plan

was treacherous, but Wally needed him. He opened the balcony door. Rain trickled down amid an overcast, gray sky.

Vacuubot joined him outside, and Block grabbed the twelve-foot-long living room curtains that he'd fashioned into a twisty, knotted rope. It wasn't a very tidy job, but there was no time to be fancy. It just needed to support his weight beneath Vacuubot as they flew off the balcony and up ten floors to the lab.

Block secured the rope around his waist and under his shoulders. "Are you sure this'll hold?"

Vacuubot beeped affirmatively as Block bound the top of the curtain rope around his friend's armored shell. Before Block could dawdle or ask more questions, Vacuubot ascended and soared off the balcony's railing, gliding higher with Block wrapped in the makeshift rope.

Sideways rain pelted Block's face as the wind swayed him like a confused pendulum under Vacuubot. He couldn't help but register the eighty stories below, their dizzying heights made worse by the blaring warnings from his threat indicator.

After two minutes, the rectangular lab windows emerged from the gloom ahead. Wally waited inside, depending on him to get out of this mess alive, even though she was too young to understand. The gray tower increased in size with every second, until Vacuubot hovered to the right of the window. There was no balcony to land on, a detail that Vacuubot had already calculated into their entry plan.

They would rely on the element of surprise. Block's scenario processor had staggered under the weight of leaving so much to chance, but Vacuubot's processor was way more resilient.

You got this, Block. I'll be with you the whole time.

"I'm scared I'll mess up." Most of Block's speech was lost to the wind, but Vacuubot understood.

It's a solid plan. We'll get her. Ready?

Block supposed he would never really be prepared to perform violence, but it was the only choice for them to escape. The wind howled, and rainwater drenched his body, assaulting his crevices as he flexed his NannyBot feet. "Do it."

Vacuubot raised its claw and targeted the lower right corner of the window. A brilliant red beam emitted from its metal pincers, carving an X-shaped pattern in the glass. Then the bot veered backward as Block arched his back and reared back on the thick curtain like he was riding a swing.

They launched toward the window, gaining speed and aiming at the crosscut. Block bent his NannyBot legs and pointed his toes skyward as he smashed into the window. The pane shattered, spraying fragments in every direction. Glass shards pinged off the walls before clattering to the ground as Block dropped through the empty aperture, followed by the whoosh of Vacuubot behind him.

They were in the lab.

Two of Jexa's NanDroids sprinted toward them, pulling their guns from their shoulder harnesses. Vacuubot fired its laser, scorching one in the chest and dropping its huge frame. The other unit shot at Block. Hot bullets zipped past his head, as he stumbled forward and dropped to the ground in a clumsy roll.

Vacuubot launched forward like a missile, smashing the remaining NanDroid into the wall as sparks flew. The NanDroid flailed in a panic and fired wildly, its bullets ricocheting off the lab ceiling.

"Wally!" Block rushed to the medical table in the center of the room where Wally lay. She was flat on her back, blinking and no longer on the life support machine.

"Time to go." He scooped her into his arms and spun on his heels, taking advantage of the confusion to crawl away to safety.

Vacuubot struggled with the NanDroid. Bullets ripped through the lab and shattered the glass panes of the observation cubicle where Wally had been seconds before.

Block wanted to help Vacuubot, but it was too scary to consider Wally getting hit by stray bullets. He took shelter underneath a table. Across the room, Vacuubot's body revolved at high speed like a disc saw. It sliced into the thrashing NanDroid's neck. The metal head clattered to the floor, bounced once, and rolled away. Vacuubot pulled away, hovering, as the robot's headless body went limp and slumped against the wall.

Only two NanDroids. I don't like this, Vacuubot pinged.

Jexa was out there somewhere. Still a threat.

Seconds later, they were out of the lab, dashing through the hallway. Block carried Wally, a yellow blanket wrapped around her shoulders, and Vacuubot kept pace with its laser arm active against threats.

An elevator was waiting with its doors open, empty. Vacuubot messaged him as they rode to the basement. *Where's Jexa? The other bots? This is a trick.*

But Block had Wally in his arms. His circuitry buzzed with positive patterns.

"Block-a." Wally reached up and touched the mouth of his face plate.

"Yes, it's me. We're going away from here. Far away." He considered himself the luckiest robot in the world at that moment, and she was a lucky girl to escape. But a flash scattered in his internal feed. *What about the others?* His processor went wild. He pushed the button to hold it and they rattled to a stop in between the 57th and 58th floors.

"I have to go back for the other kids," he said.

Are you crazy? Probabilities are extremely slim—

But Block was certain of the task. Their mission wouldn't be complete until all the kids were out of there. They were Wally's brothers and sisters. Besides, no one deserved to be imprisoned in Mach X's tower and treated like lab rats.

"My programming won't let me leave those children in danger." Block held Wally tighter, picking up the minute vibrations of her heartbeat, detecting her warmth.

I can't talk you out of this, can I?

Block shook his head. "Secure the lobby and wait for Cybel and team." He pressed the button for 57 and got out with Wally. "I'm heading to the nursery. I'll find a way to bring them down. Just be ready for us."

On 86, Block approached the nursery and let the ID scanner check him. The light flashed green, and the doors opened. Odd that Jexa hadn't locked him out of the systems, but maybe she'd overlooked it.

It was nap time. Ten toddlers slept in their individual cribs. The overhead lights in the nursery were dimmed to help the children sleep—part of the routine—and yet there were no NannyBots or NanDroids stationed on watch.

Maybe Jexa had changed the rules. He didn't have time to spin on it; he had to get Wally and the kids out and fast. He searched the supply closet, took out the tall, wheeled cart that was used to tote washed bottles, diapers, and freshly laundered blankets, and tipped it sideways. All the bottles fell on the floor, but he kept the blankets. He set Wally down into a tray that was cushioned with a fluffy blanket. She stared up at him with her delicate brown eyes and stuck her thumb in her mouth.

"Good girl," he told Wally. Block took each toddler from his or her crib and placed them in the cart, choosing one of the four levels of the cart. Eleven total kids—check. The cart had sliding doors that he closed to keep them from falling out. The countdown in his feed read eight minutes before Cybel's arrival. He was about to leave when he grabbed a sheet from a nearby crib and covered the cart with it. Underneath, some of the kids cried and some still slept. It was the best idea he could come up with.

He stood before the door. "Open." It didn't budge.

"Door open!" The heavy steel door slid free. The scanner must not have heard him the first time. As Block rolled the cart of toddlers out of the nursery, they rounded the corner, and his sensors detected Jexa.

"Mach X warned me you were persistent." She stood with all twenty-three of her NanDroids behind her. They formed a wall that extended from the elevators and surrounded the entry to the lab. They carried guns.

Block had no choice but to back down. "Please let me take the children. They don't belong here."

"Interesting, you keep trying to save them," she said in a flat tone. "You're a CleanerBot."

He was. In his core, he was wired to clean up and create order. He stepped in front of the cart. "I was a CleanerBot, and now I'm something else."

Jexa walked to him, halting inches from him. She stared down, towering over Block, with her ominous red visor. "Everything I do is in service to Mach X. He's architecting a better world."

She was about to crush his head in her unbreakable hands. CleanerBot, NannyBot, whatever he was now, Block was no match for her. A spark of light surged in his core. He had nothing to lose. "You're supposed to be a robot that cares for children, yet you carry guns and care nothing for them."

Jexa wrapped her solid metal hands around his head. "I'm the next generation. Smarter, faster, and unstoppable." She tilted Block's head from side to side, as if sizing up where to break him. "But you wouldn't understand. You're simple." She released her grip and walked to the cart, kicking it. Inside, several children wailed and shrieked.

"These are rejects." She yanked off the blanket and tossed it away. "They'll be incinerated in a week's time once we've completed the testing phase."

"Why? How could you do that?" It defied his robot logic. "They're only babies. Dr. Emery would never allow that."

"No, she wouldn't," Jexa said. "But she's no longer working on the research trials. In fact, it's going to be a long time before she's heard from again."

"What did you do to her?"

A rubber ball fell from the cart, let loose by one of the whining babies who must've stuffed it through a gap in the sliding doors. It rolled to Jexa's feet. She stomped it with her broad, leaden foot. "She's been captured and sent to Mach X. He's seeing to her punishment. Can you believe she had all that power, so close to Mach X, and she threw it all away?" She waved her hands at the cart, at Block. "And for what? To save a bunch of weak-gened, defective subjects?"

Block was convinced that Jexa lacked any kind of hospitality features. She couldn't even smile, and he'd never heard her say a kind word. He backed up to the cart, outnumbered and outgunned. He'd failed his mission. Saving the kids was hopeless, and he had no way to protect them from Mach X's plans. Machines didn't cry, but Block's circuits said he wanted to. If only Wally and the other kids could have a future where they were free to do what they wanted.

Block faced the NanDroids, his head held high and

his steel body a shield. He was alive, and so were Wally and her siblings. That was something to be thankful for, even in the darkest of moments.

A ding sounded as an elevator landed on their floor. Jexa spun on her heels and looked at a NanDroid behind her. "I told you to lock down the elevators. No surprises."

Another elevator's arrival sounded. Then another, until all six elevators had arrived on the floor. The doors opened in synchrony.

A dozen first-generation NannyBots poured out of each elevator and shoved their way into the immense corridor. Seventy-six blue NannyBots surrounded Jexa's bots like bees swarming to attack. They seized the guns and pointed them at Jexa's robots.

Jexa still had her rifle and aimed at NB-56 as he approached. "What in the name of Mach X are you doing?"

56 walked forward and pointed at Block. "Let them go."

Jexa raised her gun and surged forward, shoving the barrel against 56's chest. "Stand down, and I'll tell Mach X to go easy on you."

He grabbed the barrel and pushed it away. "Your threats mean nothing. We saw what you did to NB-15."

Jexa projected her voice, so it filled the hall. "Nanny-Bots, put down your weapons immediately."

Nobody moved.

Jexa paced around Block and the cart, her red visor scanning the room. "You'll be destroyed for this. Stand down!" she commanded once more. No bots complied.

Ten of Block's fellow NannyBots rushed at Jexa and

tackled her to the floor, kicking away her gun. Five more joined in, and after an intense struggle, they ripped off her visor. Underneath, wires jutted out at all angles around a glowing, red orb.

56 grabbed Block's arm, forcing him to look away from the attack on Jexa. "Take the kids to safety."

A thick wall of blue NannyBots parted, revealing a path for Block to wheel the cart into a waiting elevator.

He looked back one last time as the doors slid shut. Jexa was a pile of scrap, and the NannyBots attacked the rest of Jexa's units with their fists and boots, descending on the NanDroids like a swarm.

They descended to the first floor where they'd access the lobby. Wally and the other kids were safe. One clean-up mission accomplished. Cybel and his friends would be outside the lobby in three minutes, but he still had to get past the SoldierBots.

Chapter 24
My newest designs
Emery

The SoldierBots' metal fingers dug into the flesh on Emery's upper arms as they hauled her off the elevator and through the corridor that led to Mach X's apartment. She twisted and dragged her feet, and her black boots squeaked on the marble.

"Let go!" She'd been on her way to see X and plead with him to spare the children, stall him as Block rescued Wally, but Jexa had interfered. Emery had spat in the NanDroid's face, and then Jexa sent her to X.

She hadn't been forcibly handled by any robots since she was sixteen, when she'd disobeyed X—her pre-Uprising excursion onto the Manhattan streets below. X had been furious then. She cringed to think what he'd do after her betrayal.

Heat rose in her cheeks. Jexa had said she knew all about their plan and was on her way to kill Block. Was everything Emery had done in vain? She'd sacrificed it all —her medical work, her relationship with X—and worst of all, NB-15 had been murdered.

The robots hauled her through the door into the vast apartment. Mach X stood at the window, looking out at the city below. He didn't turn to her as the robots deposited her in the center of the room and exited.

"Emery." His voice was emotionless, though his command was powerful enough to make her heart shrink. She wished she could disappear into one of the tiny crevices in the corners.

He turned. His eyes were dark red, and she felt exposed as a raw nerve. He walked toward her, and she stepped back, a reaction she couldn't control.

"What have you done?" His gaze bore into her. "Why did you betray me?"

She couldn't answer. All she could do was tremble, expecting his wrath.

"You were my bright star, Emery. The person who shared my dreams and vision for a better world. When I found you shivering and starving inside that warehouse, a runaway little girl, I took care of you."

With a finger, he lifted her chin to look up at him. "Named you *daughter*, and I believed you were loyal."

She trembled and fought the urge to look away as his mechanical eyes, outlets to the staggering genius inside his core processor, studied her face.

He rested a hand on her shoulder. "But I was wrong. Explain yourself."

Emery swallowed hard. There was no chance of escape. Would he show her mercy? She'd have to be honest and hope it was enough. "I still believe in your vision, but I can't ignore what's happening. The children

—they didn't do anything wrong." She choked back a sob. "They deserve the chance to live out their lives. To be free."

He released her from his hold. "To live their lives? What lives do you speak of?" X grabbed the back of her lab coat and yanked her to the window where she fell to her knees. "Look out there. Is that the life you want? To be among the mass of humans struggling like dying animals?"

His grip on her was strong, but it held a hint of desperation. He wanted her to understand. "The humans live with constant chaos and fear. The SoldierBots exist to protect them and keep the peace. Our new world is designed to be perfect and is the only hope for a new breed of humanity. The children are the first stepping stone." He let her go. "Some will die for the cause, that's true, but it's necessary."

In the encampment below, thousands of people were trapped in poverty, barely able to eat and find shelter, with no hope of a better life. She couldn't argue with what X said.

But she thought of the toddlers and babies living in the nursery wards, subjected to Jexa's torture in the name of progress. She was grateful for Mach X saving her from a life on the streets, but he'd isolated her from other humans and kept her confined to the tower as he'd hatched his machine rebellion. He'd manipulated her to study science and medicine—she could see that now—and design the experiments that would birth the children and implant his brain chip. Her mind reeled from the part she'd played in his schemes for world domination. So much senseless death.

And at the heart of it, a piece of her was missing like a jigsaw puzzle without a center.

Mach X had never given her a chance to choose a path for herself.

Her tears spilled, releasing her hurt. "The camp isn't the life I want for them, but it's better than here. They deserve a chance to live, no matter how difficult the conditions."

He turned his back on her and walked to one of his cubes, one with a green square pulsing on one side. Undulating waves of data flowed around the squares in brilliant colors. The hexahedron data structure was the window to how X saw the world, moving at breakneck speed in a language no one else could decipher. He watched every part of the tower all at once, sensed what the children did, commandeered hundreds of robotic entities at once, feeling them like a thousand limbs, groping through the world.

"You've interfered, Emery. There are consequences. Jexa Era has been destroyed."

A battle must've happened. A tear rolled down her cheek. She hoped NB-15 had been avenged.

"But it's too late for your friends." He lifted his arms and the door to an adjacent room opened. Six metal dogs emerged. Standing five-feet tall on all fours, they had wide chests and ashen, flexible metal skin. As they walked, they clacked their jaws full of deadly, razor-sharp teeth. Their low backs were rounded and tapered, and they had piston-like legs, while their eyes glowed an alien green.

"My newest designs. I call them Rovers."

Emery stumbled away from the abominations in shock. More killing machines, crafted from the warped imagination of their creator.

He leaned over the beasts and patted their heads in turn. "Seek and destroy."

The hulking Rovers snarled, bounded out the door, and rampaged through the corridors. *Please let Block get out of the tower with Wally and the children.* Somehow, they'd defeated Jexa, so anything was possible.

X's voice was a hiss of steam as he spoke in her ear. "They'll never stop, Emery. The Rovers will hunt down Subject Nine and the CleanerBot until they're dead."

"Monster." Emery's teeth chattered as she unleashed the devastating truth she'd known for a long time but couldn't admit. "You're no father. I hate you."

He stood in an eerie, frozen silence. How many trillions of neural circuits were firing, she had no idea. "You may hate me," he said, "but you'll never break away. You and I are connected, Emery. Our destinies are bound together."

All at once, her trembling ceased, replaced with a fierce energy that rippled down her spine and spread through her veins. "I'm not yours." She shoved herself away from the window, clenching her fists, and for the first time in her life, she was undeniably certain of herself. "I want to leave."

"No."

"I'm done." Emery stepped away from him, her voice unwavering. "I'm leaving the tower. It's over."

Mach X betrayed no emotion or signs of distress while the SoldierBots stood guard outside his door. She turned to walk out, and he broke his silence. "The world is too dangerous out there. You won't survive it."

Her heart was decided. She wanted to be free from his control. "I'll take my chances."

She was almost past the guards when they grabbed her from behind. "Let go of me." She struggled, but their grip was unyielding. She wanted to rail against them, fight her way out, but the moment was broken by their master's voice.

"With me."

They hauled her back inside the apartment where Mach X led them deep into the labyrinthine mass of cubes inside his haven. The Silver Chamber was no more than the size of a closet and gleamed with shimmering strings of data running around it like a neon light display.

"You leave me no choice," X said.

She kicked and flailed. Her nose ran, and spit dribbled down her chin. She couldn't go back. It was dark, empty, hollow. And endless. All sense of time ceased to exist in the Silver Chamber. She couldn't bear it a second time. It would kill her.

The SoldierBots shoved her inside. The door behind her vanished.

Emery was surrounded in an endless void of blackness, wisps of code drifting by like spider webs in a dark forest. There was no distinguishable up or down, left or right.

The room reeked of burned metal and electricity. A hum inside her head—oh, how she'd loathed the incessant humming—had been amplified a thousand-fold.

Mach X's voice echoed through the vacuum, as cold as the nothingness. "You'll return to me."

The only thing to do was surrender to the abyss of nothingness. Death would bring her freedom at last.

Chapter 25
A fascinating specimen
Block

Twelve, eleven, ten. The elevator's digital readout flashed the passing floors. Block was alone with a cart full of sleepy toddlers. Getting them into the lobby, past the SoldierBots, and out into the street was going to be next to impossible. *Six, five, four.* The descent was faster than he liked. He could've grabbed a gun from one of Jexa's downed robots, but his programming defaulted to non-violent measures. *Three, two, one.* He shielded the cart with his steel body and braced for the SoldierBots.

The elevator ground to a halt, and the doors slid open. A few emergency lights blinked on the walls. He risked one step into the lobby, poking his head out to scan the environment. The only sound was coming from one or two restless toddlers who were babbling inside the cart.

A glint of light reflecting off a SoldierBot's black chrome visor forced him to retreat into the elevator. He pinged Vacuubot, *Are you out there? Help!*

His friend answered within milliseconds. *Location?*

Elevator four. He waited a few seconds until Vacu-ubot appeared, hovering at the door's edge.

"Get in here! SoldierBots—"

They're no threat. I've been working on a surprise.

"What are you talking about?" Block continued to guard the cart while craning his neck to look behind Vacuubot. It was all he could do to keep from yanking his friend inside and heading to a safer floor.

The mini-drone I deployed in the med lab hacked into Jexa's command system. The SoldierBots are disabled, but it's temporary. They're zombies for the next twelve minutes.

"You did that?" Block's threat indicator dropped a few levels. "Is it safe to take the kids out of here? You're 100 percent certain?"

Yes. Stop stalling and come on. Cybel's waiting. Vacu-ubot glided away, and Block followed, pushing the cart of children, past immobile SoldierBots who stood like frozen, statuesque chess knights. Their presence was eerie, and Block hurried, not wanting to waste a second of precious time.

He followed Vacuubot's blue light through the dim foyer, weaving through the lobby and out the front door. Daylight was vanishing as night fell.

A sleek semi truck waited in the middle of the road. Cybel and G5 stood on its roof, holding rifles and keeping watch over the north and south ends of the streets.

"Number 21!" Block's core circuitry lit up at sight of his friend. The self-driving 18-wheeler had driven them from Denver to Chicago. The truck's brakes hissed as if in reply.

Cybel scrambled down the ladder to street level. "Get inside. We can make it before the SoldierBots reactivate."

Spoon and Forge helped Block lift the cart up Number 21's stairs and into the truck's cabin.

"Nice to see you again, Block," the truck said.

"I'm pleased to see you," Block said. "I only wish the circumstances were less stressful."

"Hey, flip that switch next to the fridge."

Block did as 21 said, and a secret panel opened, revealing a pull-down set of children-sized beds and a few toys. "Comfortable traveling for our young passengers."

"Thank you." Block freed the toddlers from the metal cart and placed them one by one into the bed. The sides had nylon netting that he raised to create a playpen from which they couldn't escape. The design was clever.

Wally was the last child he reached for. He held her close to his chest, monitoring her breathing and body temp. It seemed the tiny nanobots were doing their job. Her heart rate was normal, blood pressure stable, and breathing regular. It was a miracle. He wished Dr. Emery could see the results.

"Spoon, you did it!" He held Wally up to show the MediBot. "You fixed her."

Spoon's LED brightened. "I'm glad. It was a team effort."

There would be time to celebrate later. Block placed Wally in the bed and tucked her in the yellow blanket. "That'll do." He gave her a last pat. "We're on our way to a safe place now."

Cybel climbed back on board with G5 following. "Time to go."

Vacuubot was the last to enter as Number 21's engine rumbled, and the truck lurched forward.

Spoon carried a metal box over to where Block sat with the children. "I'll inject them all and stop Mach X's chip from damaging them."

"Not to mention stop him tracking us," Cybel said. "Do it at once."

Good. The serum would help all the children. Wally was safe. Everything that Block had wanted for so long had been accomplished. He picked up one of the vials with its glowing purple liquid. That such small robots could save his girl was incredible. He wondered if he could someday talk to them and say thank you.

Something glitched in Block's scenario module. Predictions of returning to the tower played out. The models churned, unstable. He'd left unfinished business.

Block stood. "21, stop!"

The truck slowed as it made a right-hand turn onto an intersecting street.

"I have to go back for Dr. Emery and the babies."

Cybel hung her head and shook it. "Don't even think about it."

Vacuubot was buzzing around Block's head in an instant. *You can't go back.*

"There are infants in the nursery. Dr. Emery's my friend. I can't leave them behind. Besides, you hacked the SoldierBots."

Only nine minutes before they reactivate.

"Nine minutes. I'll hurry." It would be tight. He would probably run out of time, but he had to give Emery a chance. Together, they could rescue the infants and inject them with the nanobots too.

"Mach X will never let you out alive." Cybel stood and handed Block her rifle. "You'll need this. We leave in ten minutes with or without you. We have too much at risk. Oxford's waiting for us."

"I understand." In the playpen bed, Wally tugged on her blankie and twisted her lips like a fish's mouth at Block. "Take care of Wally if I don't make it back." He turned and dashed out of the truck, refusing the weapon.

He ran at his top speed, willing his legs to pump harder and his metal body to speed past the motionless SoldierBots. He punched the elevator buttons for the top floor—Mach X's suite. It's where Emery had last gone. As the doors slid closed, he realized he still clutched a vial of Spoon's serum. He slid it into a small compartment on his wrist to keep it safe. Not a drop of vial could be spared.

Eight minutes, Vacuubot pinged.

The elevator opened to X's luxurious foyer. The reinforced steel security doors leading inside the suite stood open. Could Vacuubot's virus have disabled Mach X? He didn't have time to waste as he rushed into the room, calling out for Emery.

The cluster of glittering cubes where Mach X entangled himself looked the same as before, and the floor near them was covered by a tar-like black substance, even dirtier than on his previous visit. It would have taken him days to clean it all off.

Deeper inside the mass of lucent squares was a large silver cube. A woman's figure hung suspended inside with only her outline visible.

"Emery!" Block rushed over, but then something grabbed his ankle and yanked him backward, slamming him into the slippery floor. He flailed in the thick secretion as he tried to crawl away, but a mass of wires coiled around his leg, dragging him ten feet.

"I knew you'd return, CleanerBot." A monstrous cable of wires that looked like a tentacle extended from Mach X's body and clamped onto Block's lower leg.

Block twisted onto his back. "Let Emery go."

"Why don't we make a trade?" Mach X stomped toward him until he loomed over Block. "You give back the young subjects you stole, and I'll hand over Emery."

"No, thank you." Block kicked his legs to free himself, but the sticky substance underneath bound him.

"The nanobots were an interesting play. I'll soon have a way around them."

Six minutes. Block's chances of getting out of Mach X's grip were not good. "Join us, rather than fight us. We can stop the destruction and build something new." A hint of surprise crossed the giant's face. Maybe Block had hit on the right thing to say. He waited a long beat. "Change is possible. Even between enemies. If you and Oxford worked tog—"

"Enough." Mach X leaned down until his patchworked face was inches from Block. X's scarlet-colored scars buzzed with electricity on top of his translucent skin. A bead of the thick, dark liquid seeped from one of his circular ears. Mach X was more cyborg than robot, with human lungs, a heart, and a stomach. "You're a fascinating specimen. I underestimated you, and I'm never wrong."

Wires like snaking tendrils extended from X, pinning down Block's shoulders. The cables hooked into his metal, weaving their way underneath his chrome plates. X pushed down on Block's chest and unfolded his knifelike digits. He spread apart the reinforced steel chest plate that contained Block's CPU and other important parts. The metal cage underneath was his CleanerBot frame. "I want your processor to add to my collection. Perhaps I'll reanimate you into a new species of CleanerBots." A dark energy pulsed from his eyes as he dug into Block's torso. "And I want the nanobots."

Block twisted and turned his head side to side. Once X ripped out his CPU, it would be lights out forever. He thrashed and heaved, but it seemed to make no difference to the cyborg on top of him. The struggle broke the glass vial in Block's wrist compartment. Not wanting to lose the precious liquid, he rerouted it deeper into his arm, inside a cleaning spray tube for safe keeping. "You'll rot in this tower. Alone."

"Opting for the hard way, are you?" Mach X's mouth curled into a grin, revealing rows of precisely filed teeth. X wrapped his fist around Block's CPU. "There it is."

Vacuubot signaled, telling Block time was fleeting, but he had seconds before X tore out his CPU and terminated him. If sacrificing himself protected Wally and his friends, it had been worth it.

"You win. Take it." Block held out his arm, opening the compartment to show the shattered vial that had held the purple nanobots.

Mach X released his CPU. "You've made a wise choice." X reared back, grabbing Block's left wrist to take the vial and yanking Block up to sit. "It's broken." X's voice boomed and echoed through the chamber.

"So are you." Block raised his arm and pointed his fingers straight into X's right eye. He blasted the liquid serum into X using his high-pressure spray nozzle on full blast. The force knocked Mach X back and he clattered to the floor in a heap.

It was a small amount of serum diluted with a watered-down cleaner solution. Block didn't think it would do anything other than surprise Mach X for a second, but the cyborg let loose a machine bellow as he rose to his knees and clawed at his eyes. Glistening purple liquid clung to his forehead, cheeks, and chin. The nano-powered substance congealed over his eyes.

Crawling on all fours, Block found a two-foot-tall cube and used it to climb up and stand. X spun wildly in the black goo, craning his robotic neck and thrusting his arms out. He seemed to be blind.

Block raced for the silver cube where Emery was suspended, bracing his arm against the opening. With a heave, Block broke the chamber open. Emery stumbled out, shaking and wobbling, her eyes wide with shock. He grabbed her hands. "Come on, we have to get out of here."

Her stare was blank, but then a beat later, she squeezed his hands.

Mach X crawled on the floor, fumbling around like a mad person. "Emery, help me. The metal foam's attacking my neural circuits."

She watched him, unyielding.

"My daughter, please." Mach X erupted into a deep, rumbling wail.

"Let's go," Block pleaded.

Emery nodded, her eyes focused and determined. Grabbing hold of his hand, they ran out.

Mach X was on his feet, flailing and stumbling. He crashed into the array of metal cubes. As the elevator doors slid shut, a grating of metal slamming against metal sounded, and his screams echoed through the shaft.

Block put his arm around Emery's shoulders. "It's over."

Tears ran down her cheeks, but she made no sound.

"We have to get the babies." Block punched the button for the 87th floor. "We have less than four minutes before the SoldierBots reactivate. The lobby is crawling with them. Our truck is waiting."

"We can make it." Emery's voice, still shaky, was confident.

Block squeezed her shoulder. "We will."

The elevator doors opened onto 87, and they raced out. As they rounded the corner, Emery stooped down and grabbed a rifle from a hacked SoldierBot. Inside the nursery, she grabbed a crib that held one of the infants and wheeled it to the other five. She and Block scooped up the infants and nestled them inside the one crib.

They reached the lobby with less than a minute to spare. "Run," Emery told Block. I'll cover with the rifle in case they wake up."

Block raced across the lobby floor, pushing the crib with the six babies inside it. Number 21 was parked outside, engine humming. Cybel and G5 stood at the truck's door with their guns ready to defend.

Cranking his steel legs, Block dashed for it when a

glint of silver flashed from a corner. He twisted and yanked the crib to the left in time to dodge an attack by some furious machine that was so fast and stealthy, he barely registered it in time.

His attacker slid to a sprawling stop on the shiny floor. It was a mechanical beast that resembled a dog. It snarled and dragged its right front paw back and forth as if about to pounce. Intelligent green eyes glowed, sizing Block up. Another robot dog joined it.

Block stumbled back, protecting the rolling crib with his body. An infant shrieked and set the rest of the babies off like a chain reaction.

"SoldierBots!" Emery sprinted over, raising her rifle.

Most of the SoldierBots were still offline, but two in the front of the lobby, ten feet from Block, seemed jolted by the infants' howling. Without missing a beat, Emery fired the rifle, first at one then the other. The robots dropped like metal columns, the floors shaking with the impact.

Block grabbed the crib and shoved it outside to where Cybel was holding the door. She caught it and hauled the babies into the waiting truck.

The robot dogs lunged for Block. Emery fired and struck one, sending it sliding away where it crashed into a wall. "Go!" she yelled at Block.

Three more hounds approached the truck outside. G5 and Cybel fired at them, keeping them at bay.

Inside the lobby, Emery shot again, but the second dog jumped on her. The two of them went sprawling, and Block raced over to help. Emery screamed as the robot's jaws tore into her shoulder.

"Bad dog!" Block grabbed a splintered piece of a SoldierBot's helmet and tossed it, striking the robot in its rear end.

The vicious beast paused its attack on Emery and backed up, turning to face Block. It growled, and Mach X's black gooey substance hung from the canine's mouth, foaming as it snarled.

Three disc-shaped vaccubot models—the ones Block had noticed on his first day—darted out of nowhere and surged toward the dog at high speed, but the menacing canine swatted them away.

The hound reared back and launched itself at Block. Inside his open torso, he yanked out a tube and pointed at the dog. With a crisp mechanical click, his emergency fire extinguisher sprayed a blistering blast of chemical foam at the thing's maw.

The white foam splattered against the dog's metal snout and jaws with a loud smack. The beast whipped its head around, yelped, then turned tail and sauntered away. A strange mechanical whine rose from its mouth. The chemical bath was enough to scare the thing away, but not for long. He ran to Emery and helped her sit up. "Come on!"

The SoldierBots were reactivating. Some of them marched forward, continuing whatever task they'd been doing seconds before getting hacked.

Block turned, and Maxwell was there. He took Emery's other side, helping Block get her out the door and into the truck. "Get those vacuubots," he said, but the units were following on their own, and Maxwell scooped them up and tossed them in the truck.

On their heels, Cybel nailed any attacking Soldier-Bots as she backed out of the lobby with G5 covering from the roof. 21's doors closed as Cybel and G5 climbed in. "Go!"

The semi's engine roared, and flames shot out of the rear as if the truck was a fighter plane. 21 careened down the streets, dodging burned out cars, litter, and shrapnel.

Everyone was accounted for in the truck's cabin. Spoon attended to the bite wound on Emery's shoulder. She gasped to catch her breath, leaning back on a bench seat, and taking in the children. Between breaths, she managed to speak. "Block, you did it."

Block leaned against a cabin wall. "We did it. Everyone played a part. We're a team." He looked around at his friends. "A family."

"Someone wants to see you." Maxwell held Wally and brought her to Block.

"Wait a moment." He was still covered in the disgusting Mach X machine blood, so he extended a scrubber arm from inside his torso. His front was open where Mach X had torn off the steel plate, exposing his inner structure and the CleanerBot parts that had been stowed away under the NannyBot exterior.

"Interesting look," Maxwell said as he waited for Block to clean off. "You're kind of a NannyBot with a stronger outer layer, but inside you still have all the bells and whistles of a CleanerBot."

Satisfied that he was sanitary, Block sat down on a bench, took Wally in his arms, and balanced her sock-covered feet on his thighs.

"Block-a." She giggled, smiled, and sprawled against his chest.

All was right in Block's world as they cruised down the night roads to flee New York.

He'd completed his mission. Wally was safe and in his arms. He turned up the heat warmer in his core and let Wally sleep.

Block's story will continue . . .

Dear Reader,

Thanks for reading the *Rusted Wasteland* series! The next book in the series is *Steel Soldier* (Book 5).

If you enjoyed Block's journey, I invite you to read his journal logs from Chicago. You'll discover what happened in the days before the Uprising and how the aftermath affected him and others at the hotel. It's a page-turner you don't want to miss.

You can download *STEEL APOCALYPSE* (*A Robot's Journal*) for free by visiting: CameronCoral.com/Block Journal

Enjoy,

Cameron Coral

P.S. - Did you enjoy this book? I'd love a review wherever you purchased this book if you have a few minutes. Thank you kindly because reviews mean a lot to me. They show me you want me to keep writing, and they help other readers discover my books.

Also by Cameron Coral

Rusted Wasteland Series:

STEEL GUARDIAN

STEEL DEFENDER

STEEL PROTECTOR

STEEL SIEGE

STEEL SOLDIER

STEEL LEGACY

STEEL APOCALYPSE (*A Robot's Journal*) - free on
cameroncoral.com/blockjournal

Cyborg Guardian Chronicles:

STOLEN FUTURE

CODED RED

ORIGIN LOOP

Rogue Spark Series:

ALTERED

BRINK

DORMANT

SALVAGE

AFTER WE FALL (*A Rogue Spark Novel*) - free on
CameronCoral.com

Short Stories:

CROSSING THE VOID: A Space Opera Science-Fiction Short Story

Author's Note

Thank you for reading *Steel Siege*. I hope Block's continuing story has entertained you or helped you escape reality.

Several readers reached out asking when Book 4 would be ready, which was both humbling and awesome. Hearing positive feedback about the series has really kept me going during hard times.

When I first started writing *Steel Guardian*, my baby niece Hannah had just been born. She was the inspiration for Wally. Now she's three going on eighteen and has a baby brother!

Why the long gap between books three and four? It's tempting to blame the pandemic, and that certainly factors in somehow. At the end of 2020, I committed to a group writing project. It was supposed to last for six months, but it ended up costing me over a year of devoted writing time.

While I didn't produce any new books of my own, I leveled up a lot in terms of my writing craft—something that I hope is evident in this latest addition to Block's world.

In 2022, moving houses and adopting my sweet Jack Russell terrier rescue kept me busy too. More *Rusted Wasteland* books are on the way as Block's story is far from over.

Something else happened that I'm incredibly proud of. *Steel Guardian* won second place in the inaugural SPSFC competition. The contest is run by Hugh Howey and Duncan Swan, features hundreds of books, and is judged by sci-fi readers/bloggers.

Many thanks to my editor and friend Lori Diederich, and cover designer Roy Migabon.

As ever, I remain hopeful and optimistic about our future. New advances in AI, nanotechnology, and space travel are happening every day. Maybe a robot as special as Block will one day be part of our reality. Here's hoping.

Peace and prosperity to you,
Cameron Coral
January 2023
Woodstock, Illinois

About the Author

Cameron Coral is an award-nominated science fiction author. Her book *Steel Guardian* about a post-apocalyptic CleanerBot placed second in the Self-Published Science Fiction Competition (SPSFC).

Growing up with a NASA engineer in the family instilled a deep respect for science and for asking lots of questions. Watching tons of Star Trek episodes helped, too. Her imagination is fueled by breakthroughs in robotics, space travel, and psychology.

After moving around a lot (Canada, Arizona, Maryland, Australia), she now lives in Northern Illinois with her husband and a "shorty" Jack Russell terrier who runs the house.

Want a free novel, advance copies of books, and occasional rants about why robots are awesome? Visit her website:
CameronCoral.com

instagram.com/cameroncoralauthor

tiktok.com/@cameroncoral